POPPA'S WAR

A NOVEL

Alberta Tolbert

Wandering in the Words Press

To
Morgan, Zyion,
Jassmon
Best
Alberta Tolbert

PUBLISHED BY WANDERING IN THE WORDS PRESS

ISBN-10: 0-9967878-8-7
ISBN-13: 978-0-9967878-8-8
First Edition

For Vic
For everything

AΩ

Silence may be as variously shaded as speech.
— Edith Wharton

1

Spring—Minnesota's miracle—was late, unwilling or unable to challenge a winter laden with winds—cold, harsh, and bitter like Poppa's words that lingered in their house on the hill. Alicia Drake, with her elbows on the wooden sill of her bedroom window, leaned into the lilt of song birds and gazed at the wild purple mayflowers nudged through the soil. They promised change. The scent of sun-warmed purple lilacs filled her with hope on her eleventh birthday.

She bounced down the stairs and paused to listen. Only the hum of conversation and clatter of cups accompanied the smell of coffee wafting from the kitchen. Ahead, white lace living room curtains billowed in a gentle breeze, dusting fern fronds in their wake. To her right, two identical, high-back, rose-patterned chairs flanked a floor lamp. To her left, on the coffee table, a rainbow of colors spilled from her sister Gina's crayon box next to a drawing of the American flag: thirteen stripes and forty-eight stars in perfect rows. Gina was nowhere in sight.

In the kitchen doorway, Alicia took a deep breath and, using her eyes like pencils, traced the kitchen: the open porch door and, across the room, the sink and refrigerator on either side of the cellar steps. Three canisters with decals of clustered, ripe apples and pears lined the base of white cupboards next to the electric stove. Empty bowls and filled ashtrays anchored a rectangular wooden table pulled slightly away from the open north window. Above everything, the red electric clock read 8:45.

Everything seemed in order.

Grandpa Anton, his back to the dining room doorway, sat with his antique mustache cup in one hand. His reading glasses hugged the tip of his nose, and his head bent over the May 30, 1946, edition of *The Minneapolis Morning Herald.*

Ready to head to the cemetery, Grandpa removed his glasses and tucked them into his good, white church shirt. "Another year passed. It doesn't get any easier, Ilse."

"I know, Pa," Momma said.

Momma sat with her back to the window where blue sky, brilliant after so many grainy gray days of rain, blinded Alicia and prevented her from seeing Momma's face. Alicia scooped a bowl of oatmeal from a kettle on the stove and sat in Poppa's chair facing the porch door. She pushed away an overflowing ashtray, topped with a crumpled Lucky Strike cigarette package, and Poppa's plate of congealed eggs mixed with ashes. "Morning," she said. "Where's Gina?"

Grandpa turned to her with a startled look, almost as if he didn't recognize her. The lines at the corner of his eyes were deep; sadness had seeped down his face. He attempted a big smile for Alicia that didn't fool her even a little.

How's the birthday girl? Feeling old?"

Alicia shrugged.

"Isn't Gina coloring her flag?" Momma passed the sugar bowl to Alicia. "Go easy, Princess." Alicia's eyes adjusted to the light. Momma, too, was ready for the cemetery. She wore her shoulder-padded, blue maternity suit that matched her sad eyes, and she had drawn her long, auburn hair severely to the nape of her neck. "Gina wants you to open the birthday card she made for you. She's worried you won't like it."

The white folded paper smelled of TABU, Momma's good perfume they were forbidden to touch, much less use, but Momma seemed not to notice. On the outside, a huge, yellow sun filled the card's corner, and a red robin, singing with his beak in the air, perched next to a nest tucked in the crook of a green tree branch. Inside, rainbow colored daisies framed the greeting in Gina's careful penmanship.

HAPPY BIRTDAY
TO
MY FAVERIT SISTER

"And your only sister." Alicia smiled inside and out. Sweet little pixie Gina, whose feelings were so easily hurt Alicia feared a strong wind or strong word might blow her away.

The porch door slammed, shattering Alicia's thoughts. "Alicia what the hell have you done with my medal?" Poppa's anger buzzed like an angry hornet. Dressed in his Army uniform, Poppa seemed too large for the doorway; his hands grasped the door frame as if he might pull it away from the wall.

She cringed, a motion that had become so familiar around Poppa that she barely noticed.

"I looked on my bureau, the closet, everywhere. Don't you understand? I need my Silver Star for protection at the cemetery."

Alicia made a move to get up.

"No! You!" He pointed his finger at her. "Sit still."

"Ed," Momma said with a sigh. "Not today of all days. Can't you calm down for once?" With palms pushing against the table for support, she rose out of the chair.

"Wait up, Ilse," Grandpa said. "Why don't you take the butcher knife and cut some flowers for Johan's tree?"

Momma hesitated, and with a shake of her head took the knife, its blade glinting in the light. She glanced over her right shoulder, and then she made her way out the door.

Grandpa folded the newspaper. Deliberately and precisely. "Ease up on the girl, Ed. I'll not have you cursing in front of Ilse or the girls in my house. I'll go and find your Silver Star before you have a conniption." He stood and walked away with slow, measured steps.

Poppa paced the worn kitchen linoleum with the same cadence that Alicia heard on so many winter nights. She slouched down, her head grazing the top of the ladder-back chair.

"Dammit, Alicia, you been messing with my foot locker in the car shed? You and that *Clara*?"

"N-no, Poppa." Behind her, he placed his calloused, mechanic's hands on her shoulders, small beneath his grip. Hands she used to think of as strong, protective. Before the War. He was gentle at first. Then he squeezed harder. "Give up the medal, and I'll go easy on you."

A spider crept down the radiator pipe; walls closed in; each faucet drip echoed like a hammer to metal.

You're hurting me!

Poppa had never hurt her before. Not ever. Except with words. His hands squeezed harder. She strained to hear the song birds, but in the deadly sound of silence, Alicia's world shifted, changed in a way she could never have imagined.

He bent close to her face. "I know you hid my medal," he said in a low, barely audible whisper. The hands squeezed harder. "And I know Clara told you to do it." He straightened up, and his huge, dark shadow loomed across the table, dwarfing Alicia. His raised voice drowned the refrigerator's vibrations and stung her ears. "I told you to stay away from her. She's big trouble for me. Are you listening to me?"

Alicia leaned away from his yelling until her neck ached from the strain.

"Ed, back off." Grandpa stormed across the kitchen. "I found your medal on the living room rug underneath the coffee table. Poppa turned, snatched the medal from Grandpa's outstretched palm.

Caught in some kind of nightmare, the urge to flee overwhelmed Alicia. She shoved the chair back with her legs, and it crashed into Poppa. He whirled back to her, lurched forward, grabbed her wrist, and jerked her across the kitchen to the dining room doorway. On one side of her, Momma's good china and silverware decorated the lace-covered dining room table, already set for Alicia's afternoon birthday party. Frilly, yellow, leftover May baskets overflowed with candy corn and peanuts. A vase held pink flowering almond branches—her favorite. On the other side, Poppa's face distorted in anger.

Grandpa blocked the doorway and placed his right arm across Poppa's chest. "I said … let … her … go."

Poppa yanked Alicia closer. The veins in Poppa's powerful neck bulged when he raised his right arm as if to strike Grandpa. Alicia was afraid to struggle—or move even at the sound of a thud followed by the crack of breaking glass.

The kitchen door slammed, but only Alicia seemed to hear. Momma ran to them with the butcher knife still clutched in her hand. Her face was white as the irises falling to the floor.

"What's going on here? Have the two of you gone crazy?"

A piercing wail halted them like children in a game of frozen tag. "Alicia, help me," Gina cried.

They all turned to look. Beside the living room coffee table, broken pieces of a mirror littered the floor around her sister's bare feet. Alicia jerked free and ran to her. Gina's face was bleached white, and the blue of her eyes had disappeared into the black of her pupils. She swiped her face, turning tears into blood. "Am I going to die like the soldiers? Like Uncle Johan?" Gina sobbed.

"No, you aren't going to die. It's just a little blood." Alicia lifted her sister from the glass shards. Gina's arms and legs wrapped around Alicia, clinging to her sister like a second skin and refusing to let go. Tiny red polka dots of blood dotted Alicia's white nightgown.

Grandpa eased the butcher knife from Momma's grasp and placed it on the dining room table. He knelt in front of the girls and unwound Gina's arms and legs. He wiped her tears with his big blue handkerchief. "What happened? You can tell us. Nobody is going to yell at you." Grandpa glared up to Poppa.

"I went upstairs and got Poppa's medal from his bureau." Gina glanced around at the floor before she looked up to Momma and Poppa. "Then I went back upstairs and got Momma's silver mirror so I could see the medal when I pinned it on my dress. But I tripped on your magazines, Grandpa." She pointed to his stack of *Reader's Digests* strewn across the rug. "The mirror broke … I'm sorry, Momma … I tried to pick up the pieces …"

Alicia opened Gina's clenched fist. A tiny blood-smeared shard stuck out of her palm. Tears flooded Gina's eyes.

"Why did you want to wear your Poppa's medal?" Grandpa gently pulled the shard from her hand.

Poppa moved closer as if to hear the answer.

She hiccupped. "I wanted to be a hero like Poppa and Uncle Johan and wear it to the cemetery for Decoration Day. To show Uncle Johan how brave I am."

"Your Uncle Johan is in heaven," Momma said.

Gina shook her head.

Alicia willed an unspoken warning to Gina. *Don't say what you've been telling me since last Halloween, that Slick is really Uncle Johan.*

"Stop it, Gina!" Poppa yelled. "Stop it. Johan is dead and he's never coming back."

Grandpa stood and again faced Poppa. "I don't think any of us need a reminder of that. Least of all today." Outside, a cloud passed over the sun, and color faded from the walls. Silence, gray and heavy, seeped into each corner and ushered Poppa, wordless, through the kitchen, out the back door. Grandpa followed, as if making sure he left.

2

Alicia gently tugged her nightgown away from Gina's stranglehold. "I'll help her, Momma. Come on Gina." She gathered Gina's paper and crayons from the coffee table and led her sister upstairs to the bathroom.

The smell of Grandpa's shaving soap lingered in spite of the open window. Alicia moved Grandpa's straight edge razor and shaving mug to the sink's edge, took out two washrags from the white cabinet above the claw-foot tub, and from the wooden medicine cabinet removed a small, brown glass bottle of mercurochrome.

What's wrong with me—that makes him so mad at me all the time?

"Noooo!" Gina hid the bloody hand behind her back.

Ignoring the protest, Alicia ran cold water over one washrag and handed it to Gina. "Bite down. And don't be such a baby. When we're done in here, I'll help you make a paper medal. And you better stop talking about Uncle Johan." She rinsed the other washrag in warm, soapy water and grasped Gina's hand to clean the cuts. Gina tried to wiggle away, and the cold washrag fell from her mouth.

Alicia held Gina's hand and wiped the cuts, checking for glass splinters. A pink page from Gina's pocket-sized Rainbow Tablet sat on the windowsill. It was dated with today's date and numbers one through fourteen, and it gave Alicia an idea to distract her sister. "You know all the cars you count from this window going by on the highway?"

Gina raised her head and nodded.

"Since the War ended, Joe says cars, lots of them from all over the United States, stop at his gas station. Instead of just counting cars, we could list license plates from all of the different states that you see—starting with Poppa's Minnesota plates. But you have to see them—no cheating." Alicia leaned over the sink, soaked the washrag in warm water, and then rinsed soap from Gina's cuts, knowing the worst was still to come.

Gina had a faraway look in her eyes. Grandpa always said he could hear the wheels turn in Gina's head.

"Me and you? Friends? Like you and Clara?" she asked.

Alicia disappeared into her own thoughts. *Like me and Clara. Used to be.*

"Sure. Maybe we can get all forty-eight states before school starts." With Gina temporarily distracted, Alicia opened the mercurochrome bottle, removed the glass applicator, and quickly swabbed the cuts, blowing on Gina's palm to ease the sting.

"Ow." Gina waved her orange-dabbed palm, blew on the cuts, and frowned at her sister.

"Let's make this our secret sister thing. Can you do that?" Alicia whispered.

The word "secret" must have clinched it for Gina; even her eyes smiled.

"Okay, then. Come on. We'd better hurry if we're going to make a medal for you and get dressed for the cemetery. And you can pick up empty shells after the soldiers are finished with their gun salute."

Gina scrambled onto their unmade bed beside her Raggedy Ann doll propped against the white headboard. Dried globs of gum clung to the back of the metal post on Alicia's side. On the white paper, Gina drew a copy of Poppa's Silver Star medal: a palm-sized, five-pointed gold star—colored yellow because she didn't have gold—a small silver star in the middle—colored green because she didn't have silver—with a red-, white-, and blue-colored paper ribbon. "Is Alphie going to be there?" she asked without looking up.

"I don't know."

"Then Slick better be there, too. Alphie's mean, and I don't like him."

Alicia smiled at the medal as she carefully cut around the star points and placed it on the dresser between Gina's Kewpie doll—a gift from Uncle Johan—and Momma's old powder puff box. Still dismayed at how quickly new problems popped up with Poppa, Alicia scooted to the foot of their bed and parted the sheer white curtains. If only her birthday wish for the new red Schwinn bicycle would come true. She imagined herself riding out to Clara's farm after the long months of Poppa's forced separation.

Gina joined her sister and wrapped her small arm around Alicia's shoulder as if reading her feelings. Alicia's thoughts turned away from Poppa—for a while.

"See that daddy robin?" Alicia pointed out the window to the nest in the elm tree where the heads of two baby robins stretched for the worm dangling from the male robin's beak. "He looks just like the one you drew for my birthday card. Someday you're going to be a famous artist."

Gina crawled off the bed, and Alicia followed her to the front of their dresser. "Those freckled babies don't look like robins. Do you think we look like Momma and Poppa?" Gina pointed to their reflection in the cracked mirror.

Alicia and Gina looked like twins separated by four years: same tall, willowy frame as Momma's, same curly auburn hair, same crystal blue eyes, same spray of freckles across their noses. Gina was a happy-go-lucky chatter-box. Alicia wasn't.

"Time to get ready for the cemetery." Alicia picked up an old, half-used tube of Momma's Fire Engine Red lipstick and almost touched it to her lips. Not worth the trouble it would cause. Instead, she removed the rags from her hair and brushed the unruly curls that seemed to have a mind of their own.

If I look like them, then who is the real me?

"Gina, do I look older? Different?"

"Nope."

Anger-tinged words slipped out. "What do you know? You're only seven." Alicia was mad a lot lately, and she worried that, maybe, she was more like Poppa than she wanted to be. In the mirror, Alicia saw the hurt reflected from Gina's face. "I'm sorry I sounded mad. I didn't mean it." She hugged Gina.

"I'm sorry, too." said Gina's muffled voice. "It's my fault Poppa got so mad and yelled at you. I heard him, so I hurried to tell him I had his medal and I tripped and ..."

"Shh." Alicia wiped tears from Gina's face. "It's okay. Poppa sometimes yells at me. Now for your medal." Using a safety pin, Alicia secured the paper medal to Gina's brown and white polka dot dress and covered it with Gina's brown sweater.

"If you girls are done getting all dolled up, it's time to leave for the cemetery," Grandpa called through the closed door.

Alicia inhaled a deep breath. The scent of lilacs with their promise of hope had faded away.

Gina skipped ahead to Grandpa's car, leading the procession of Drake women. Side by side, Alicia and Momma followed.

"Is your wrist okay?" Momma asked.

Alicia nodded, denying the still-throbbing red bracelet of finger marks and sore shoulders that Momma knew nothing about. She wondered why she lied for Poppa. Or was it Momma she lied for?

"Oh no," Momma said. "The flowers. I forgot them. I can't seem to remember anything anymore ..."

Alicia ran back to the house for the Mason jar of white irises on the concrete porch steps. Momma continued walking with her hand resting on the small of her back. "Uff da," Alicia heard her say as she slid into the front seat of Grandpa's old Chevy. Alicia hurried to the car, placed the jar on the floorboard between Momma's swollen feet, and climbed into the backseat beside Gina.

On either side of the graveled road to the cemetery, barren cornfields with black soil finally drying from the early May rains stretched to the horizon, and the azure sky covered it like a translucent bowl.

"Today's the last day for frost in this part of Minnesota. I'll be planting the rest of my garden this week," Grandpa said. "Can I count on you girls this summer?"

"I might be playing with my dolls," Gina said.

"Oh, you might, huh?" Grandpa said with a chuckle. "What about you, Alicia? What are you going to be doing?"

Nothing *is what I'll be doing all summer.* "I'll help again this summer, Grandpa."

"Johan would be so proud of his gardener niece," Grandpa said. "If he were still alive ..." A hush fell over the car and rode with them to the cemetery until Grandpa parked at the end of a long line of cars.

A group of uniformed veterans—Navy, Air Force, Marines, and mostly Army—milled outside the entrance beside the flagpole that leaned against the wire fence. A veteran blew into his bugle and shook it. Poppa and three other veterans, rifles in hand, stood behind him.

Grandpa checked his pocket watch. "We have enough time," he said.

With the jar of white irises in hand, Alicia followed Grandpa into the cemetery and along the road used for funeral corteges.

"Good crowd," he said. "To be expected this soon after the War."

Mimicking the stripes on Gina's flag, ribbons of white petunias and red geraniums stretched from one end of the cemetery, between weathered old alabaster tombstones and new marble ones, to the other end. The aroma of freshly mowed grass hovered above it all. Here and there, Grandpa patted headstones as if greeting old friends—some so old that names and dates in Norwegian were nearly erased. At the family plot, Grandpa knelt beside Uncle Johan's memorial evergreen tree, now almost as tall as Gina, and placed the jar of white flowers. An eagle circled. Its wings cast for a moment the shadow of an arm across Grandpa's shoulders.

The family had learned of Johan's death on Christmas Eve 1943, and as the memory came back to Alicia, the May morning turned upside down in some topsy-turvy fashion—the warmth gave way to the winter cold of that night.

The moon and starry sky had lit the street for Momma, Grandpa, Gina, and Alicia. Snow crunched beneath their boots.

"More snow's coming before midnight," Grandpa had said.

Inside the small, white, Vinji Lutheran Church, the pine scent of the Christmas tree rose over friends and neighbors gathered in pews close to the front, near the floor furnace. Beside the organist, a deacon hovered, checking now and then the heat of the electric bulbs to make sure they didn't ignite the tree.

The congregation had risen and was singing "Silent Night" at the end of the service when the double doors beneath the bell tower slammed opened. The north wind rushed into the church. Heads turned, one by one, into the frigid air.

Mr. Oldenburg, depot agent and telegraph operator, walked up the aisle with a telegraph in his hand. He brushed against the Christmas tree, and a red glass ball crashed to the floor. Tinsel draped his sleeve. Pastor Anderson left the altar to meet him. They spoke in hushed tones. The outer doors slammed shut; altar candles continued to flicker, and a chill refused to leave the church.

Keeping his head bowed, Mr. Oldenburg walked to the pew where Alicia's family sat.

Grandpa rose and stood straight as the soldier he had been in the First World War. His hands shook as he reached for the telegraph and read it. The yellow paper floated to the floor. "My boy, Johan. His ship was lost at sea. Our family will be leaving now."

Snow, huge flakes of Christmas snow, blanketed the world outside, muffling sound. A perfect silence. Wrapped in her own sadness, Alicia had seen Uncle Johan with his arm around Grandpa until the swirling snow covered Johan and he had disappeared.

Now, even beneath the clear May sky, Alicia shivered.

"Alicia?" Grandpa's voice pulled her back to the present.

"Look at Johan's tree."

"Huh?" A cluster of wild, white crocuses tied with a blue ribbon lay beneath Johan's tree. From Clara. For a moment, just a sliver of time, Alicia allowed herself to imagine Clara and Johan married. The way they had planned. Struck by the loss she felt, she surveyed the area, hoping to see Clara, but instead, across the cemetery where the veterans would stand, she spotted Clara's brother, Alphie. He elbowed his way through the gathered Gold Star Mothers and crouched next to Gina. She shied away.

"Time for the ceremony," Grandpa said. "And to help Gina." When they reached Momma and Gina, Grandpa stepped behind Alphie.

Twelve o'clock. Men removed their hats and held them to their hearts. The veterans marched into the cemetery with the unfurled stars and stripes snapping in the prairie wind. At headstones or memorials of every soldier who had served in the Spanish American War, in World War I, and in World War II, veterans planted small American flags and saluted. When they returned to formation, rifles were raised, and a twenty-one-gun salute echoed across the prairie. Momma held Grandpa's hand as the bugler played taps.

When the veterans stood at ease, the scramble for empty cartridges began. Alphie lunged in front of Gina, but Grandpa had collared him by the back of his shirt. "Alphie, aren't you a little old for this? What are you? Seventeen?" Assured Gina had a shell or two, Grandpa released his grip.

Alphie's knees smacked the ground. "I'll get even," he muttered.

The odor of spent shells lingered. "Where's Poppa going?" Alicia asked.

Poppa walked fast, almost running to his car, and drove away; gravel sputtered in his wake. Now that she thought of it, his medal hadn't been visible on his uniform, and his hands shook as he'd held the rifle before the twenty-one-gun salute.

"Let's go show Johan my medal," Gina said. She tugged her sister's hand to the family burial plot. Along the way, Alicia caught a glimpse of Clara leaving the cemetery through the north gate. At Johan's tree, Alicia unpinned the paper medal. Gina placed it beside the small American flag and Clara's bouquet of flowers. Facing the tree, she saluted just like the veterans. "You were right. Uncle Johan does like my medal better 'cause I made it myself."

"I'm sure he does," Slick said.

Startled, Alicia jumped.

Gina dropped her shell casings. "Uncle Johan! I … I mean Slick." She tilted her head back and forth. "You look different."

A blue suit and tie replaced the mechanics uniform Slick wore to work at Poppa's Tire and Auto Repair Shop. "Didn't mean to scare you, Alicia. Hi, Squirt." Slick handed Gina the dropped shell casings. His smile remained, but his blue eyes looked sad. "Way too many graveside flags for a town this size." Slick touched the tip of Johan's tree. "So this is his memorial tree."

"How come you call me Squirt like Uncle Johan?"

"'Cause you are a Squirt." He lifted and swung Gina around, nearly bumping into Grandpa and their neighbor, Bill Watson, approaching on his blind side. "Sorry." Slick lowered Gina to the ground and shook Grandpa's hand. "Anton." Slick nodded towards Bill's cane. "Bill, your leg bothering you again?"

"No, just probing for gopher holes." As Bill smiled, the dimple on his chin deepened like the movie star Kirk

Douglas's, except Bill's cheeks were ruddy from the sun and probably the bald spot on top of his head was, too. The girls knew Bill, "Crazy Legs" Watson, had been a star running back for the University of Minnesota Gophers until he broke his leg, which never healed properly. Grandpa warned them to *never* mention it.

"Is that your crazy leg?" Gina asked, standing slightly behind Alicia and peeking around her.

Grandpa shook his head. "Tsk, tsk." He hid a smile behind his hand. "I wondered how long it would take Gina to ask."

Bill laughed and danced a little jig.

Gina's laughter bubbled with the warmth of a spring morning as she imitated Bill's dance.

"Alicia," Bill said, "I came to tell you Donna is filling in at the hospital for a nurse whose brother just got mustered out, but don't worry; she won't miss your party."

Alicia had no plans to worry about some dumb birthday party with a bunch of old people. Her friends avoided her house like it was quarantined with measles because of Poppa's anger.

"Anton," Slick said, "Ilse is waiting in your car. I think … she's worried … Ed … "

Grandpa sighed. "Come on girls. Me and Ilse got a lot to do before the big shindig." He, Bill, and the girls left for the car, but Slick stayed behind.

Grandpa slid into the driver's seat of his car. "Ilse, we'll see if we can find him." Gina clutched her shell casings and slid to Alicia as they drove the streets of Fullerton in silence. The second time they drove home, Poppa's car was parked in front of the car shed.

"At least he came home. This time," Grandpa said. "He has restlessness about him like an old dog pacing the yard to stay ahead of the pain in his belly. I'll try to reason with him. No sense his ruining the birthday party."

Inside the kitchen, Poppa, no longer in uniform, was dressed in his mechanics coveralls and seated in his usual chair beside the radiator. The Silver Star was nowhere in sight. Alicia's empty stomach argued with her desire to get away from Poppa's recognizable simmering anger. He turned his package of Lucky Strike cigarettes upside down and tamped one out. Only the fizz of the striking match made a sound. "What's Ilse doing? I hear her talking to Bill."

"Gina and I are coming inside," Momma called from the porch. "Alicia, look at this beautiful cake." She carried an angel food cake with eleven candles stuck into the swirled white frosting. "From Donna. Bill just brought it over. She must've saved her sugar ration coupons to make this. I'm lucky to have her for a friend."

"What did you and Bill talk about?" Poppa asked. "Are you going behind my back? Does he want you going back to work for him? With the baby coming … that discussion is finished."

Like every time they argued since Poppa had insisted Momma quit her job as bookkeeper for Bill's store, Alicia pretended not to hear. Momma placed the cake on the counter top, gripped its edge, and looked out the window. Away from Poppa.

Gina's eyes darted from Momma to Poppa, and Alicia detected a new wariness in them.

"I got two shells, and nobody is happy," Gina said.

"Well, I'm happy for you." Poppa bolted out of his chair, took Gina's hand, and led her out of the kitchen.

Alicia wanted to go to Momma, to say the right thing, to remove the sadness that covered her like a shroud. Unable to help, she looked to Grandpa.

"Ilse," he said, "Ed just needs some more time. It's a big adjustment coming back home. Days like today are filled with memories. Good and bad. Come, let's sit outside a bit. Enjoy spring before it's gone."

3

The afternoon hours seemed like days. Gina buzzed in and out of their bedroom like an annoying fly. "I stuck my finger in the frosting on your cake. It's yummy. Why can't Clara come to your party? She was here last year. Is Slick coming?"

Alicia told her sister to go away.

She was five pages into *The Bobbsey Twins Treasure Hunting* when Gina came back, her eyes dancing. "I know a secret from you."

"I don't care." Alicia raised her book to ignore Gina, who again went away, but her mind drifted back to the bicycle she had so desperately wanted for her birthday. The Schwinn bicycle in the Gambles Store window: red with white pin striping—the one actress Jane Wyman was holding in the magazine. Her dream had burst like a soap bubble when she overheard Momma and Poppa talking about money. Again. Today, she only wanted to survive the birthday party without showing too much disappointment.

The porch screen door creaked, and Momma's and Gina's voices called to her, along with the smell of roasting, clove-studded ham that wafted through the floor opening around the radiator pipe. With a sigh, she closed the book and put on her new blue dress.

"There you are." Momma's cheeks were flushed, and her eyes smiled for the first time in a long time. "Let's go outside and see your birthday present."

"Outside?" Behind her back, Alicia crossed her fingers for luck.

"Yes, outside." Momma said.

Linked hand in hand, Gina led Momma and Alicia through the porch to the top cement step where Momma called to Poppa. Gina bounced up and down. When a bicycle wheel protruded from the open car shed door, Alicia jumped down the steps and raced to the sidewalk's end. She stopped short when she saw the bicycle: old, painted black—not a brand new shiny red Schwinn.

I should've known better than to make a silly wish on the first star.

"Come and see your birthday present." Poppa pushed the bicycle up the lawn towards Alicia. "Ain't she a beauty? I bought it at Graffie's Trading Post and fixed it up for my girl. Look ... new pedals, shiny new black paint. I cleaned up the chrome handlebars, too." He offered the bicycle to her. A smile filled Poppa's face—a real one.

Disappointment swirled in Alicia's stomach and reached the back of her throat with a biting sour taste.

No bicycle *would've been better.*

She held her hands back as if the metal would burn if she touched it. She wanted to turn away, but Poppa's smile kept her in place. Momma stepped between them and took the bicycle from Poppa. "Good as new. You like it, don't you?" Her eyes connected with her daughter's. "So close to the War, new ones are hard to come by and they cost so much ..."

Grandpa stepped away from the house, approached Momma's side, and eased the bicycle from her hands. Quietly, he said, "Take it for a spin. I'll help you get started. You don't want your Poppa to think you don't appreciate his present, do you?"

Sometimes Grandpa seemed to know what she was thinking, and today, she didn't like it.

"Thanks, Poppa." They were the only words she dared let slip her tongue.

Grandpa wheeled the bicycle across the grass to the driveway and steadied it. Alicia climbed on and put her feet on the pedals. Wobbling and weaving, she rode down the driveway, gripping the handlebars for dear life, determined to ride in spite of tears of disappointment that dampened her cheeks and blurred her vision. She steered to the grassy side of rain-deepened ruts on the graveled Depot Road until she reached the corner where the old hotel—home for retired Great Northern train men—met the tarred road. There, she turned, relieved to be out of ruts and gravel. More confident of her ability, she rode along Main Street, deserted except for two cars parked outside Hugo's Pool Hall.

The afternoon sun beat against the closed green shades of Bill's Mercantile. Across the street, two brown and white dogs ran up the steps into the shaded band shell in an otherwise empty park. Gaining speed, Alicia cruised by the Cozy Café, the Farmers State bank—guarded by a concrete eagle—and around the corner. She zipped onto Center Street past Sorenson's Hardware, flanked by Agnes's Dress Shoppe and Poppa's Tire and Auto Repair Shop. Only the green and white Quaker State Oil sign remained outside the two closed bay doors of Poppa's shop. She rode in and out of the shade of the elm canopy that seemed to be holding hands over the street. Exhilarated, she pedaled faster. The breeze lifted her hair, and curls swirled around her face. Her heart raced in her chest. Nothing existed or mattered—just the ride.

"Hey, brat," Alphie yelled. "Where'd you get that old bicycle? The dump?"

His brown plaid shirt was half-hidden in the shadow of evergreen trees that shaded the church yard. Cigarette in hand, he waved.

The bicycle tilted towards the tarred street. Alicia jerked the handlebars, over-corrected, tipped, and slammed into the graveled shoulder. She ended up wedged under the back tire. Mockingly, the pedals and front tire continued spinning.

Alphie sauntered across the street—his black hair slicked back, his beady eyes laughing.

He wants to make sure I'm hurt.

"I guess I got my revenge for the shells," he said.

Alicia bunched up her face, determined not to cry in spite of the pain. "If Slick or Clara were here, you wouldn't dare to do this."

With an exaggerated effort, he looked around. "They ain't here now, are they? How 'bout you fighting your own battles?" He tossed the lit cigarette and strolled away.

Tiny rosebuds of blood bloomed on her scraped arm—elbow to wrist. She pulled herself to her knees, the pebbles biting into skin. Upright, she straddled the bicycle to determine the damage: handlebars were twisted right of center, rust dotted the metal fender where black paint had been scratched off, and the right pedal was bent. Her left shoulder ached as she pushed the bicycle towards home. A piece of her dress hem was caught in the chain and churned in rhythm with the worry in her head.

What is Poppa going to say?

Poppa and Momma were sitting on the shaded lawn bench. Alicia swallowed hard and pushed the bicycle to them. "You're hurt," Momma said. "Let me help …"

Poppa put his arm across Momma's chest. "Sit still, Ilse. She's a big girl." With two steps, he reached her. With his back to Momma, he grabbed the bicycle from her grasp and let it fall to the grass. He leaned close to her ear. "You clumsy oaf. I worked hard on this." Poppa drew his head back and stared at his daughter. "Did you do this on purpose?"

Alicia had no idea of what to say or do. She blinked back tears.

"Get in the house!"

Upstairs in the bathroom, Alicia felt the sting of Poppa's accusations more than the scrapes and bruises.

How can he think that about me?

She tossed her ruined birthday dress down the clothes chute and went into her closet to find something to wear to her party. The only dress, ironed and on a hanger, was last year's church dress that she hated—orange like the mercurochrome streaks on her knees and arms. She wished to shrink into a corner. But … she slowly descended the stairs.

"Poppa?"

He jerked forward in Grandpa's rocking chair. "Son of a bitch! How many damned times have I told you not to sneak up on me?"

His face was so white that his dark blue eyes looked like holes in his head. Locked in place as if her shoes were nailed to the rug, Alicia waited.

"I fixed the bicycle. If you're going to ride, there are rules. *My* rules, and they are iron-clad."

She let her breath escape; at least she still had a bicycle to ride, and she could deal with Poppa's rules.

"Number one." He held up his clenched fist and raised a finger. "Ride only when you've finished your duties."

Duties?

Baffled, she leaned closer as if better hearing might provide better understanding.

A second finger. "Stand up straight when I'm talking to you. Gina's your responsibility for the summer. School's over, and your Momma needs help with the baby coming soon."

A third finger. "You can wear dungarees only when you're riding or working with Anton in the garden. Otherwise, I want you looking like a young lady. I want none of that Rosie the Riveter stuff in my family."

With each raised finger, Poppa's voice had become harsher, steel-driven. The too-tight sleeves of Alicia's dress rubbed against her scraped arm, but she stood straight as a board.

The fourth finger. "Number four. Stay in Fullerton. No crossing the railroad tracks, no crossing the highway, and no riding out to Clara's farm behind my back."

Alicia had harbored a hope—however small—that somehow the bicycle meant she could ride to see Clara. The room grew smaller; she felt as trapped as if she'd been locked in the front hall closet—the one with the inside doorknob missing.

He paused. "Oh, yes," he said. "Number five. Never lie to me again." He turned up the radio volume, and a curtain of noise fell between Poppa and daughter.

"Yoohoo," a woman called. "Somebody open the door for me. My hands are full."

Relieved, Alicia dashed into the kitchen and pushed the screen door open. Sarah Olson came inside, bending forward as if butting a strong head wind. Hairs slipping from her graying bun created parenthesis beside her wide smile. When she stood, she was taller than everyone except Grandpa. "There's the birthday girl! I made your favorite JELL-O. Lime green with carrots and shredded cabbage and a dollop of mayonnaise—just like the party last October, when your Poppa came home from the War."

Alicia grasped the edges of the glass cake pan. A tremor passed through her. Memory jolted her back to that day: Poppa's homecoming party. It seemed a lifetime ago, or, perhaps, the life of another person.

Poppa had returned the night before Halloween 1945. That night, Sarah had placed a similar pan of JELL-O on Momma's dining room table, set with good dishes, gleaming silverware, and a sour cream raisin pie—Poppa's favorite—served as centerpiece. "I thought Ilse and Ed would be here by now." She looked around, disappointed. "Clinton, Iowa, isn't that far, for goodness sake. Joe will be by later. He's lost his glasses again. I swear that husband of mine would lose his head if it wasn't attached."

Grandpa had smiled as he checked his pocket watch. "They'll be here any minute now, I figure. Gina, careful of the stove. I don't want you burning yourself." All afternoon, anticipation—like Gina—danced around the kitchen as friends and neighbors brought food to celebrate Poppa's safe return from the War. Mason jars of Grandpa's dandelion wine were dusted, opened, and ready for a toast.

Alicia caught the whirling dervish that was her sister. "We're going outside to wait for Momma and Poppa before you break something and get in trouble with Grandpa. Clara, you coming, too?"

Outside, the musky smell of fall filled the air, and the scent of burning leaves drifted to the girls. A few leaves still clung to branches that glistened golden in the fading sunlight. Dirt beneath the tire swing swirled up into small dust devils as Alicia and Clara took turns pushing Gina. Her small hands wrapped around the thick rope.

"Poppa made this swing for me when—"

"I know, I know." Gina rolled her eyes. "When you were seven like me. Do you have to tell that story so many times?" Gina slowed the swing with the tips of her shoes and looked up at her sister. "I'm not 'posed to interrupt. Sorry." Her face brightened. "But can you 'member me about Poppa one more time?"

The truth was Alicia mostly remembered what Poppa looked like from his and Momma's wedding picture: long, curly, dark hair that slipped across his forehead, eyes that smiled right out of the photograph, and an arm around Momma's shoulders, holding her so tight she tilted towards him. She barely remembered Poppa's big hands, which swallowed hers like oversize mittens, and falling asleep to his stories. All these details she had told Gina over and over. "He's like a big teddy bear," she said at last.

Clara had retreated to the iron lawn bench and, with her back to the fading sun, a halo had formed around her long chestnut-colored hair. Clara's posture was rigid, and suddenly, the air seemed to go out of her.

"Gina, swing by yourself for a while." Alicia sat down beside Clara. Both of Clara's eyes, one brown, one blue, conveyed a message Alicia couldn't comprehend. "Are you all right?"

The sun fell deeper into the horizon before Clara spoke. Her voice sounded far away. "I saw Johan last night—maybe it was a dream—but it felt so real." The wind held its breath, waiting for Clara to speak. "He was wearing his blue Navy dress uniform." She reached deep into her pocket for a small framed picture. "This one." She pushed a strand of hair behind her ear. "He told me he is afraid for you—for your family." A flock of blackbirds flew out of the tree overhead, momentarily darkening the sky. "Johan said he's coming to help you."

Like what I saw that Christmas Eve?

Alicia dismissed the thought as quickly as it entered her mind and focused on Clara, who appeared so determined, so full of belief in what she said, that a growing panic seized Alicia. Momma and Grandpa had worried, still worried, that Clara would never recover from Johan's death. Alicia's hand covered Clara's. "You don't need to worry. Poppa's home now, and everything will be fine."

"Alicia. Clara," Gina shouted. "Momma and Poppa!"

A cloud of dust followed Grandpa's 1936 Chevy down Depot Road. In the driver's seat, Poppa honked the horn and flashed the headlights. Gina slid the toes of her shoes in the dirt, stopped the swing, and bolted to the driveway's edge.

"I'll go tell everyone they're home." Clara disappeared into the shadows of the wild plum trees, dry twigs crackling underfoot.

Momma opened the passenger door and floated from the car. Her cheeks glowed in the low-slung sun, and golden streaks glistened in her hair. Momma had never seemed prettier or happier. She smiled at her daughters.

Poppa picked up Gina, put his Army hat on her head, and twirled her around. "You're beautiful, Gina. Just like your Momma. Alicia, come over here. Let me see you, too." He crouched down and put Gina on his knee.

Alicia didn't recognize the man who called her. Confused for a moment, she approached Poppa with butterflies in her stomach. "Your hair is gone," she said, remembering his wedding picture.

"Hair grows back." Poppa laughed a deep, happy laugh. "I'm the same old Poppa." He took her hand. "You're going to be tall like Anton and beautiful like your Momma."

A warm blush settled on Alicia's cheeks. "You're home, Poppa. Really home."

"Doesn't anybody want Poppa's party?" Gina asked. "It's a surprise, Poppa, and besides, I'm hungry." She led the way up the lawn, past two smiling jack-o-lanterns on the concrete steps, and past Grandpa, holding the porch screen door open.

Behind Gina, Poppa stopped to shake Grandpa's hand. "Anton, you old dog. How the hell are you?"

"Poppa," Gina whispered loudly, "nobody swears in Grandpa's house."

"Glad to see *you* made it home," Grandpa said.

Alicia watched from the bottom step. There was a chill between Grandpa and Poppa that Alicia didn't remember.

The smile slid off Poppa's face as if he had been struck. "Jesus, Anton, I'm sorry. I wasn't thinking. I was sorry to hear about Johan. He was a good man."

"Coming through. Hot, hot dish." Donna, Bill's wife, set the speckled blue roaster on the stove. Without her nurse uniform, Donna was tiny, delicate like her collection of porcelain birds perched all over her house, but "prairie strong," Grandpa said. Donna reached up, firmly grasped Poppa by his arms, and stood back as if examining him. "Ed, you're looking good," she said. "Bet you're hungry for my famous tuna hot dish."

"I'll eat anything not a C-ration," Poppa said. He shook Bill's hand. "I'm thinking about buying Gus Peterson's repair shop. Ilse wrote me that he closed up after he lost Jack on Iwo Jima."

"No business talk tonight," Sarah insisted from the dining room doorway.

"As bossy as ever, I see," Poppa teased. "You still have all those mangy cats?"

"Well, Ed, I can see you haven't changed either," Sarah said with a laugh. "It's good to have you home." She wrapped her arm around Poppa's shoulder, led him out of the kitchen, and ushered him through a small crowd of friends and neighbors into the dining room. She returned with a smile on her face and a tray of empty dandelion wine glasses.

When Clara returned, she carried a depression cake from Mrs. Oldenburg, a Gold Star Mother, who wasn't up to coming to the celebration. Before the War, her son, Will, and Johan had grown up together, best friends—had enlisted at the same time, and had perished on the same ship. Sarah took the cake from Clara. "This must be a hard night for her. As well as for Anton. And you." Sarah's arm encircled Clara's shoulder. "Ilse is playing the piano. You girls, shoo. Anton and I can handle everything in the kitchen."

"That's 'People Will Say We're in Love,'" Alicia said. "Momma played it when she was really missing Poppa … and now she's playing for him."

Alicia and Clara stood in the doorway between the kitchen and dining room. Alicia surveyed the party: Gina's WLCOME HOME POPPA banner hung from the built-in buffet door knobs, bowls of Poppa's favorite food covered the table, and people sat on chairs that lined walls of both living room and dining room or stood behind Momma at the piano. Laughter and clinking glasses punctuated the music. Poppa waltzed a smiling Gina around the dining table to Alicia and Clara. He stopped abruptly, stumbled, and nearly dropped Gina. His face was white, his jaw set hard. "You!" He pointed at Clara. "No, it can't be … how?"

"Momma! Poppa's squeezing me too tight."

Momma raced to the doorway, unwound Poppa's arms from Gina, and eased her into Grandpa's arms. "Ed? You remember Clara Benson, don't you? She and Johan were engaged."

Poppa looked puzzled and shook his head as if fighting to clear his mind. "Clara?"

Momma wrapped her arm around Poppa's waist, led him to the piano bench, patted the seat next to her, and repeated the song. Donna joined them, put her hands on Poppa's shoulders, and sang. The crystal notes floated around the room, and the gift of speech returned.

The heavy stomp of Poppa's work boots jolted Alicia back to the present—her birthday party. The green JELL-O in the pan quivered. Poppa hovered in the doorway. "The War's best forgotten," he said. The spring sun still shined outside, but inside, a chill swept the room.

4

Alicia pedaled her bicycle in slow, easy figure eights from Poppa's car shed to Depot Road, in and out of shadows of powder puff clouds.

"Alicia, you're making me dizzy." Grandpa lifted his straw hat and mopped his brow with his blue handkerchief. "Stop riding in circles like some lost baby robin."

She laid her bicycle beneath an elm and walked down a seemingly endless row of flowering peas to him.

"What's the matter?" he asked.

"I feel like a bug trapped in a glass jar. Riding round and round Fullerton." Careful not to speak up, she mumbled, "I wanted a bicycle to get away. Not this." She tugged at her starched blouse collar that chafed like Poppa's rules.

Has it only been a week?

Grandpa placed both hands on the top of his hoe, as if studying her. "Assuming that jar didn't have a lid, where would you go?"

The truth buzzed around like the gnats Grandpa swiped away with his hat. "Clara's farm, Grandpa. I miss her."

"So do I. Give it a while. Ed used to be a fair man. Let him get over whatever it is about Clara that bothers him. In the meantime, tell you what …" He reached into his pocket. "Here's a half dollar." He handed her a radish-filled colander. "Why don't you take Gina to Graffie's Trading Post and get me a packet of pumpkin seeds; last year's molded. You can have a bottle of pop with the change." He smiled. "Clara's working today."

Gina sat at the kitchen table with Sarah who grabbed a radish, rubbed the dirt from it, and popped it into her mouth. "I was just leaving. Ilse's resting. Oh, this radish is sweet. Anton's a magician with that garden. What are you up to now?"

Alicia was barely done explaining before Gina had raced out of the kitchen and retuned with her Rainbow Tablet and her pencil with the well-chewed eraser lodged behind her ear. She whispered to her sister behind an open hand. "You never know when you might see a new license plate."

On the hot, half-mile walk to Graffie's, mirages rippled across U.S. Highway 16, suggesting lakes that appeared and disappeared before their eyes. On the other side of the highway, a graveled county road paralleled the town dump and county gravel pile. A mile beyond, the old road crossed over Cutters Creek, and eventually, after another mile, ended at a T, crossing in front of the farm where Clara, Alphie, and their folks lived. The girls continued walking along the highway shoulder, pausing for a moment in the shade of the railroad bridge. A lonely whistle of a freight train lingered and faded as if it had never been there. Ahead, Graffie's Trading Post was on the right side of the highway.

A weathered, fake log building anchored the highway next to a tall rusted pole and a sign—GRAFFIE'S TRADING POST—hung by one side and had hung that way for as long as Alicia remembered. Burlap sacks with faded chicken feed logos covered unused gas pumps. A car made a right turn out of the parking lot.

Gina pointed after it. "Another state for us. I was right! What is it? What is it?"

"Texas."

"Tex-as." Gina tried it on for size.

"I'll spell it for you inside," Alicia assured her sister.

Beneath a faded, green and white striped awning, the trading post screen door hinges squeaked. They stepped inside. Alicia waited for her eyes to adjust from the brilliant sun to the dimly lit store. A black fan attached to the metal stamped ceiling rattled as it lazily moved the stale, cigar-smelling air. Horizontal boards secured axes, scythes, hoes, rakes, and shovels—both garden and snow—to the wall between the doorway and the cash register. Long aisles of scarred, wooden tables held a jumble of items—hammers, screwdrivers, pliers, used toasters, mismatched dishes and silverware, an oil lamp, and antique sepia photographs of persons unknown. All their orange tags had prices lined out and cheaper ones scribbled beneath. Seed packets were scattered about. Guns mounted on a knotty pine wall behind the cash register stood guard, and knives were locked in the glass counter.

Alicia set the pumpkin seed package on the glass counter, yellowed with age. An enticing jar of penny candy—root beer barrels, licorice sticks, jawbreakers, and wax guns filled with sweet, orange liquid—stood next to the register. "Mr. Graffie?" She spun the half dollar around on its edge so the landing would clatter on the glass. When that didn't attract any attention, she raised her voice to the drawn curtain dividing the trading post from his living space. "Mr. Graffie. I want to buy seeds for Grandpa and a Coca-Cola for me and an Orange Crush for Gina."

Graffie parted the curtains and ducked his head to pass through. He was a big man with a big voice to match. Gina used to think he was the giant in *Jack and the Beanstalk*. A gentle giant, but not without his faults—he liked to know everybody's business and wasn't afraid to pass on information if it suited him—according to Grandpa.

"I thought Anton saved seeds from year to year. Is your Grandpa all right?" Graffie asked.

She nodded.

"Darndest thing. I thought I heard him talking to Johan when I delivered rabbit fencing yesterday. He was in the shadow of those wild plum trees he grows, so I wasn't sure if I heard right." The cigar in the corner of his mouth bobbed as he talked. "How do you like your bicycle? I gave your Poppa a good deal."

"I like it fine." She wasn't about to tell Mr. Graffie that Grandpa sometimes talked to Johan as if he were alive and standing next to him. "Can I please have the bottles of pop? We can't stay long. Uh, Grandpa needs the seeds."

Graffie popped the caps and slid the bottles dripping with icy water across the counter. Alicia hooked the bottlenecks between her fingers, grasped the seed packet in the other hand, and wove her way through the maze of black metal tables and chairs in the café side of the trading post to the wooden booths.

Gina, standing, was barely visible over the tall booth. Slick towered behind her, sipping on a cold Coca-Cola of his own.

"Alicia, Slick told me Alphie tried to steal some cigarettes, and Graffie kicked him out for a week." She reached for the Orange Crush and sat down. "Clara was here, and she said to stay."

Alicia scooted next to Gina. "Slick, did Poppa go home? Is that why you're here?" She hoped she kept worry from her voice. Her bicycle was home, but Poppa might come looking for her and catch her with Clara. She rubbed her finger over a carving on the wooden table: ED AND ILSE—FOREVER.

"Nah. He went to Marshall to get a fan. Graffie didn't have one. The shop is like an oven. He'd cleaned up some oil spills with gasoline, but the smell was so strong, I cleared out." Slick cracked his knuckles. "Won't do any good to warn him. He says he's not in the Army anymore, and he's not taking orders from some snot-nose kid."

"Your nose was snotty the first time I saw you," Gina said.

Alicia rolled her eyes.

"Remember? Me and Alicia were trick 'n' treating and you were all covered with snow. I thought you were Johan's ghost." She whispered the last sentence.

Last Halloween, the day after Poppa's homecoming party, an early blizzard had smashed into southwestern Minnesota and dropped three feet of snow on Fullerton and the logs for the Halloween weenie roast. Trick or treat was cancelled, but Momma still bundled the girls in winter coats over their matching black witch costumes with instruction to only stop at Donna's and Sarah's houses. As usual, they first went to Donna and Bill's house. Not all of the streetlights were on when they high-stepped through deep drifts from Donna's to Sarah's. Since it was Halloween, after all, Alicia wanted to scare Gina a little bit, so she made a creepy owl sound just as a black cat streaked across the street.

Gina screamed.

"It's only Whiskers—Sarah's cat." Alicia quickly reassured Gina. And herself.

Next door to Sarah's house, a streetlight flickered, lighting up a dark car beneath it that had its back half wedged in a huge drift. A tall, coatless, snow-covered figure leaned against the car.

"Let's get out of here," Alicia said.

"No. I want to go to Sarah's house for more trick 'n' treat candy."

Alicia tugged Gina's sleeve. "C'mon."

Gina held back, resisting. Her feet slipped, throwing her backwards into a snow bank. "Ow."

The tall, snow-covered figure, a man, walked towards them. "Can I help?" he asked.

"No," Alicia said. "We can take care of ourselves. Who are you, and what are you doing out in a snowstorm?"

"My name is Slick, and I need a job. I heard a man called Ed Drake needed help in his car repair shop."

"That's our Poppa," Gina said.

"Then I guess I found what I was looking for." He'd lifted Gina over his shoulder like a fireman. "Lead the way," he'd said.

Gina took a long sip from her Orange Crush. "And I didn't get my candy either. But I'm glad it was you."

"Me, too, Gina," Alicia said.

She'd only known Slick since he'd started working for Poppa last November, but there had been something familiar about him from the very first.

Graffie's back door squeaked open. Golden sunlight framed Clara until the door swung shut and she disappeared from sight. Near-darkness again filled the café. A moment later, she glided to their booth, slid in beside Slick, and placed a blue velvet box on the table. "For your birthday, Alicia." The look in Clara's eyes told Alicia how much she had missed the birthday party.

Gina leaned close to the box.

Alicia lifted the top; inside was a folded white handkerchief, delicately crocheted with white lace and embroidered in blue: FRIEND. Alicia cradled it in her hand, surprised at its weight. "It's so beautiful, Clara, thank you."

"Wait. There's more," Slick said.

Carefully, Alicia unfolded the handkerchief and revealed a silver necklace cradled in the folds.

My first piece of real jewelry.

"That's from Johan. And me," Clara said.

Alicia glanced up.

"It came the Christmas he was lost at sea," Clara said. Tears floated in her eyes. "His letter said I'd know when to give it to you. Take it out. It's a Celtic cross. I think the closed knot means family and love. At least it would to Johan. Here, let me." She reached for the necklace, opened the clasp, and draped the cross around Alicia's neck.

Alicia pressed her hand over the cross for a moment. She felt warmth encased in a sweet feeling of being held close, being rocked, being safe. She slipped it under her blouse, knowing not to let Poppa see it, but she couldn't have explained why. "I'll treasure this forever."

Clara and Slick passed smiles back and forth. He spoke, but his words were lost in Gina's words.

"Clara, can me and Alicia come out to your farm and build a castle? Like last summer? It's magic, Slick." Gina's eyes widened, matching her smile. "It had big, big walls made of stone." She gestured, nearly knocking the bottle of Orange Crush off the table. "And a ballroom and fancy dishes and furniture *and* even a special room to feed Clara's royal kittens. It was fun, and Alicia played with me all the time. Now, Alicia says we can't go this year." Gina's smile left her face.

Alicia sometimes wished for the times she had spent at the castle, too. Neither Momma nor Grandpa had explained to Gina why Poppa had forbidden them to be around Clara. If Gina knew what Alicia believed to be the reason, her sister's sense of fairness would lead her to say something to Poppa, and that might bring Poppa's anger down on Gina. So far, he left Gina alone or used her as an example of how much he could love an obedient daughter. With Gina sad about missing the castle times, the burden of guilt rested heavily on Alicia's shoulders.

Slick seemed to sense the growing sadness lurking over the booth. "Squirt, what's in that tablet you always have?"

"Can I tell them … please?"

Alicia smiled and nodded.

Gina opened the Rainbow Tablet and gave Slick the list of six state license plates: Minnesota, Iowa, South Dakota, Kansas, Illinois, and Wisconsin. "Alicia and me go to Joe's gas station and talk to him. You know he tells stories 'bout the olden days? He's older than Grandpa," Gina added. "His hair is as white as the white crown on his gas pump. Not the red one; that's for Grandpa. Anyways, we wait for a car from a new state, then we write it down, but we don't tell Joe 'cause it's our sister secret." Gina looked dismayed as if having second thoughts. "I guess it's your secret now, too." She looked from Slick to Clara and back. "Can you keep a secret?"

"Don't worry," Slick said. "Your secret is safe with us."

"Okay. Can you spell Texas for me? I'm only going to be in second grade."

"Got your pencil? T … E … X … A … S."

Graffie's one-winged, crazy cuckoo popped out of the clock, bouncing while he cuckooed thirteen times—always the same number, no matter the hour.

Maybe it's time to leave.

Grandpa entered the trading post from the back door, shielding his eyes and hurrying to their booth.

Uh oh.

Clara scooted closer to Slick to make room, but Grandpa remained standing.

"Clara, Slick." He nodded a greeting. "Alicia, your Poppa's back in town. You girls get in my car before he sees you with Clara. Slick, I'd like a word with you."

When Alicia reached the door, she remembered the pumpkin seed packet was still on the table, so she ran to get it. She saw it in Grandpa's hand but paused when she heard Grandpa ask, "Is Ed acting strange at work?"

Grandpa must have seen her because he held a hand up to Slick and turned to his granddaughter. "Skedaddle," he said.

5

The next day brought no relief from the heat. The June sun climbed to the middle of the sky over Grandpa's garden. He was on his knees beside his newly planted pumpkin patch.

"Phew, it's sweltering." The underarms of his blue shirt were ringed dark with sweat. "Glad we're done for the day. Give me a hand, Alicia."

She took his calloused hand and helped him stand.

He swiped a mosquito from his neck. "Why don't you pick some strawberries for dinner? We got a bumper crop."

"Okay, Grandpa." She walked past her bicycle leaning against the red barn now being used for a car shed. On the west side of the shed, horseradish plants surrounded the strawberry patch like sentinels. Plump, red, juicy berries glistened in the sun.

Alicia's colander was nearly full when she heard the rumble of Slick's jalopy in the driveway. She ran to the corner but slowed when she saw Poppa in the passenger seat. She waited until he went inside the house and then cut kitty-corner across the grass to intercept Slick on his way back to his car. "I need to ask a favor," she said.

"Sure thing, but let me help." At the outside faucet, he turned the handle so a gentle stream of water poured over the colander. "What is it?" He scooped some wet berries, popped them into his mouth, and wiped the red juice from his chin with the back of his hand. "They're good."

Alicia tried to be patient but was afraid of being overheard through the open dining window above the faucet.

"Can you get a message to Clara? I hate that her folks don't have a telephone yet."

"Did something happen?"

"Yesterday when I got home from Graffie's, Momma was at the kitchen table, crying." Alicia's shoulders drooped. "She never used to cry, but now … Anyway, she had empty, dusty jelly jars lined up in front of her. She said strawberry jam is the only thing that will get her through the long Minnesota winter, and she's been saving rationed sugar, and she's afraid the strawberries will all die on the vine." Alicia steadied herself, pushing back the sadness and anger roiling in her stomach. "Slick, Momma looked so sad. I told her I could help her like Clara used to do, but she said I'm too young for the boiling water and hot sealing wax. I'm not." A note of defiance laced her last words. "I hate it when I can help but everybody treats me like a baby."

"Shh," Slick said. He tilted his head towards the sidewalk corner. Off to Alicia's side, not twenty feet away, Poppa stood, arms locked across his chest.

"If you haven't washed the taste off those strawberries, get them inside. Seems there's no hot meal. Don't know why there can't be a decent meal for a working man." He did an about face and disappeared around the corner. The slamming of the screen door reverberated across the yard.

Unconsciously, Alicia rubbed her wrist. The pain was gone, but the memory lingered like a nightmare.

Slick's hand on her shoulder turned her back to face him. "Alicia, Ed's having a hard time now, but Clara and me are here to help you. I'll go talk to her Ma and see what can be done to help Ilse." He frowned. "Are you all right?"

Alicia nodded, unwilling to speak. She watched him walk to his car and drive away, wishing that she, too, could leave.

"Get in here. What's taking you so damned long?" Poppa yelled through the open dining room window.

Alicia hurried through the porch, into the kitchen and set the colander of dripping berries in the sink. Grandpa sliced cold meatloaf with a butcher knife. The kitchen smelled of onions and potatoes frying in bacon grease. Poppa sat in his chair with a fork in one hand and a knife in the other, ready to attack his empty plate. Across the table, Momma snuffed her cigarette in the full ashtray. Gina's head swiveled back and forth between them.

"Wash up, Alicia," Grandpa said. "Get the milk bottle from the refrigerator and sit up."

With the lightest of footfalls, she obeyed.

Momma sipped her coffee and set the cup down. It rattled against the saucer. "Ed, when are you going to understand that I'm not like one of those women in the *Ladies Home Journal*? I never was, and I don't want to be. I want my life … I mean my job back. After the baby's born. I don't understand … I liked working, and you never minded when Pa owned the store before his heart attack and Bill bought it and I kept Bill's books until you came home." Momma's hands gripped the sharp edge of the table. "How else would you've had enough money to buy your shop?" She shook her head, rose from the chair, and disappeared into the dining room.

"Hell and damnation!" Poppa yelled. "I want the life back that I had before the War, too. Now who's going to fix that?" He shoved away from the table and followed Momma into the dining room.

Gina's face was the same white color as when she'd cut her palm on Decoration Day. "Momma, Poppa," Gina whispered. Wide-eyed, she looked ready to bolt.

"No, Gina, don't go in there." Grandpa reached across the table and put his hand on his granddaughter's arm. All the air seemed to leave him.

With shouts and muffled cries coming from the living room, just staying in the kitchen wasn't a good idea. "Grandpa, me and Gina are going outside and have a picnic." Alicia wasn't certain he heard.

She turned off the stove burner, scooped fried potatoes and cold meat onto her plate, and doused everything with catsup.

She led a hesitant Gina outside to the bench in the northwest corner of the yard underneath the towering maple. The scent of freshly mowed grass tickled her nose. Alicia sat cross-legged on the bench facing the porch door, and Gina copied her on the opposite end of the bench. The white dinner plate sat between them.

Eating with her fingers, Alicia licked the dripping catsup. "Mmmm. Blood."

Gina dropped her slice of meat.

"No, Gina, I'm sorry. I'm being silly. It's just catsup."

"I know." Gina said, but she examined a piece of catsup-coated meatloaf and wiped almost all of the catsup away with a slice of fried potato.

Alicia set the empty plate aside. Down the hill, Joe, standing between his gas pumps, waved. The girls waved back.

Gina turned on the bench, dropped her legs over the edge, and swung them back and forth. She seemed miles away. "I'm going inside to see Momma." Gina didn't look frightened, just horribly sad.

"Gina, wait." Alicia took off her right shoe and anklet to retrieve the shiny buffalo head nickel hidden under the arch of her foot. She held it above Gina's head, just out of reach. "Want to share a Hershey Bar?"

Gina tilted her head and puckered her lips the way she did when Momma said she was behaving like a little imp. "Okay. Ifff we get a plain one."

Alicia groaned for her sister's benefit. "Nope. Changed my mind. Hershey Bar with almonds or nothing." She raised her foot as if to replace the nickel.

Gina placed her hands on her hips and insisted. "Plain." A small smile twitched the corners of her mouth.

"Gina, you look like Momma did before Poppa ..." The rest of the sentence died in her throat. She swallowed hard. "I was just teasing you. Take the nickel. Buy the candy bar you want." Gina ran down the hill.

But the image of Gina's sad and confused face as Momma and Poppa argued loomed large, cutting Alicia to the bone.

If only Poppa would let me and Gina go to Clara's farm and build the castle one more time. Or if we could travel back in time when everything used to be so much easier.

Alicia's thoughts swirled around as if buffeted by the warm, westerly wind. No solution came to mind—only one big problem: what Poppa would do if she disobeyed him. She was tempted. What if he didn't find out? She shuddered; the memory of the wrist pain lingered. Alicia knew that she could ride the two miles to the farm and be back before Poppa came home after work.

Is it worth the risk?

Poppa slammed the porch door. Hard. Seemingly enveloped in a fog of anger, he stomped across the lawn, taking the shortcut between the car shed and wild plum trees and disappeared.

Alicia breathed a sigh of relief.

Gina ran up the hill and handed her sister the Hershey Bar—with almonds.

Alicia hugged Gina who felt so small and warm in her arms. Gina was the only thing that hadn't changed since Poppa came home, and Alicia intended to keep it that way. "You can eat all of it. I ate too much blood."

This time, Gina giggled. She took small bites, licked the almonds clean, dropped them on the grass, and licked melted chocolate from her fingers. An aroma of warm chocolate clung to Gina.

If there's a way around Poppa, I'll find it.

Inside the window-shade-darkened house, an oscillating black fan gently circulated warm air around Grandpa, who dozed in his rocker by the silent console radio. Momma slept on the sofa, her knees drawn up to protect the pink baby blanket she clutched to her stomach.

Alicia couldn't leave Gina with both of them sleeping. An idea popped into her head: Momma's best friend. "Let's go visit Donna," she whispered.

"Why?"

"Shh. You're old enough for your first grown-up tea party."

Gina shook her head. "Nope. We're going to Joe's and wait for cars from new states. You promised." Her arms crossed in front of her chest.

And Momma think's I'm stubborn.

A promise was a promise, but if she could convince Gina to change her mind, then she wasn't breaking a promise. Not really. And maybe, just maybe, Clara could find a way for Gina to go to the farm. "When I have tea parties with Donna," Alicia said, painting the best word picture possible, "she lets me pick a bird from her collection and hold it. The red-headed woodpecker is my favorite. Then she fills her very best blue-bird painted plate with cinnamon Cry-Baby cookies, and you drink milky tea from her English tea cups. And if you're very, very careful, you can play her music box."

Alicia faked a worried look. "Maybe you're still too little …"

"I can do it. I can do it."

Grandpa's head lifted, he gave a muffled snort, and his chin went back down, grazing his chest.

Outside, Alicia and Gina followed the path beside Grandpa's garden and crossed the street to Donna's beige stucco house. Budding red rose bushes grew along the porch front, and potted plants the colors of the rainbow flanked the front door.

From the white porch swing, Donna greeted the girls and held up a half-knitted yellow baby sweater. "I hope I finish before the baby comes. It's yellow because we don't know if it's a boy or girl."

Gina climbed onto the swing, picked up the yarn ball, and squeezed. "Poppa ordered a boy from heaven."

Donna sighed. She was still dressed in her white nurse uniform with white hose and shoes.

"Are you going to work?" Alicia asked.

"No. I just got home from the hospital and decided to enjoy the sunshine. Any reason why you're asking? Is Ilse okay?"

"Yes. She and Grandpa are sleeping, and I was wondering … could you and Gina have a tea party? Right now?"

"I'm big enough," Gina said. "Look. There's Missy." She put down the yellow yarn ball and went down the porch steps to capture one of Sarah's cats.

Donna raised one eyebrow and leaned into Alicia. "I take it you have something special to do?" she whispered.

Alicia nodded.

"Well, I guess it's time to teach this young lady the finer points of a tea party." Donna rose from the swing and smoothed the front of her uniform. "Come inside, Gina. I'll take you home after our little party and check on your Momma at the same time. "And you," she pointed her knitting needles at Alicia, "don't do anything foolish."

Alicia waited until Donna closed the door before she darted home, jumped on her bicycle, and scanned the neighborhood for watchful eyes. Seeing only deserted yards and roads, she pedaled from the driveway, turned left onto Depot Road, raced down the hill, across U.S. Highway 16, and onto the graveled county road. Toward Clara's farm.

Alicia's legs pumped hard and fast on the flat road. Fullerton seemed as far away as the sun that warmed her back. She inhaled the sweet clover smell of freedom. Echoes of Poppa's harsh words blew away in the wind. A mile from Fullerton, the flat road gave way to a steep incline down to Cutters Creek bridge that spanned the normally docile water now running high from early May rains. Off her bicycle, she hesitated; riding down this hill in Grandpa's car made her stomach lurch. There were other roads to Clara's farm, but all of them meant backtracking too close to Fullerton.

Determined to finish the ride, she climbed back on her bicycle, inhaled deeply, and tried to pedal slowly, but the bicycle accelerated. Shoes off the pedals, she clutched the handlebars with a vice-like grip. The bicycle sped downward over the wooden plank bridge and halfway up the other side. Fearing a roll back into the bridge or creek, she jumped clear, landed on her knees, stood, checked herself, brushed gravel from her dungarees, picked up the bicycle, and pushed it the rest of the way up the hill.

Next time, I'll ride faster down and make it all the way up the other side.

Tall grasses swayed along the last mile of flat road until Alicia rode straight into the driveway of Clara's family farm. She got off the bicycle and wheeled it past the slowly churning windmill and water trough beside a single light post. Clara's white clapboard house stood a stone's throw from a gray, weathered barn where two black and white Holstein cows chewed grass. A brown and black cow bird mingled with the cattle. Clothes hung on a line connecting the house to a chicken coop. Hens clucked from nests hidden in tall, silvery cottonwoods outlining the backyard. Drawn by the smell of freshly baked bread, Alicia knocked on the screen door.

6

Clara stepped outside onto the stoop and quickly closed the door behind her. "Alicia? What are you doing here?" Worry clouded her face. "Is something wrong at home?"

Alicia shook her head.

Clara studied her. "Does Ed know you're here?"

"I … I'll be home before him," she said with more bravado than she felt. "I came to ask your Ma if she could help Momma with the strawberry jam. And to see our castle."

"Slick was here a bit ago and told us about your Momma and the strawberries. Ma said she'd gladly help for as long as it takes. She and Pa are still grateful for Anton's help the summer that Pa sliced up his leg with the scythe. Graffie closed the Trading Post yesterday for a couple of days and went to an auction of prisoner of war camp equipment up by Ortonville. So I'll be home to help Pa with chores. Alphie's, well … Alphie."

"I remember. That's the first year we built the castle." That summer had been filled with warm, yellow butterfly days under clear, cloudless blue skies. Fluff from the cottonwood trees floated down like summer snow. Loose sheaves of hay gathered from a wagon soon outlined walls that, for Alicia and Gina, morphed into rooms made of rough stone—cool to the touch. Tree canopies formed ceilings. Chips on Blue Willow dishes disappeared when Clara placed them on an apple crate that turned into a gleaming dining room table. Royal cats drank cow's milk from a silver bowl that shined in the dappled sunlight. And one-half of an old rain barrel became a chair for the prince—if he ever came into the ballroom. They had danced across the ballroom floor, dressed in Momma's beautiful, old, sequined dresses and hats with tall, pheasant feathers, to music made by the breeze floating through the leaves.

"The castle? Come with me." Clara led Alicia down a familiar path behind the house into the grove of cottonwoods where the castle had once stood. Today, hay that had outlined tall walls was dried and scattered; splintered wood from the rain barrel littered the grass; strutting roosters replaced the orange, black, and gray barnyard cats; chipped dishes littered the rotten wood well cover. Overhead, two crows circled, cawing.

Motionless as the towering cottonwoods, Alicia blinked, trying to make all of it reappear, but she knew better. The enchanted castle was gone. That part of her life was lost forever. Her future stretched in front of her—vast, shrouded, uncertain, frightening. As if coming out of a fog, she registered Clara's arm around her shoulder and her own hand clasping the Celtic cross.

"If Gina were here, she would see the castle just as you both saw it last year." Clara's voice dropped. "It's wrong for Ed to steal this from Gina." She tilted Alicia's chin to meet her eyes. "But for you—a new beginning. Meet me Monday afternoon by the bridge over Cutters Creek."

"I, I don't know if ..."

"Please try. It's important." Clara vanished into the cottonwood trees, her shadow merging with tree shadows.

Above the graveled county road leading back to Fullerton, a crow took flight from a fence post, soaring into a limitless sky towards a waning sun that had moved too fast, too far. Alicia pedaled harder and harder, gulping air. At the hilltop north of Cutters Creek, she stood level on the pedals, soared down the hill, over the bridge, and all the way up the other side. The bird, now only a black streak across the sky, turned and disappeared. Her legs and chest burned as she raced to beat Poppa home.

She rode into the driveway and crossed the lawn to the faucet, washed tell-tale pebbles and gravel dust from her bicycle, walked to the bench, and plopped down. The maple tree shaded her sunburnt cheeks.

I did it! Poppa doesn't know! Why does Clara want to meet me? Do I dare try again?

Grandpa came around the north side of the house to the bench and leaned his spade against the tree trunk. "Phew," he said. "I thought I was seeing things when I looked out north by the gravel pile. 'My,' I said to myself, 'if I didn't know better, I'd think that was Alicia, hair flying, racing the devil home.' You know anything about that?"

"Grandpa, I rode to Clara's to get help for Momma's canning. Her Ma is coming tomorrow." She looked away, hoping that might stop Grandpa's questioning.

His eyes caught hers and held them. "Slick stopped by earlier and told us. Any other reason you risked making your Poppa mad?"

She couldn't lie, at least not to Grandpa. "I wanted to see Clara and the castle we built. Please don't tell Poppa."

Alicia looked away and then artfully shifted the conversation. "Where is Gina? Is she back from Donna's tea party?"

"She's inside playing the piano with Ilse. Pretty clever method of getting away from your sister. I set a pork roast to cooking. Meat's getting harder to come by. Meat shortage? Not sure the government knows the War is over." Grandpa sat down hard, almost a stumble onto the bench. "He pushes Ilse to cook, but he knows she can't cook a lick. Doesn't have any trouble wolfing my cooking down. Gotta clean up the kitchen." He started to rise, sighed, and sat back down.

"Grandpa, you rest. I'll take care of it." Alicia had never heard Grandpa say anything bad about Poppa. Ever.

Why now?

The smell of roasting meat filled the kitchen. In the sink and on the counter tops were the unwashed noon dishes and all of the cooking kettles. The frying pan was still on the grease-splattered stove. Carrot skins, potato peelings, and onion skins cluttered the cutting board. Empty coffee cups were pushed to the middle of the table. Alicia unhooked the dishpan from its place behind the cellar door, filled it with hot, soapy water, and put cups, plates, saucers, and silverware to soak. Half the kitchen mess was hidden beneath bubbly water. She found a dishrag draped over the faucet and held it under her nose to see if it smelled clean.

She carried the filled ashtray to the galvanized slop pail on the cellar steps but found it filled to the rim with barely room for ashes. Grandpa had forgotten to empty it. She struggled to lift the five-gallon pail, and some liquid spilled. She grabbed one of Momma's dish towels hanging on the cellar door knob and wiped the steps. "Oh no. One of Momma's good ones."

While the dishes soaked, Alicia tossed handfuls of vegetable peels onto another dish towel. She carried them halfway down the cellar steps to the outside door, walked past the coal chute, and threw them into the bramble of gooseberry bushes. Back inside, she rinsed the dishes and scrubbed down the stove and table. At the sound of Poppa's car, she scrubbed the kitchen table for the second time to scour away the worry that Grandpa would tell Poppa of her ride.

Poppa laid what looked like a stack of newspapers in one of his boxes on the porch. "So far, so good," he said.

"Poppa, look how clean I got the kitchen." She spied the stained dish towel hanging on the cellar door knob and quickly moved to block it from his view.

"You want praise for doing your job? Are you crazy?" He gestured around the room with his arm. "It ain't finished. Dry the dishes and set the table. Time you learned some womanly duties. You're going to be like your Momma was before I left for the War. If it kills me." He left the kitchen. "Now where's Gina?" he called. "Where's my girl?"

"I'm your girl, too, Poppa." Alone, she stuffed the stained dish towel behind the radiator.

7

The breeze blowing into the kitchen from the porch ruffled the corner of the newspaper Poppa held in front of his face. He slammed the newspaper down, a recognizable anger simmering. "Joe is spreading rumors about me. He's trying to steal business from me."

Silence hovered like the odor of the frying fish. "Ed, what's gotten into you?" Momma turned to Poppa and snuffed her cigarette in the ashtray. "First you think Joe's rubbernecking on the shop phone and now this? You've known him since we were kids, for Pete's sake."

"People change."

Grandpa placed the platter of fried fish in the middle of the table and sat down. "Ed, you know Joe can barely add oil to an engine, much less fix one. He's happy pumping gas and shooting the breeze with anyone who stops to buy gas."

Only sounds of chewing, rattling of knives and forks, and clinking of cups and glasses challenged the tension-laden silence. Alicia hid her piece of fried bullhead behind a small mound of mashed potatoes. She had felt sorry for the flopping fish after Grandpa cut off its head. Its glassy, marble-like eyes burned in her memory and turned her stomach; unable to eat, she slid her chair closer to Gina's plate to pick out the fish bones.

"Alicia, how many times do I have to tell you to sit still at the table?" Poppa asked. He grabbed Gina's plate and forked through the fish. "Ilse, can't you do something about her? Look how quiet Gina sits."

Wide-eyed, Gina appeared frozen in place.

Alicia's cheeks burned.

Little Miss Perfect Gina. I'm never good enough.

"Ed …" Momma pleaded.

"All that girl ever does is try to please you, Ed." Grandpa's voice was angry, but he wasn't shouting. "I don't know what the hell gets into you sometimes."

"Momma," Gina whispered, "Grandpa said a naughty word."

Poppa laid down his fork and clutched the table's edge. The milk bottle teetered. "Anton, I'm her Poppa, and I'll raise her how I see fit. I can't stand a girl who fidgets like she does." He turned to Alicia. "How is everything going to get set back to normal if *you* don't follow my rules? Women wearing pants … working men's jobs. Goddamn it. Where's it going to end?" His head swiveled as he looked through the silence at Momma, Grandpa, Alicia, and Gina. "Are you all against me? Why can't you see things the way I do? Everyone in this damn town treats me like I'm some kind of stranger." Poppa stormed out the door, but his anger lingered like the smoke from his smoldering cigarette.

"Pa, you said to give him time. But how much time does he need?"

Alicia bolted from her chair; Momma's hand reached out, but Alicia twisted away from her. Outside, she swiped away tears.

Even if I obey his rules, he still yells and gets mad at me all the time. It doesn't matter. So why not go?

Alicia shouted to the empty yard. "So what, Poppa? I'm going to meet Clara."

Afraid a call from Momma or Grandpa would snap her back to the house like a giant rubber band, she jumped on her bicycle, and without pausing to look right or left, sped down the driveway, onto the graveled road, across the highway, and onto the road to Cutters Creek. The sun melted away her worries with each turn of the pedal until she reached the south hill overlooking the bridge. Ahead, heaven and earth touched in a world of blues and greens. The enormity dwarfed Alicia.

She rode on an old horse-trodden path, shouldering the ridgeline until she reached a gray, elephant-sized glacial rock surrounded by a sea of small, yellow prickly pear flowers. Here Clara sat, leaning back on her hands, face to the sun. A foot-high, pyramid-shaped rock glimmered in the light next to where Alicia laid her bicycle; she bent to capture its brilliance with her fingers.

"I'm glad you decided to come." Clara smiled—the smile that seemed to cause everyone to smile back—except Poppa. "Did you have any trouble getting away?"

Alicia shook her head.

"Good. Still, we'd better hurry."

At the hill's crest, Clara pointed to an oxbow in Cutters Creek. "That's where we're going." They descended together, sometimes slipping, sometimes sliding down the slope thick with willows and cottonwoods, until they reached the rocks jutting into the creek. Other willows grew horizontally out of the bank, their exposed roots reaching finger-like into the water. Shoes and anklets off, they waded into the stream. Minnows swam around their toes; an emerald green dragonfly cruised by; a bullfrog sang to them; green leaves danced in the breeze.

It's another world—a peaceful world.

Seven Monarch butterflies landed on Clara's arm: a tapestry of orange and black. One of the butterflies floated from Clara to Alicia, paused above her outstretched hand, and then flitted away to join others on purple milkweed pods.

"Ever think how hard it must be for a butterfly to get out of its cocoon before it becomes a beautiful butterfly?" Clara asked.

Reality wormed its way into her thoughts. *Poppa.* "Clara, why am I here?"

Clara spoke, but the water gurgling over rocks obscured her words. She led them through ankle-deep water, tracing the shoreline for nearly a mile until they reached a shaded grotto. Alicia glanced back. The bridge had disappeared. Clara picked up a scarred stick shaped like a long wooden staff curved on one end. She waved it back and forth in a slow arc, and a foot-long black snake with yellow ribbon stripes slithered out of the tall, bluestem grass. At first, the snake barely moved when Clara picked it up. Then, in the blink of an eye, the snake's markings vanished; its body enlarged, two, maybe three times; it coiled around Clara's arm.

Alicia screamed and closed her eyes, shutting out the fearful image. Then absolute silence. Alicia slowly opened one eye and then the second. Clara was in the same place, rubbing under the jaw of the same small, gentle garter snake.

Clara extended her hand with the snake. "Take it."

Alicia shook her head. She touched the Celtic cross necklace beneath her blouse.

I can't make that happen. I don't know how.

"You will." Clara spoke to Alicia's thoughts.

The air smelled of rain. A flock of blackbirds soared overhead and sheltered in the cottonwood trees. Thunder rumbled like a herd of ghostly buffalo chased across the prairie. "I need to go," Alicia said.

Back on the graveled county road, rain drops splattered Alicia's head, arms, legs, and bicycle. She looked back toward Clara, but rain had lowered a gray curtain.

Ahead: Fullerton and Poppa. Larger, colder raindrops pelted her, forcing their way through her clothes and soaking them. Strands of wet hair fell into her eyes, blocking her vision as she crossed Highway 16 and rode into the driveway to the car shed.

Poppa stood under the overhang. Cringing, she dismounted and pushed the bicycle to him. He stepped towards her, tore the cigarette from his mouth, and snuffed it with his heel. Rain poured over the brim of his hat and down his collar. "Out to Clara's farm, were you?"

"No, Poppa." He didn't ask if she had seen Clara, so it wasn't a lie. Not really.

He stepped closer. His eyes were as dark as the blackening hail clouds. "Her two different color eyes … always staring at me like she knows."

Alicia waited, shivering for an eternity while Poppa seemed far away.

"What kind of notions is she putting into your head about me?"

Alicia's answer was lost in a strong gust of wind that bent a nearby sapling to the ground.

"Inside." Poppa grabbed Alicia's arm in a vice-like grip and pushed her through the open car shed door. Dark shadows hovered. Rain lashed the windowpane. "Hell will freeze over before I let you ride that bicycle again!"

Outside, thunder cracked the sky.

8

Alicia struggled to lift her smashed bicycle from the car shed floor. A barrage of pain constricted her arms. Poppa's shouts chilled her like balls of hail pounding her skin. She tried to call out, but words caught in her throat.

"Wake up. Wake up." Gina shook Alicia's bruised arm. "Momma and Poppa are fighting."

Silver lights pierced her nightmare like bolts of lightning. Outside her bedroom window, the sky was clear, cloudless. Poppa's loud voice seeped around the closed door from Momma and Poppa's bedroom. He had finally come home.

"I saw you talking to Bill this morning. How many times do I have to say this? No wife of mine is going to make me look like I can't support my family."

"Ed, things changed while you were gone. You don't seem to realize that."

"Hell I don't," he shouted. "Well, in case you haven't noticed—I'm home now, and things are going to change back."

"Ed, quiet down—the girls."

Alicia leaned her ear to the wall separating the bedrooms. Momma lowered her voice but spoke loud enough for Alicia to hear. "Bill bought the lumber yard yesterday, and he really needs a bookkeeper. He said I could work from home."

The silence was louder than the shouts.

"Ed, we have to do something. Except for our War bonds, our savings are gone; the shop still isn't making enough money; the baby will be here soon."

"You think all of this is my fault? Goddamn it, Ilse, I'm trying."

"No, Ed, I don't think that. It's just . . ."

"They're not fighting," Alicia said. "Just talking loud." Still, she grabbed the thin blanket she'd kicked away during her nightmare and pulled it over Gina and Raggedy Ann. Poppa's bedroom door slammed shut, shaking the house. "Everything will be better in the morning. You'll see." Alicia may have convinced Gina, but not herself. In the kitchen beneath their bedroom, Poppa paced. The smell of cigarette smoke rose into her bedroom as it had on countless winter nights. Only when she heard the slam of Poppa's car door, did she fall asleep.

***

Alicia awoke to an empty bedroom and examined the fingerprints that laced her upper arm. She was glad that Gina wasn't around to see them. Caught between belief and disbelief, her mind swirled: yes or no; meant to hurt or not? One question remained constant.

When did I become so awful?

In the back of her closet, she found an old blue blouse with sleeves that grazed her elbows. After spending yesterday's long rainy afternoon in her bedroom pretending to be sick, she could no longer hide. One thing was certain: today she was going to do her best to stay out of Poppa's way.

The house was silent, meaning Poppa had left for the shop. In the kitchen, Momma was on her knees underneath an ironing board, pinning two sides of an old white sheet together to form a cover.

"Help me up," she said.

Alicia steadied the rickety wooden ironing board with one hand and helped Momma with the other.

"Uff da." Momma slowly straightened up. Her swollen feet bulged over the edge of Grandpa's slippers.

"Where's Gina?" Alicia asked.

"She and Pa went to Graffie's for a new hoe. Hungry?" Momma had lined up ten pints of strawberry jam on the stove like prize jars at the county fair. "It sure was nice of Clara's ma to help. I gave her a few jars, too."

"I could've helped. I'm not a baby anymore."

"Why are you so ornery all the time? You never used to be like that. What's gotten into you lately?"

Alicia's retort balanced on the tip of her tongue until she realized Momma's eyes looked like those of a rabbit caught under Grandpa's wire fence. "I'm sorry, Momma. I just feel … I don't know …" Since her birthday, she had become stubborn as an ox, according to Poppa; cranky, according to Momma; no fun, according to Gina; only to Grandpa was she all right. Alicia smiled inside, thinking of the Goldilocks story, but truth was, she felt boxed in with no way to push back—or not even really wanting to push back—and now, her bicycle was gone, her escape taken away. Alicia sighed, not willing to say all of this to Momma. Especially after last night.

"I'll make a jam sandwich," Alicia said. "Then can I iron the pillowcases for you?"

"I'm sorry, too," Momma said. "It's … Thanks. I'd really appreciate that. I didn't get much sleep, and I need to lie down for a while." Slowly, silently, Momma vanished.

Alicia breathed in the fresh outdoor smell of pillowcases dried in the warm morning sun. She dipped her hand into a chipped bowl and sprinkled all five pillowcases with water. She rolled them up and covered them with a damp towel, and then plugged in the iron and waited for it to heat.

Two car doors slammed. Gina rushed into the kitchen, skidding to a stop at the ironing board.

"Yippee, me and Grandpa are going to make monster donuts." Chocolate outlined Gina's smile.

"It's a scorcher out there. More like August than June." Grandpa wiped his brow with his handkerchief. "Catch, Alicia." He tossed a package of spearmint gum to her. "Wash up, Gina."

He carried the kitchen table across the linoleum floor to the white stove and set a heavy kettle of grease to heat. Gina put a cloth mat, wooden rolling pin, donut cutter, and bowl of chilled donut dough on the table. Grandpa flattened the mat. With his ghostly, flour-dusted hands, he moved the rolling pin back and forth across cream-colored dough until it was thin and smooth.

Gina cut perfect circles with the donut cutter, and Grandpa set aside odd shaped dough to fry later as monsters. The lard sizzled and spit as Grandpa slid dough from the spatula into the grease kettle.

"I'm going to take some monster donuts to Poppa, Alicia. Want to come with me?"

"No. I'm busy," said Alicia, intent on the pillowcase on the ironing board. Facing Poppa was the very last thing she wanted to do.

"Please," Gina whispered loudly. "Alphie was at Graffie's, and he said he's going to make me give back the soldier shells that belong to him. I don't like him." She crossed her arms over her chest.

Alicia looked over the top of Gina's head to Grandpa. His face was turning red. He turned off the stove burner. "We'd better go teach that hooligan a lesson, Johan."

What am I thinking?

With Grandpa talking out loud to Johan, it would be a bad idea for him to go hunting for Alphie. "That's okay, Grandpa, I'll take her when you're done frying donuts." Worry hovered around Alicia as she smoothed a white pillowcase over the ironing board, dipped her fingers into the bowl of water, and splashed the iron. The droplets sizzled and danced. She slid the hot iron from side to side, edge to edge, corner to corner.

If only I could iron away my problems as easily.

Gina brought a fried donut hole to her sister; it smelled of warm cinnamon. "Say ah," Gina prompted.

The flavor filled Alicia's mouth with sweetness.

"You like it?"

"It's the best ever!"

A fake seriousness played across Gina's face. "I gotta get back to work."

Cooling donuts stretched out on a brown paper sack; monster donuts and donut holes outnumbered regular donuts two to one. Monster donuts were fried without a second rolling. Grandpa turned off the stove, set the hot kettle of grease on a cold back burner, and plopped down on a kitchen chair. His shoulder sloped as if carrying a great weight across his back. "I'm all played out," he said.

"Grandpa, I'm almost done ironing. Me and Gina will clean up before we leave for Poppa's shop."

"Thanks. I'm going to take a little snooze until it's time to cook the noon meal."

She placed the hot iron on the stove between the burners and away from Grandpa's grease kettle. Gina pushed a chair to the sink, filled the dishpan with warm, soapy water, and, up to her elbows in suds, washed the dishes. Alicia wiped down the table and went outside to shake the rolling pin cover and mat. She carried all the jars of strawberry jam down the steps into the cellar and lined them in two straight rows on wooden shelves next to Grandpa's workbench.

Four trips later, Gina was waiting for her by the cellar door. "Can we go now?"

Reluctantly, Alicia agreed. She separated the donuts—plain from cinnamon-sugar-coated—into two brown paper grocery bags. Gina tightly clasped a third sack.

"What's in there?" Alicia asked.

"My Rainbow Tablet and pencils. In case we find any new states for our list."

When they reached the sidewalk along Center Street, Gina handed her grocery bag to Alicia with instructions to be careful. She hopped ahead into imaginary hopscotch boxes on the chipped sidewalk. They passed budding mock orange bushes shielding the Jensen house, purple irises and white petunias in Sarah's front garden, and a brown and white dog chasing its tail in the church yard. Dread was Alicia's only companion until they reached Poppa's shop.

Poppa's painted wooden sign, *Ed Drake Tire and Auto Repair*, nailed over the shop's original sign, hung above the front entrance of the red brick building. A battered metal sign with a twelve-inch Esso man pumping gas propped an open window. A green and white, metal Quaker State Oil sign and an orange and blue Purolator Oil Filter sign flanked the open bay door in the building's side. Stacked along the back bay wall were boxes, five gallon oil cans, and tires wrapped around tall vertical rods in front of shelves full of used car parts. Suspended light bulbs made rainbows in the oil spills on the concrete floor. A faint smell of gasoline lingered, and a hubcap reverberated as Slick pried it loose from the wheel.

"Hi, Alicia, Squirt. Ed's out front. What's in the sacks?" he asked.

"Monster donuts," Gina said. A smile hovered in the corner of her mouth. "May-beee one for you, too."

"A monster donut? Does it eat me if I don't eat it first?"

"No, silly. I'm going to find Poppa. Then you can have one."

Alicia hung back. The rear end of Joe's '36 black Ford Coupe balanced on two jacks; its back tires lay flat on the oily floor. Mr. Oldenburg's Studebaker was on the wooden frame over the oil changing pit with the hood up. Poppa's tool kit was spread across the front fender with five wrenches lined up like soldiers.

Slick wiped his hands on a rag. "Clara wants you to meet her at Cutters Creek this afternoon about 1:30. She's done working at one o'clock."

Alicia glanced at the wire covered wall clock: 10:10. "I can't. Poppa took my bicycle away. Did she say why there and not Graffie's?"

I might be able to sneak to Graffie's.

"I know he did. I told her. She's gonna wait there for a while. I can drive you ..."

"No. If Poppa caught me riding in your car, especially to meet Clara …" She cringed. First hurtful words, now marks on her wrist and arms … What might he do next? "Never mind. Let's go have a donut. Gina made them with Grandpa." Alicia hesitated at the door to the shop front.

Slick stopped behind her, his hand on her shoulder. "You all right?"

"Yes." Another lie added to her accumulating collections of lies and half-truths. She followed Slick across the threshold.

Gina, perched on a tall wooden stool behind the battered wooden counter, motioned Alicia and Slick to her. She pointed to the open pages of the *Minneapolis Morning Herald* spread out before her. "It's like a paper tablecloth."

Across the counter from Gina, Poppa smiled and lifted a sack. "What did my good girls bring for their Poppa?"

Alicia eyed him cautiously. His hand, lightning fast, reached into the sack. Alicia lurched backwards. His hand came out, clutching a donut. He tossed it into his mouth and mumbled through his chewing, "Slick, try a monster."

Gina climbed down from Poppa's stool and handed Slick a sort of dinosaur-shaped monster donut.

He turned it over and over in his hand and then chomped on a head-like part. Mmmmm," he said. "One less T-Rex."

Gina giggled.

Sarah pushed the front door open. "Hello, everybody. Gina, I was looking for you. Missy's kittens opened their eyes this morning. Come and see them."

Gina nodded.

Poppa opened a donut sack and held it out for Sarah.

"Don't mind if I do. I'm on my way to see Ilse. Missed her at Ladies Aid last Thursday. The Church Sunshine Committee wants to know if she needed any help. By the way, is Joe's car ready?" Sarah's words always pushed against one another, hurrying to get said.

Poppa's smile disappeared; his face hardened as if chiseled from rock—so quickly that he seemed like two different Poppas.

Alicia touched her bruised arm.

He went to the stool Gina had vacated, sat, and began turning the pages of the newspaper. "Tell those busybodies Ilse will manage. Alicia will see to that." A yellow butterfly flew in through the open window and landed on the donut Poppa had just set down. "About the car. I said I'd get to it when I had time. First I have to put new spark plugs in Frank Oldenburg's car. He and the misses are leaving for the cities. They have a new granddaughter."

"That's fine. Any idea about our car?"

Poppa swiped at the butterfly that was unwilling to give up its prize. "I *said* I'd get to it when I could. I don't have the right size brake linings. I'll go to Marshall tomorrow and pick some up. That good enough for you?"

"For Pete's sake, Ed. Don't blow a gasket." She put her hands in the air. "We're in no rush. It was just a simple question." She left the shop, taking all sounds with her.

Poppa stared at the newspaper in front of him. Suddenly, he wadded the paper into a ball and heaved it into an empty oil drum. "They think they'll trick me. Hiding information. Well, they've got another think coming." Poppa's hunched shoulders were a sure sign of simmering anger.

"Poppa," Gina spoke softly, "I'm thirsty."

His eyes glazed, and he stared at Gina as if she had just floated through the open door.

Alicia stepped between Gina and Poppa. "Gina, I'll get you some water from the town pump." She shoved the remaining two monster donuts into the sack with Gina's Rainbow Tablet. "Poppa, I'm taking Gina to the school yard to play."

"Yah, yah."

Slick caught Alicia's eye. "Ed, I'll put in the spark plugs and tune up Gus's car if you want to drive to Marshall for the brake pads this afternoon."

"Make sure to use your own tools."

Alicia closed the door on Poppa's words. With Poppa gone for the afternoon, she could easily walk the mile to Cutters Creek.

Relieved, she and Gina crossed the street to the school, where smells of orange peels and chalk dust lingered all summer long. The yellow butterfly danced lazily ahead, guided them to the pump, and rested on the long handle as if waiting for a drink. Gina cupped her hands to catch water for the butterfly.

Something Clara would do.

"I want to swing," Gina said. "Remember when Poppa came home, you had to push me all the time." She hoisted herself on the rubber swing seat and clutched the metal chains. "Now I can pump myself and read and stay in the lines when I color. There's Slick. Slick! Watch me!" She pumped, higher and higher, her feet pointing to leaves on a low branch.

Slick crossed the street. "Hold on tight, Squirt," he said. From the look on his face, Alicia realized bad news followed. She met him halfway on the sidewalk. "Ed found brake linings in a miss-marked box in the bay, so he's not going to Marshall. Sorry."

Alicia shrugged. She should've known getting away was too good to be true.

Gina dragged her shoes in the sand until the swing slowed enough for her to leap from the seat. She stumbled, corrected herself, and scooped up the brown sack. She jammed it behind her and pointed. "Alphie. He's mean and he stinks." She clung to Alicia's blouse.

Slick laughed out loud. "That's his aftershave. He thinks the girls like it."

Alphie sauntered across the graveled road that divided the church from the school. "Got my shells, Brat?" he said to Gina. He threw down his cigarette butt. Alicia pirouetted between Alphie and Gina. Slick moved in front of both girls.

Alphie smirked. "You sure are brave when my friend is around. How's that crappy bicycle doing?"

Slick put his hands on Alphie's chest and shoved. "Cut it out. Haven't you got anything better to do than pick on a girl? For God's sake, Alphie."

"C'mon, Slick. I was kidding around." The hard look in his eyes revealed the lie.

"Alphie, wanna lose a game of pool? I'm going to the pool hall for a hamburger. I'll buy, you freeloader." Slick jostled Alphie across Center Street, paused at the corner of Main Street, turned back, and motioned for the girls to leave.

When Slick and Alphie turned the corner out of sight, Alicia spoke. "Come on. Hurry up."

No hesitation from Gina. They ducked behind the schoolhouse, wove in and out of the row of trees fencing the softball field, and emerged in Oldenburg's apple orchard.

Alicia glanced back a time or two. "I know someplace Alphie won't find us, but before we go, you have to promise *never, never* to tell Poppa or Momma I brought you there. Not even Grandpa. Or go by yourself." Alicia's destination, Bill's lumber yard, had been her escape from Poppa until her birthday bicycle—the one locked in Poppa's car shed.

"I'm not a baby, anymore! I'm seven and I can keep a secret."

The lumber yard was located at the south end of the apple orchard, separated by a graveled road and a storage lot. The lot held charred wood, oil drums for burning trash, weeds, and an unlocked door. Alicia had discovered the door last October when Mrs. Oldenburg let her pick windfall apples for Grandpa's pies for Poppa's homecoming party. Her tongue puckered at the thought of tart green apples yet to come this summer.

Alicia checked right and left, assuring herself that the back lot remained empty. Both girls ran to the windowless wooden door, and Alicia twisted the knob. It turned, but the rain-swollen door refused to budge; she leaned her shoulder against it. Nothing. She pushed again with her back, using her legs for leverage until a narrow crack opened. Alicia slipped through, reached back for Gina's hand, and pulled her inside. Sunlight poured into the open roof area in the middle of the building. Haphazardly stacked lumber filled rectangular openings on two levels accessed by wooden stair steps leading to a catwalk. New wood smell filled the air.

They climbed to the second story landing, which was laced with cobwebs. Gina leaned over the rickety railing at least twenty feet above the concrete floor.

Alicia shuddered and yanked the back of Gina's shirt. "Stop that! Maybe I shouldn't have brought you here. It's too dangerous. We're going down."

"No, please … let me stay. I'm sorry." Gina ripped a yellow sheet from her Rainbow Tablet and handed Alicia a pencil—a peace offering for her sister.

"Then be more careful!" Alicia pushed an empty nail barrel out of the way into a railing corner and joined Gina on the landing, their feet resting on the top steps. Alicia attempted to doodle but only filled the paper with chicken scratches—Grandpa's words. Poppa's swift mood changes left her dizzy, off-balance, unsure what to do. Finally, through the haze of her worries, Alicia realized Gina was crying. "Are you sad 'cause I yelled? I was so scared you'd fall."

Gina shook her head. "It's all my fault."

Alicia was immediately alert.

"Momma never smiles anymore, and she doesn't say we're her princesses. I asked Grandpa this morning if I cost a lot of money, and he laughed and said I did, and now Poppa is running out of money." Tears soaked a pink page, her list of states.

Gina had heard and understood last night's argument. Alicia touched the cross necklace, scooted closer, and wrapped her arm around her sister. "Grandpa was teasing you. That's why he laughed. Put your stuff back in the sack, and we'll go home and make a new list. Did you write down the Ohio license plate that we saw at Joe's last night?"

Gina nodded and wiped her nose on her sleeve. "I'm glad you're my sister."

"Me, too," Alicia said.

9

On the way home, Gina's chatter drifted in and out like a distant radio broadcast obscured by the static of Alicia's guilt and worry. Momma was preoccupied, even distant at times. Grandpa always seemed tired. Clara's castle remained out of reach. And words to comfort, to explain things to Gina, flited away as lightly as the butterfly in Poppa's garage.

How can I explain what's happening when I don't know myself?

Clara's reasons for meeting at the creek remained a mystery, but Alicia had reasons of her own. Whether they were to seek Clara's help or to seek the peace of the creek, she didn't know.

One thing for certain, with Poppa staying in Fullerton, she would have to be quick and cautious. Alicia hung back at the car shed and encouraged her sister to check on Momma. As soon as Gina's back was turned, Alicia went to the car shed door and twisted the handle. Locked. Just as she had suspected. There was another way; Poppa kept his keys in a glass ashtray on his bureau. All she had to do was wait for him to leave for work.

All through dinner, Alicia kept track of the slow movement of the hands on the kitchen clock behind Momma's head. She sat as still as possible and ate everything on her plate, hoping to fade from Poppa's usually watchful eyes.

His plate empty, Poppa lit a cigarette and sat back in his chair. Alicia sensed the anger still churning inside of him.

Poppa interrupted an uneasy silence. "Joe didn't even have the guts to come himself."

Momma bent her head over her plate and studied the mashed potatoes she listlessly stirred with a fork.

Poppa's voice grew louder. "He had to send that scarecrow of a wife to check up on me. No woman should be taller than her man," he said, as if imparting a truth and ignoring the fact that Momma was two inches taller than him. Poppa's chair careened behind him when he stood, but Grandpa caught it before it hit the floor. Within seconds, the noon news from WCCO blared from the radio in the living room.

Alicia contemplated just how much to say. "Sarah said she was only asking about the car. She said no hurry. They could wait." She purposely stopped the story there and stared a warning to Gina. For once, her sister kept her mouth shut.

Momma lit a cigarette. The match flared and fell to her uneaten plate of food. "Sarah came over after she saw you girls." She inhaled and blew the smoke out. "But she didn't say … Pa, I'm getting so tired of his … Isn't there something we can do? Is it ever going to end?"

Grandpa placed his hand on Momma's arm, but she pulled away, picked up her package of Camel cigarettes and her matches, and went outside.

Alicia snuffed out Momma's lit cigarette, wishing she could make Momma's sadness disappear as easily as the cigarette's light. "Grandpa?" She, too, wanted an answer.

"Well," Grandpa said, "those dishes aren't getting done by themselves. Gina, your turn to dry. Alicia, bring the dirty dishes to the sink." He hoisted himself from the chair with a sigh, brought the dishpan from behind the cellar door, and filled it with hot, soapy water. "Ed better be thankful for the customers he has."

Gina pushed a chair to the sink and dried silverware, cups, and glasses. She reached for a big bowl, but it slipped from her dish towel and crashed to the floor. She shrieked. Cherry red shards flew across the linoleum and landed like blood splatters. Wide-eyed, Gina jerked back—the chair teetering before Grandpa steadied it.

Poppa stomped into the kitchen. "Do you always have to be so clumsy, Alicia? Now you're making me miss the news."

"Poppa, I'm sorry. It sorta slipped," Alicia lied for her sister. "I'll clean it up."

"You bet you will. Now I'm damn glad I took that bicycle away. You don't deserve it. Gina, go play. Your sister will clean up her mess and finish the dishes."

He started to turn away when Gina said, "But Poppa, it's my turn. Grandpa says I'm his little helper." Pride slipped into her words.

Poppa whirled around with a cold hard stare at Gina. Alicia froze. She had never seen Poppa look at Gina in that way.

Only at me.

His eyes, his whole face looked like it had with Sarah at the shop just hours before. Alicia rushed to her sister's side. "Do what he says, Gina. It's okay. You can take my turn tomorrow."

Poppa started across the linoleum, but Grandpa quickly lifted the barefoot Gina from the chair. "Stay there, Ed. I'll bring her to you." He carried her over scattered shards into the dining room. "It's not right," he said, coming back into the room. "The way Ed treats Alicia. Making her a scapegoat for his troubles." He had the faraway gaze that meant he was talking to Johan.

Alicia worked silently so Poppa might think she had disappeared. As if he cared. When finished, she grabbed Grandpa's butcher knife and went outside past shriveled lilacs—their fragrance of hope a dried up, distant memory. She crossed the lawn to the double rows of peonies and slashed stem after stem of pink, rose, and white blooms until she had eight—a bouquet for Momma. She shook the flowers, and a rain of black ants fell to the grass.

If he doesn't care, why should I?

"I'm going to meet Clara and that's that." Saying the words out loud made the decision real.

Minutes dragged until Poppa crossed the yard in front of her and wordlessly climbed into his car. Alicia hurried into the house, quickly filled a Mason jar with water for the peonies, placed the bouquet on the dining room table, and slowed as she approached the living room. Elm tree shadows swayed gently on the walls, but all was quiet. She crept past Grandpa, who was dozing in his rocking chair, and went upstairs, walking on the side of the steps to avoid their creaking. She peeked into her bedroom where Momma and Gina napped beneath lace curtains billowing in and out in rhythm with their breathing.

Certain her plan would work, Alicia entered Momma and Poppa's bedroom, went to the bureau, and tipped Poppa's glass ashtray for keys. Empty. She opened the top drawer, and near the rear, found a key. She hurried through the house, glancing at the kitchen clock. After quietly closing the porch door, she bolted across the lawn to the car shed door and inserted the key. It slid in but failed to unlock the door. She kicked the door, and a starling flew from its nest under the eaves.

Now what?

Time was running out. Frustrated, Alicia pocketed the key, walked to Depot Road, turned left down the hill to reach the highway as if she had no care in the world. She pretended she was going to Graffie's, hoping to convince anyone who might be watching.

About to make the forbidden highway crossing, she heard the familiar rumble of Slick's car. He pulled to the side ahead of her and leaned to open the passenger door. His jalopy smelled of pine from the paper tree dangling from the rearview mirror and the stale odor of Alphie's cigarettes.

"Get in. I'll give you a ride to Clara."

"Okay."

I have to take the risk for Gina.

Slick's car roared onto the highway. "I'll stall Ed from going home. He's been mad all morning since Sarah left. Now he's saying people are treating him different since he came back from the War. Far as I can tell, no one talks about the War with him. Just about their car trouble." He turned towards Alicia.

"Look out!" she screamed. A large dark hulk wandered across half the highway and collapsed. Slick slammed on the brakes and skidded onto the graveled shoulder, narrowly missing the animal.

"It's a dog!" Alicia reached for the door handle, but Slick pulled her back.

"It's probably hurt and might not be friendly. I'll check first." He killed the engine, jumped out of the car, and ran to the dog.

Alicia refused to heed his warning. She got out and moved to the back fender. Two cars, one from each direction, honked loudly and swerved to avoid Slick and the dog. After the cars passed, Alicia ran behind Slick and peered around him. She thought it was short-haired and black, but its coat was so matted with mud and blood, she couldn't be sure.

Slick knelt and slowly extended his hand. The dog's tail thumped once. "She's in pretty bad shape, looks like. Watch out. I'm going to check for broken bones." He probed. The dog remained motionless. "Don't feel anything broken."

Alicia knelt, extended her hand, let the docile dog smell her, and then caressed its head. "Shh, you're going to be okay." With a small cry, the dog lifted its head; warm chocolate eyes pleaded for help.

"I thought she might've been hit by a car, but with all these cuts, looks like she tangled with a lot of barbed wire," Slick said. "Better get her off the highway before we all get killed."

A greyhound bus raced past. The driver blasted his horn, punctuating Slick's warning. Slick ran to the car's trunk and returned with a blanket. The dog cowered and whimpered as Slick eased his blanketed arms under her and lifted.

Alicia ran across the highway and opened the car door. He laid the dog and blanket on the back seat. Alicia climbed in beside the animal. She spit on her hankie to wipe away some of the dried blood and mud on the dog's chest, but a wound re-opened. Blood flowed in small rivulets.

Slick's jalopy engine roared to life, spinning the shoulder gravel. His tires squealed in the half-circle turn on the highway.

Alicia lurched and grabbed the front seat. "Where are we going?"

"The shop. Ed has a first-aid kit."

Alicia felt the key in her pocket to reassure herself that she hadn't lost it. The dog's heavy panting rocked the car until Slick slowed on Main Street around the corner from Poppa's shop. "When we get inside, you follow along with what I say, all right?" She nodded, knowing why; she wasn't allowed in Slick's car.

Slick drove into an empty bay, carried the dog into the front, and set her down near the floor drain. Poppa looked up, startled.

"I was driving to Graffie's for the wrench you wanted when I spotted Alicia on the hill behind your house," Slick said. "She flagged me down and pointed to the ditch and this dog. I brought both here. Figured you'd take a look at the dog."

Poppa squatted beside the dog. He spoke in a low, soothing voice and glided his hands over mud-and-blood-crusted hair. "Her nose is hot and dry. Not good. Slick, get a bucket of water, some clean rags, and my first aid kit." Poppa motioned to the other side of the prone dog. "Alicia, me and Slick will hold her steady and you clean the cuts. Careful now."

Alicia rinsed the cuts, and the dog barely flinched. Mud ran brown to the floor drain, followed by blood, exposing a deep wound five inches across her right front flank.

"Keep going," Poppa said.

Alicia cleaned a half-dozen smaller gashes on both sides.

"I thought maybe she got caught in some damned trap, but looks more like barbed wire. Wonder where she came from." Poppa uncapped a bottle of peroxide. "Alicia, get back." He poured peroxide on the cleaned wounds. Again the dog remained still.

Alicia, Poppa, and Slick stood, surrounding the dog. Clean, she seemed to have shrunk in size. Her ribs were like washboards.

"It's a female, mostly black lab," Slick said, 'but she's half starved—a good fifteen pounds underweight." He checked her teeth. "She's not quite six years old." The dog stretched her neck, attempting to lap muddy water as it trickled towards the drain.

Alicia spotted a soup bowl Poppa had forgotten to bring home. She filled it with water, and knelt in front of the dog's mouth. The dog lapped greedily.

Poppa knelt beside Alicia. She looked for tell-tale signs of returning anger. Instead, he placed a warm hand over hers on top of the dog's head. "Easy. Not too much at first. Don't want her heaving. Good work. I don't think she's infected. Yet. In the War I saw …" Poppa's head jerked as if backing away from unsaid words. He stood and helped Alicia to her feet. "I don't know if she'll make it. That one cut's pretty deep." The dog's sad eyes seemed to understand Poppa's words.

She attempted to stand but crumbled to the floor.

"Poppa, we have to try to save her." Alicia wanted to plead, but she didn't know if that would make it better or worse. The silent seconds stretched endlessly.

"I'll come at night and tend to her, Ed," Slick added.

Poppa shrugged his shoulders. "I don't know … she's pretty weak." He looked from Alicia to Slick. "All right, we'll try, but I can't make promises. You're going to have to keep the dog a secret from Momma, Gina, and Anton. With the baby coming so soon, I can't have anyone getting upset if I have to put the dog down."

Poppa's warning was too big for Alicia to comprehend.

"I think Ed means if the dog isn't going to live," Slick said.

"If we're going to do this, then we'll do it right. Alicia, in addition to your other duties … ah … chores, you will be helping me feed and care for the dog. Slick, take Alicia and get the two Army blankets from my foot locker in the car shed." Poppa tossed Slick a set of keys. "Hurry up about it. She's shivering bad."

Inside Slick's car, Alicia spoke. "You lied to protect me. Why?"

He answered, but the words bounced off the windshield and out the open car window. Alicia focused on the image of her and Poppa working together to save the dog.

He'll be so proud of me.

She vowed to return the stolen key.

"You're a million miles away," Slick said. "I saw that happy look on your face when Ed told you 'good job.' He ought to say that more often."

Now he sounds like Grandpa when he talks to Johan about me.

She smiled to herself, admitting it felt good to hear. Slick killed the engine and coasted to a stop at the driveway's edge on the Depot Road shoulder, preventing Momma from hearing the jalopy's loud muffler or seeing his car behind tall elms. They dashed between the wild plum trees and made their way around the backside of the car shed and past the strawberry patch to the side door.

Sunlight filtered through the grimy south window, and cobwebs connected one wooden beam to another. Slick picked up Alicia's bicycle and leaned it against the wall. Poppa's green foot locker was wedged under a make-shift workbench in a far corner. Using a second key, Slick unlocked the foot locker, lifted the lid, moved to block Alicia's view, and laid two blankets on the packed dirt floor. He quickly slammed the locker lid and locked it. "Hurry up. She needs these."

"What was in Poppa's locker?"

"Not much. Army stuff: Ed's Silver Star, some pictures of Army guys standing in front of a bombed out building."

He stopped in front of the shop and handed her the blankets and key ring. "I still have to go to Graffie's for Ed. I'll drive out to Clara's and tell her what happened."

Filled with anticipation, Alicia ran into the shop. Poppa was mopping an empty floor.

"She's behind the counter," Poppa said.

Relieved, Alicia plumped a single blanket into a round nest, coaxed the dog onto it, and draped the second blanket over the counter stool. "Poppa, here's your keys." She reached into her pocket, careful not to bring out the stolen key.

He removed a single key and handed it back. "For the car shed. Get your bicycle out. You earned it."

She clutched the key and ran outside into the sunshine.

10

Fireflies flickered. It was the in-between time: neither day nor night. Alicia was running out of time; soon her decision would be made for her. Through Slick, Clara had urged Alicia again and again to meet at Cutters Creek, but for the past two weeks she had worked beside Poppa, caring for the dog and daring to hope he had changed. Yet months of experience made her cautious and not trusting. She closed the porch door, and as her eyes became accustomed to twilight, saw Poppa on the bench across the lawn, an obstacle to her plan. Bathed in the porch light, she knew Poppa could see her.

"Alicia," Poppa called. "Come and sit with me."

Reluctantly, she approached him with a glance down the hill. Joe's lit red and white gas pumps glowed.

How long before he closes?

A cooling breeze ruffled the elm leaves above them. Poppa's arm rested on the bench back, and he patted the seat next to him. She sat. He leaned close to her and pointed to the northwest sky. "See the Big Dipper? Follow it up to the North Star."

Alicia gazed skyward. She leaned closer to him, basking in his attention, and let her eyes follow his pointed finger.

He's like a real Poppa.

Apprehension slipped away into the darkness, quickly replaced by emptiness—a longing.

Why can't he always be like this?

Poppa took a deep breath. "All the smells: the night air, freshly mowed grass, Anton's flowers … smells like home.

Nothing like a June night in Minnesota with my girls. Sure missed you. I figured when I got back, you'd be the same as the picture I carried." A deep, sad sigh left Poppa.

Alicia remained silent, alert, wondering where the conversation was headed. Poppa never talked about the War. For a while, he kept his eyes on the sky as if scanning the Milky Way. Then he removed his arm and lit a cigarette; the match glowed briefly and faded into the darkness. A moth circled the porch light.

"That Clara," he said, finally. "Funny her having two different colored eyes. Reminds me of a girl I saw over in Germany. About her age, too." The moth ricocheted from porch light to porch light. "Do much riding after church?" he asked.

The mention of Clara caused a wave of apprehension. She remembered Poppa's swift change with Sarah over Joe's car and all the times his anger struck like a bolt from the blue. She searched for possible offenses she might have committed since the noon feeding of the dog. Nothing came to mind—unless he knew she had taken her bicycle to Joe to fix the tube in spite of his warnings to stay away from the station.

She had been so careful. After church, she had waited until Poppa left to listen to a Cubs and Cardinals baseball game on the shop radio before she wheeled her bicycle down the hill. Joe hovered nearby while she added air that hissed out faster than it went in. She had followed him into the station and helped him remove the tube; it resembled Grandpa's patchwork quilt. Joe had offered to try one more patch but made no promises.

"No," she answered Poppa, hardly remembering the question. "I helped Grandpa pick and shell the peas we had for supper." Maybe she could get his mind to something else.

Poppa sat silently for a while. "You're doing a good job with that dog. Her wounds are scabbing over except for the big one. It was so deep, it'll take a while. Way she follows you around the shop—like she's your shadow." He smiled. "You're going to make a good momma someday. Not one of those *modern* women." He tossed the cigarette butt on the grass and crushed it with his heel.

It's now or never.

"Can I, I mean, can we keep her and call her that? Shadow?"

Poppa placed his hand on her shoulder as if to support himself as he stood. "You saved her. She's yours to name. But we'll keep our little secret until after the baby comes and things settle down. You hear?"

Alicia's impulse was to jump up and hug Poppa.

Almost as if he knew she might, he backed away. "Me, Momma, and Gina are going to Marshall tomorrow to shop. Want to come along? You and Gina can each have a quarter to spend at Woolworths. We're having hamburgers at the Chat N Chew Café."

"Is Grandpa going?"

Poppa shook his head. "Then I'll stay home and feed the dog … I mean Shadow."

"I figured as much." He swatted a mosquito, and blood stained his arm. "Come inside before the mosquitos eat you alive."

Alicia's eyes followed Poppa to the porch where he carefully folded the Sunday newspaper pages and stacked them one at a time in a box. When he finished, he disappeared into the kitchen. Now she could retrieve her bicycle, and Poppa wouldn't see her push it home through the dark. A choir of crickets sang from the deepening shadows as she raced to Joe's.

Slick appeared out of the dark with two bottles of Coca-Cola.

"Thank you," she said. "Can Clara come tomorrow?" He had agreed to let Clara know Alicia could meet her at the creek the next morning—Clara's day off.

"All set. I just got back from delivering Alphie to the farm. Some guys at the pool hall thought it would be funny to get him drunk." Slick shook his head. "He's been getting into trouble since he was five …"

Alicia caught his eye and raised an eyebrow. "How do you know that?"

Slick shrugged. "I guess Clara told me."

"Johan was always bailing him out, too," Joe added. "When Alphie was five or six, he stole a carton of gum from me—not a single package, the whole kit and caboodle—and chewed up one of the packages before Johan got it away from him. I found the carton and a nickel outside the station door the next morning. Slick, looks like you're taking over where Johan left off. I miss Johan ..."

Those were more words than Alicia had ever heard Joe string together in her whole life. Sarah was the talker in the family, Grandpa said.

"I miss him, too. A lot," Alicia said. A cloud of moist, heavy silence shrouded them. Alicia searched for a happier thought, but when she realized how much Johan would've loved the dog, it was a bittersweet thought. "Slick, Poppa said we could keep the dog—Shadow. I got to name her."

"Good. That dog was meant to be here," Slick said.

Alicia's cross warmed her neck, drawing her hand to it.

"Time to lock up," Joe said. He returned, wheeling her bicycle. "The tube is holding for now. Sorry to say, that's the last patch."

Alicia held the quarter Grandpa had given her for shelling the rest of the peas when he went inside to rest.

"No need for your money here," Joe said.

Slick rounded the pump with two one-dollar bills in his hand. "Joe, get her a new tube." Alicia started to protest, but Slick interrupted. "I never did get you a birthday present, so this is it."

"I can't, Slick. If Poppa found out I was even here ..." Alicia sensed the bond with Poppa was as fragile as a soap bubble, and she was going to do everything in her power to keep it from bursting.

"This is between Slick and me," Joe said. "Ed doesn't need concern himself."

Slick squeezed the bicycle tire. "I hope this holds until Joe can find one."

"That's right. War's been over nearly a year and it's still hard to get some things. Ah, Slick, that'll be another buck seventy-nine for gas."

The next morning, Momma asked Alicia one last time if she wanted to go with. "They have so many new stores opening ... I haven't been shopping in such a long time." Alicia knew about Momma's money stashed away in an old, blue floral, covered dish that once belonged to Great-Grandmother Matea, who, Grandpa said, hid money from her sale of eggs in the same dish back when they lived on the farm next to Clara's grandparents.

"No, I don't want to go," Alicia said. "The traveling library is coming Friday and I haven't read all of my books." It was getting harder and harder to tell where truth ended and lies began.

"Ed, Gina, I'm ready to go." Momma rolled up the sleeves of her gray wool dress, picked up the accordion fan that Gina had pleated and colored, and fanned her face. "This wool is too hot for the middle of June, but with the baby coming soon, I'll have to make do. At least it will be cool in the car with all the windows down. Make sure you and Pa stay out of the heat."

"You can count on that," Grandpa said from the kitchen doorway. "It's sweltering out there." He mopped his forehead with his handkerchief and filled a glass of water from the sink faucet. A yawn stretched his face.

Gina skipped into the kitchen ahead of Poppa. "Last chance, Alicia," he said.

Alicia shook her head, aware of the shop key in her dungarees that Poppa had given to her earlier—in case Slick wasn't at the shop when she went to feed Shadow. Shadow: the name rolled silently over her tongue. Alicia trailed behind her family, watched them get into Poppa's car, and waved good-bye.

As soon as the car disappeared under the railroad bridge, she ran to her bicycle, pushed hard on the back tire, felt the air holding, and went back inside for Shadow's scraps. Grandpa was already asleep in his rocking chair beside the console radio, the volume turned low. She wrote him a note saying that she was riding her bicycle—not a lie—and for him to stay out of the heat.

Shadow was behind the storeroom door—the place Poppa hid her during the day—tail wagging, tongue lolling to one side, drool dripping in anticipation of table scraps and bones. Alicia changed the bedding, got a fresh bowl of water, and checked the gash on her velvet coat. Usually, if Poppa had time, they took Shadow behind the shop and walked around discarded rusted oil drums, well hidden by a cluster of maple trees. Shadow led the way, flushing out the occasional rabbit, but never venturing beyond the tree line and always returning to Alicia's side. Sometimes, her favorite times, Poppa told stories about the family before the War. Each day seemed like an answer to her prayers.

Is my Poppa really back?

Alicia fed the dog and led her out the back door. As Shadow was sniffing around the base of a maple, Alicia told her she was sorry that there wasn't time for a walk. The dog tilted her head, cocked her ears as if trying to understand, went back inside, turned around three times, and plopped on her bedding, seemingly resigned. Alicia hurried out the door.

She rode, surrounded by a world of greens and blues. Feathery tipped grasses rippled across the flat prairie that extended until it touched the sky.

Clara was on the wooden bridge, her elbows resting on the railing. The green of her shirt made her part of the landscape. Alicia walked up and followed Clara's gaze eastward. Cutters Creek twisted and turned, seeming to end where it began beneath jade-colored leaves that touched as if holding hands over calm waters. Clara crossed the bridge and made her way down the slope, holding chokecherry branches for support. She stopped at the creek's edge. Alicia followed. The melody of a yellow meadowlark greeted them.

They walked along the bank, brushing aside tree branches to pass through green gates of leaves. Climbing vines and unopened buds of purple flowers hid in shadows. The creek widened as it meandered through a deep glen and emerged between steep pink rock walls.

Alicia turned around to look: the bridge and all that was familiar had disappeared. Clara led Alicia away from the creek to a wide space between a tall, flat-sided rock wall and thirty-three smooth rock steps. Together, they climbed. At the top, a small glade was filled with yellow, white, and blue flowers quivering in a thunderous roar that drowned all sounds. Frightened, Alicia reached for Clara's hand and cautiously let herself be led to a blanket of green grass on the cliff's edge. The rippling creek crashed over rocks—forty, fifty feet below. A mist bow rose from the churning, cascading water. Alicia was spellbound.

Clara and Alicia crossed the glade, following in the footsteps of Lady Slippers. They passed a buffalo wallow and walked down a grassy slope through an explosion of color: scarlet, vermillion, lavender, magenta. Once again they found the docile flowing creek between rock walls. The roar of the falls reduced to the tinkling of silver bells.

Did I imagine it?

Rocks here were of a different color—the gray of a Minnesota sky before an all-day rain. Clara pointed to three turtle-shaped rocks, their noses aimed at seven worn steps beneath an archway of saplings nestled in a bed of Queen Anne's lace. Clara pushed aside low-slung branches that hid a large—tall enough for Grandpa—arched opening in the face of the rock. "We're going in."

Alicia hesitated. She had become fearful of small, dark places—fearful of being trapped. She grasped the cross necklace that had become her talisman.

"I'm going to be with you. I won't let anything happen to you, I promise." Clara vanished into the tunnel.

Alicia took a deep breath and entered. The immediate darkness overwhelmed and blinded her. She wanted to call out but knew this hushed world would swallow her words. She closed her eyes, preferring her own loss of sight to that imposed by the tunnel's darkness. With slow, measured steps, her hands on walls, she felt a growing sense of comfort. She opened one eye at a time. The walls and tunnel roof glittered like small, distant stars.

The tunnel turned sharply to the left, ending at the edge of the cavern. A solitary center in the high-domed ceiling funneled a dazzling rainbow of lights—their colors so pure, Alicia tasted them on her tongue. Melodic notes of a harp, perhaps a lute, accompanied the chanting of a wind choir. She stumbled backwards, landing on a pew-shaped rock ledge, smooth as if worn by countless people over countless ages.

Across the cavern, images of animals swayed in the shimmering lights. Alicia rose and glided through the lights over a smooth rock floor to an altar beneath carvings: buffalos, turtles, wolves, dragonflies, humans. Smells of burning leaves, lemon, a spicy mixture of cinnamon and pepper rode the wind.

What is this place?

Time passed—minutes, hours, days, perhaps years. It was a temple of solitude, of refuge, of escape, a place to be re-born. Clara touched Alicia's arm and whispered that it was time to leave. Reluctantly, she followed. Outside, clouds passed over the sun; the sky color had shifted, still blue, but not quite blue.

***

"Why so quiet?" Grandpa inquired. "It's not like you."

Alicia waited for him to ask where she'd been for such a long time, but he seemed not to have noticed.

He touched her cheek. "You look flushed. Too much sun?"

She shook her head, but Grandpa looked flushed, too. She wondered if he'd spent too much time in the sun without her there to remind him. After they finished eating, he poured a half-cup of coffee, added cream and a small spoonful of sugar, and handed the cup to Alicia. "About time they end sugar rationing, I'd say. Don't be telling Ilse about this coffee." Grandpa gave her a conspiratorial wink. She added another small spoonful of sugar.

Alicia was trying to make sense of her journey when Poppa's car horn honked and she realized she had barely made it home in time. "I'll go help, Grandpa. You can stay here. I want to see what Momma got for the baby." She was out the door, taking half her words with her.

Gina crawled out of the backseat and rushed to Alicia. "Look!" She pulled a new package of crayons and new Rainbow Tablet from a sack. "And for you." With a sweeping gesture, she presented Alicia with a Wonder Woman comic book and leaned in to whisper, "I saw two license plates, and Momma spelled them for me. Colorado and Florida. They're far away. I didn't tell her our secret. Are you proud of me? And the hamburgers were sooooo good! And we got Grandpa a new book. *Cannery Row* Momma said." Gina ran off, calling for Grandpa and waving his book.

"That girl!" Momma laughed. She looked prettier and happier than she had in a long time. A pink blush glowed from her cheek. "I can hardly believe the hustle and bustle in Marshall—cars, new stores, people, babies. It's an exciting new world." She handed three packages to Alicia. "Let's go see what I bought for the baby. I don't believe the nonsense about it being bad luck to buy things for a baby before it's born. What is the difference between that and using Gina's old baby clothes?" Sweat darkened under her arms.

Alicia spread the packages on the dining room table, and Gina opened them one at a time like birthday gifts and sorted them into neat piles: tiny white undershirts, yellow sleepers with coverings for feet and hands, small pink and blue receiving blankets, and small white bands with strings attached. "They're for our baby's belly button," Gina confided.

"Where's Poppa?" Alicia asked, wondering if he somehow knew she'd been with Clara.

"Down in the cellar," Momma said. "He's making a surprise for me, and no one except Grandpa can go down there. Gina, that means you! I'm going to get out of these hot clothes. Pa, any coffee left or did you and my girl drink all of it?"

Alicia allowed the safe peaceful feelings of the cavern to wash over her, and she dared hope for a happy family.

11

Close to suppertime, Poppa asked Alicia if she and Gina wanted to go downtown to the outdoor picture show. It seemed Bill had been shipped an extra one along with the regular Saturday night reels. "Just you and Gina," he added. "Anton's too tired to go along and sit on the ground."

Without Grandpa?

Alicia could hardly believe her ears. "Sure!" For the rest of the afternoon, she was wary. In spite of all the good signs from Poppa, habit and experience cautioned her, and she "walked on egg shells," a saying Momma used all too often.

Gina and Momma talked all through supper about their trip to Marshall. Alicia stared at the clock's hands pasted in place. She picked at her food and worried Poppa might change his mind. Alicia washed, dried, and stacked the dishes in the cupboards. She placed Momma's old quilt beside the porch door. But the sun still blazed above the horizon, refusing to set. Wound as tightly a Grandpa's old black alarm clock, she could no longer wait. She grabbed the quilt and urged Gina to follow. "You don't want to miss the *Popeye* cartoon."

"Have a good time," Grandpa called. "Enjoy the picture show."

"Be good and watch your sister," Momma said.

The words tumbled like leaves over Poppa's mumbled warning to stay away from Clara if she showed up.

"We're not going to the moon," Alicia muttered once they were outside.

"Of course not, silly," Gina said. "Nobody goes to the moon 'cause it's made of green cheese. Can we stop at Sarah's house and see how big the kittens are getting? Momma says those kittens are Sarah's babies. Did she ever have any real babies? Why not?" Gina's face took on a faraway thoughtful expression.

Grandpa would sometimes say he heard wheels spin in her brain. It had taken a long time for Alicia to convince Gina that she didn't have wheels in her head.

"But Grandpa is so smart," Gina had argued.

Alicia had heard stories that Sarah and Joe had lost twin baby girls in the influenza epidemic after the first War. With Gina so worried about death after Decoration Day, Alicia remained silent.

Without waiting for an answer, Gina skipped ahead, avoiding cracks in the sidewalk. Alicia strolled behind her and watched the sun begin its color march to the horizon. She felt the same easy freedom as when she rode her bicycle. Since the first time Clara and she had explored Cutters Creek, Alicia had noticed more things—or maybe noticed them in a different way.

Ahead, Sarah was on her knees, weeding between clumps of white daisies surrounding the stone birdbath. The air smelled of rich black soil. Sarah used her forearm to brush hair from her face, smudging her right cheek with a trail of dirt. "Give me a hand, Alicia." She pulled off the garden gloves and tossed them into the wheelbarrow. "Let's go see the kittens—if we can find them. That Momma cat spends more time hiding her babies than chasing mice, even though nobody's touched them. Protective mother, she is. Last I saw they were under my front porch."

White lattice disguised the gap between porch floor and ground, and in the far left-hand corner was a small hole in the wood, barely big enough for the mother cat. An orange tabby stared back at them. Sarah lifted a section of the lattice and hooked it upright.

"Tunnel," Alicia said.

"What?" Sarah moved so she wasn't blocking the light.

"Nothing," Alicia said.

With a loud hiss, the mother cat dashed to the scramble of kittens in a wooden apple crate turned on its side. Four orange-striped kittens, identical to their mother, rushed to nurse her long, outstretched body. A single gray kitten, smaller than the rest, toddled towards the girls. An orange flash immediately had him by the neck, carried him to the crate, and turned with a deep-throated growl.

"I guess she isn't ready for company," Sarah said with a laugh. "The friendly gray one … I call him Flicker because when he swishes his tail back and forth it looks like a candle wick caught in a breeze. Or maybe it's a her. Anyway, we'd better leave before Momma cat decides to move them again." They backed out, and the mother cat came to the lattice to make sure they left.

"You girls better head off to the picture show. Joe's been up there a while setting up the projector for Bill. Tell Ilse I'll be over tomorrow to trim her hair after Ed goes to work. Make it easier for her when the baby comes."

Barely out of earshot, Gina said, "I wish Poppa would let me have a kitty." Gina's face had looked so sad when Poppa said no cats in the house.

Alicia had nearly slipped up and told Gina about Shadow, but she didn't dare.

Gina is going to love Shadow. I can hardly wait!

The sisters walked the remaining five blocks along Center Street behind Donna and Bill who were holding hands. On Main Street, a few railroad men sat on stools, backlit in the windows of the Cozy Café. Except for the café and Hugo's Pool Hall, the buildings were dark. In the vacant lot beside Bill's store, children ran and shrieked in a game of tag. A half-circle of blankets dotted the grassy surface behind a projector that aimed its white light on the brick surface of the store.

Alicia spread her quilt next to the Christianson twins, Molly and Maggie, who were seniors in high school and talked to her about things Momma said she was too young for: the right lipstick color, high heels, colors that clashed, football and basketball games, and boyfriends.

Molly opened her compact and twisted lipstick up from its tube. "It's cherry red. The latest—everyone is wearing this color. Want to try? You can wipe it off before you go home. There goes Slick with Alphie hanging out the window. I can't figure out why a nice guy like Slick hangs out with that creep. Maybe it's because of Clara."

The cool, black lipstick tube in her hand jolted Alicia. She shook her head. The last time she had worn lipstick, it was in the castle with Gina and Clara. The fuzzy memory seemed to belong to someone else.

Gina opened her pink Easter purse and removed a black crayon and her Rainbow Tablet. She tore out a yellow sheet of paper, hunched over it, and began to draw. Words from the twins buzzed around Alicia. With a flourish, Gina revealed a picture of a large, fat rat, eyes darkened, a tail that curled like a pig's, and fangs jutting from the mouth. "Alphie," she said.

"Perfect likeness," Maggie said with a giggle.

Fireflies twittered in the growing darkness. The projector hummed, and black and white images flashed on the wall.

"Look! There's Popeye." Gina hurriedly stuffed the crayon and tablet into her purse.

"Hi, Alicia, hi Squirt, Molly, Maggie." Slick sprawled on Alicia's quilt, stretching his long legs.

Alphie emerged from the dark trees on the far side of the vacant lot, sauntered to the space between the twin's blanket and Alicia's quilt, and smoothed his hair. Gina slid closer to Alicia.

"What's buzzin', cousin?" he asked.

Molly and Maggie groaned in unison.

"Come on, Slick," Alphie said. "Who wants to watch a dumb western? Let's get some beer and go to Dead Coon Lake."

Slick shook his head and shoved some money at Alphie. "I like John Wayne. Go get an Orange Crush for Gina and Coca-Cola for me and Alicia. Something for yourself, and make sure you open the bottles."

"Make sure I open the bottles?" Alphie shook his head. "I ain't no dumb shit."

Stagecoach was half-over by the time Alphie returned and stood at the edge of the quilt.

"Down in front," someone yelled.

Bottle caps and wadded candy wrappers pelted the back of his head.

Alphie plopped on the dew-soaked grass where the Christiansons' blanket had been and passed the bottles of soda pop to Slick. "Leave the brats, and we'll go find the twins."

"Maggie says you're a creep," Gina said.

The stagecoach thundered across the screen. On the mesa above, warriors waited, their horses stomping impatiently. Gina snuggled closer to Alicia.

"Creep, huh?" Rifle shots erupted. Alphie leaned towards Alicia and whispered, "You said it, not Maggie. Dumb thing to do." Gina's drawing fluttered between Alicia and Alphie. "You want to see creepy?" His words pounded Alicia like an echo of hoof beats.

Slick grabbed Alphie's arm, pulling him off balance. "Alphie, shut up or clear out. I'm staying to the end, and then I'm driving the girls home."

"You guys make me puke." Alphie bent over, picked up the drawing, shoved it into his pocket, and tossed his lit cigarette on the grass, inches away from the quilt and Alicia.

Alicia wondered if Gina had printed her name on the drawing. Her eyes followed Alphie until his clothes blended into the darkness of the moonless sky. She knew he wasn't going to let this pass.

Alphie is so unlike Clara.

Gina snuggled against Alicia. "Slick, does the hero save the pretty girl?"

He nodded.

She yawned. "Good. Now I can go to sleep."

***

Clapping and cheering melted into the night at the picture show's end. Depot agent Oldenburg and others, whose cars had been angle parked to watch the show, turned on their headlights, lighting the tamped grass where families gathered children and belongings. Slick picked up Gina and carried her to his car. She smiled sleepily and let her head roll against his shoulder.

Alicia hadn't been in Slick's car since the day they had found Shadow. It smelled of stale cigarettes and a little of Alphie's aftershave. She was still forbidden to ride with Slick, but she hoped that Gina's falling asleep would keep her out of trouble.

Slick shut the engine off and coasted silently into the driveway. The house was dark—not even the porch light had been left on for the girls. Before Alicia opened the car door, Slick touched her arm and cautioned her to wait.

What's wrong?

He got out first, pushed his seat forward, and lifted Gina into his arms. "We'll go in together, but me first."

They walked up the lawn, climbed the steps, crossed the porch, and opened the kitchen door. Total darkness.

Alicia reached around the door jamb and flicked on the ceiling light. Poppa lunged from his chair, a carving knife poised in his hand like a weapon.

Frozen with fright, Alicia could only whisper, "Poppa!" Her heart was in her throat.

Slowly, Slick edged to Alicia's side in the doorway and halted, Gina still in his arms. "Ed, I'll trade you," he said softly. "A pretty girl for that knife."

"Who? What?"

Poppa stared at them for an eternity without recognition. Finally, he looked down at the knife in his hand and slammed it on the table as if it were a red-hot poker.

"You have my girls … thank God … I thought Clara had … I had a nightmare… "

Slick eased across the kitchen and gently lowered Gina into Poppa's empty arms, picked up the knife, held it behind his back with one hand, and with the other hand, helped Poppa to his feet.

Slick nodded to the sleeping Gina. "She needs to get in bed."

"Lock up when he leaves."

Alicia dumped the dregs of Poppa's coffee into the smoldering ashtray, waited until she heard the stairs creaking with Poppa's weight, and debated whether or not to tell Slick about Poppa's nightly pacing. Afraid to rock the boat, she only said, "We never lock our doors. I don't even know where there's a key."

"Ed keeps the shop key just inside the door."

A skeleton key dangled from a nail newly hammered into the wall, and plaster dust littered the floor. After Slick left, she swept the dust up, fit the key into the key hole, and locked the door.

Does Grandpa know?

12

Momma's screams brought Alicia to the kitchen on a dead run.

"A rat! Ohmygod! A rat." Momma held the porch screen door open, her face as white as the dish towel clutched in her hand.

Poppa pushed Alicia aside, wrapped his arms around Momma, and turned her away from the sight of a bloody, foot-long rat on the bottom step to the porch.

"I think I'm going to be sick," Momma said.

"Son of a bitch! Who in the hell would do such a thing? Joe. See? I told you he's out to get me. I'll show him the business side of my fist." Poppa shook all over.

"Calm down, Ed. You're sweating like a hog."

Grandpa eased Momma from Poppa's grasp and edged her back into the kitchen. "I've known Joe for fifty years, and he's never shot a rifle. Never owned one."

"Grandpa's right, Poppa," Alicia said. "The rat was meant to scare me. I'm sorry Momma saw it. Last night, Alphie said I called him a creep—I didn't—and he said I'd be sorry." She held back, not telling him about the picture Gina drew.

Poppa smacked his palm with his fist and let out his breath as if he had held it for a long time. "Hose down that blood before Gina wakes up. I'll get a shovel for the rat. You and me are going to have a little talk with Alphie."

Alicia pulled the green hose around the corner to the steps and waited for Poppa to bring the shovel from the car shed. She dreaded what might happen when Poppa confronted Alphie: he would tell Poppa about her secret meetings with Clara—just to get back at her—if he knew about them. Intent on her fears, she slipped on the wet steps and scraped her knee on the concrete edge. Her blood dripped on the bloody rat.

Poppa slid the shovel under the rat, carried both to the open trunk of his car, and heaved them in the trunk. He lit a cigarette and leaned against the car door while Alicia hosed away the rusty brown blood stain.

"That's enough," he called. He took another drag and then snuffed his cigarette in the gravel.

Apprehensively, Alicia crossed the lawn and climbed into the passenger seat. Poppa drove around town with dust flying on the graveled streets and tires squealing on the tarred road. "I'll find that son of a bitch if it takes me all day. This town's not that big."

A Great Northern Railroad freight train blocked Main Street just short of Hinkle's Bar. Poppa slammed on his brakes and honked wildly at the passing box cars. The train wheels clicked endlessly; the choking smell of coal smoke drifted into the open car windows. Poppa's face grew redder. When the caboose passed, Alphie was standing across the tracks in Hinkle's parking lot next to Slick's car. Poppa sped across the tracks and skidded to a stop five feet from Alphie.

"Get out, Alicia." He climbed out of the car, opened the trunk, and pulled the rat out by its tail. Ram-rod straight and with slow, deliberate steps, he approached Alphie.

The calm before the storm.

He flung the rat at Alphie's feet.

Alphie smirked. "I see your brat got my little gift. Whatcha' going to do about it, hero?

Poppa took another long step towards Alphie.

Alphie stumbled backwards but righted himself.

"She should stop hanging around Slick. He's my friend. What's a guy his age doing anyway? Her starting to …"

Striking like a coiled rattlesnake, Poppa slammed Alphie against the hood of Slick's car. His hand circled Alphie's neck—choking. "Take that damned rat back to the dump. And you'd better never cross me or my family again."

Alphie gasped for breath.

When Alicia touched Poppa's arm, he withdrew his hands, but red marks laced Alphie's neck.

Abruptly, Poppa grabbed her arm, pulled her back to the car, and thrust her inside; she craned her neck, looking out the back window. Alphie laughed soundlessly until Slick shoved him to the tar.

Poppa's fingers whitened with his stranglehold on the steering wheel. "I don't know who I can trust in this damned town anymore."

13

The sun reached its highest point on the longest day of the year—summer nearly a third gone. The scarecrow wearing Grandpa's old shirt drooped in the hot sun as if it too felt the fatigue from the never-ending heat wave. "When this one breaks," Grandpa warned, it will be a doozy.

The midday heat added to Alicia's irritation at being caught halfway between escape out the porch door and Momma's insistence that she return to the kitchen and take Gina along. To make it worse, as if it could be any worse, Poppa was waiting at the shop for his and Shadow's dinner. The grandmother clock in the living room ticked a loud reminder.

"Why does Gina have to follow me everywhere? Can't I go by myself for once?" She backed farther into the porch with the dog's sack of meat hidden behind her back. "I won't take Gina with me."

Momma leaned against the cupboard and exhaled. "Why do you have to be so ornery? You're only going to the shop. I'm going upstairs to rest. Gina, come in here and go with your sister." Alicia's argument dried up on her tongue when she saw how tired Momma looked; her eyes seemed sunken, surrounded by rings of gray. Alphie's rat had really upset her.

"You're such a pest. Sometimes," Alicia whispered harshly to Gina after Momma slipped out of sight.

Donna was sleeping after her night shift, and Sarah was busy with the Friday afternoon Sunshine Committee visits to the shut-ins. Skipping a feeding was not an option—neither was bringing Gina to Poppa's shop where she'd discover Shadow. Alicia had an idea. "Hurry up." She grabbed Gina by the arm, tugged her outside, and together, they ran down the hill to Joe's. "You stay with Joe and look for out-of-state license plates. I'll be back in a jiffy."

"But, I don't have my Rainbow Tablet."

"We'll get it as soon as I get back. Just remember them like you did when you went to Marshall."

"What if Alphie comes after me with another rat?"

Exasperated, Alicia told her sister that Joe would protect her. "Now stay here." She pointed to the stool outside the station's screen door.

Alicia sprinted up the seven blocks along Center Street with the food sacks swinging in her hand. Breathless, she pushed the shop door open. "There you are," Poppa said. "Right on time—everyday you're becoming more and more like the good soldier I need you to be when the baby comes." The praise comforted her, washed away the isolation, the loneliness.

This is how it should be… Me and Poppa.

The dog trotted to her and sniffed at the sack.

"Sit," Alicia said.

Shadow sat and nudged her nose against Alicia's hand. Alicia dumped the scraps into a bowl that Shadow licked clean. The dog's soft, dark eyes looked up for more.

Poppa tossed her a chunk of potato. Shadow caught it mid-air, gulped it down, spun around three times, and plopped beside Alicia on Poppa's Army blanket. Alicia wrapped an arm around the dog and snuggled her face into Shadow's neck.

Slick came into the front. "I got that oil pan off, Ed. Hi Alicia." He rubbed the oil streaks from his cheek with the sleeve of his coverall and knelt beside Alicia and Shadow. "You can't see her ribs anymore. Anton sure is a good cook." Shadow looked at him, tongue rolling from her mouth, a smile on her face.

The shop door opened with such force it slammed against the wall; stacked oil cans rattled in its wake. Gina stood in the doorway. "Ohhh, a puppy!" In one quick, dark motion, like ink spilling from a bottle, Shadow pulled from Alicia's arms, crossed the floor to Gina, and sniffed the bag of peanuts in her hand. Gina dumped the remaining peanuts on the floor.

Poppa stared through the open door, a look of annoyance followed by a look of anger. "Gina, is Momma outside?"

"No, she's resting. Alicia's taking care of me." Gina seemed to sense the tension-charged air, and her head swiveled back and forth between Alicia and Poppa. Worry and confusion wrinkled her brow. "I didn't have my Rainbow Tablet or my pencil, and I didn't want to ask Joe 'cause it's—"

Poppa's words slashed across Gina's.

"Alicia left you at the gas station? With Joe?" His eyes darkened.

Gina nodded and buried her face in Shadow's neck.

"Gina." His voice was ominous as the blue-black clouds gathering beyond the window. "The dog's name is Shadow, and from now on, she'll be yours, but you'll help me feed her and take care of her. Just the two of us."

Gina jumped up, ran to Poppa, and threw her arms around him. He pulled Gina's arms away from his legs, and with a long stride, stormed towards Alicia, backing her against the wooden counter.

"But, Poppa," Alicia said. "That's not fair. I—"

"Fair is what I decide. You left Gina with Joe and disobeyed a direct order to stay away from him. You know he's the enemy."

The smell of bleach rose from her white blouse beneath Poppa's sweating, squeezing hand. "Why the hell do you always have to ruin things for me?"

Gina cried out. "No … Poppa …"

Slick stepped between Alicia and Poppa. "Ed …"

Poppa whirled, red with anger, his arm raised as if to strike Slick. Stone-faced, shielding Alicia, Slick grabbed

Poppa's wrist and held it until Poppa yanked away. "Slick, keep your goddamned nose out of my family business."

Alicia cringed.

"As for you …" Poppa's forefinger stabbed the air in front of Alicia, "get out of my sight."

His love had slipped through her fingers like fine grains of sand. She darted out the door. Shrouded in hurt, she weighed her options of where to run—the cavern or the lumber yard. She chose the closest one.

Gina raced after her. "Wait up. Stop!" She gasped for air. "Why is Poppa so mad? What did I do? I'm sorry."

Alicia hesitated, stopped, and bent forward. The stitch in her side burned from running. "Nothing, Gina. You didn't do nothing. I'm the one who always does everything wrong. Go home before Poppa finds you with me. It will only make him madder at me."

Gina's mouth opened, but nothing came out; she turned away from the lumber yard door and slid behind the cover of Mrs. Oldenburg's apple trees.

Alicia climbed to the second-floor landing. She tried to sort things out, but one thing after another chased around in her mind. Poppa's quicksilver behavior left her exhausted. Poppa hated her again, and now she had Alphie to worry about, too. She dreamt of climbing on her bicycle and riding away, but she could never abandon Gina. Just the thought made her gasp. Her stomach ached with hurt and hunger, but she wasn't ready to go home to face … face what?

"Alicia, Alicia!"

Gina called to her through the fog in her head. Beneath the landing steps, Shadow's bark followed by a whine echoed her words.

"Grandpa says the sky is sick and green, and you better high-tail it home." The distant drum-roll of thunder reverberated throughout the lumber yard. Above the open roof, a menacing sky, the color of mold, had turned afternoon into night.

Grandpa's right.

She descended quickly and took her sister's hand.

"I told him you went to Sarah's house to see the kittens," Gina said.

Now I have Gina lying for me.

"When I passed Poppa's shop, Shadow snuck out and followed me. I knew this was where you'd gone."

The dog's barking grew more insistent. Shadow led the way through the orchard, along Center Street, past Poppa's shop, past the school house and church, past Sarah's house, and down the garden path to Alicia's house—a place Shadow had never been before. She constantly looked back at the girls, encouraging them to keep up.

Alicia and Gina struggled with southwesterly gusts at their backs so strong they were nearly knocked down several times. Louder and louder the thunder rumbled, bearing down on Fullerton.

After shepherding them home, the dog lunged under the porch as the first band of rain hit. The girls rushed inside. Poppa arrived a few steps behind. Rainwater poured on the kitchen floor from his drenched clothes.

"All the windows are shut." Grandpa threw a dry towel to Poppa.

As if responding to the futility of Grandpa's actions, the west porch window rattled. A worried expression crossed Grandpa's face. "Twister's coming. I can feel it. Better be ready to spend the night in the cellar."

Momma rounded the corner into the kitchen with one hand on her back and the other clutching two pillows she set on a stack of blankets. The ceiling light flickered.

"Ed," Momma said, "my back's hurting pretty bad. Having pain off and on. Could there be a worse time?"

Lightning and thunder struck simultaneously, illuminating the kitchen with a frightening brilliance.

"That one hit nearby. Get a move on, girls," Grandpa shouted above the roar of the constant thunder. "Grab those pillows from your Momma and head down into the cellar." Alicia and Gina swooped up the pillows and raced down the steps. Footsteps from Momma, Poppa, and Grandpa echoed behind them.

Schooled by tornadoes that came like demons from the sky every year, Alicia crawled under Grandpa's workbench in the southwest corner of the cellar. She hurriedly spread the blankets on the cold cement floor. Momma went down on her hands and knees, crawled beside Alicia, and leaned against the two pillows that Alicia had arranged for her. They huddled together: Poppa and Grandpa like bookends, Momma in the middle, arms encircling the girls. Each thunder clap brought the storm closer and closer. The hair on Alicia's arms stood on end. The wind shrieked like a banshee. Cellar lights flickered and went out. The dark was absolute and suffocating. Gina's sobs echoed the hard rain pelting the cellar windows. Next to Alicia, Momma stiffened. In the blue flash of lightning, her eyes squeezed shut and her face contorted in pain.

The house moaned above them. Suddenly, all the air was sucked from the cellar as if the storm was holding its breath. Then it was quiet. So quiet, it hurt Alicia's ears, until the silence was pierced by a roar so loud it shook the house above them. For a brief moment, Alicia saw nothing, heard nothing, and felt nothing.

Am I dead?

She opened her eyes and looked up, afraid she might see open sky. Or another tornado. But the living hell had passed. Their house was still above them. Even the cold rain pouring down on her from the broken cellar window assured her she was alive. Momma, Poppa, and Grandpa kept asking over and over if she and Gina were okay. Concern rode their questions. Even Poppa's.

Somewhere on the other side of Momma, Gina still cried.

"Shhh, Gina. I've got you," Momma said. "The tornado is over."

In the fading bolts of lightning, glass glittered on the floor. "Damn!" Poppa said. "Stay where you are. I'll find a flashlight." Something big and heavy crashed to the floor along with the breaking of more glass. "What's this sticky crap?"

Momma moaned.

"Where the hell's my flashlight?" Poppa demanded. "Alicia, you been down here messing with my stuff again?"

"I was using it, Ed," Grandpa said. "It's on the workbench above us. Far right corner."

The deep echo of Shadow's bark resonated off the concrete walls. A flashlight beam pierced the broken window and scoured the cellar with a blinding light. "It's me—Slick. Anybody down there?"

Momma moaned loudly.

"Slick," Poppa shouted back, "get down here. We need help."

Slick's footsteps followed the dog's padding, the flashlight beam between them. Shadow ran to Alicia, gave a small bark, and lapped her face. The dog smelled like strawberry jam.

Poppa was standing, the second flashlight in his hand. "Give me a hand with Ilse. She's under the workbench and in labor."

Momma leaned forward, still on her knees, and extended a hand to Slick, but he crawled under the workbench and lifted Momma out and slightly up for Poppa to get a hold.

"Careful," Poppa said as Slick stood and slid under Momma's other arm. "The floor's covered with glass, and she's barefoot. Get her to that stool by the steps."

They carried Momma across the concrete floor, glass crunching underfoot.

Gina reached for her sister. "Momma?"

With her thumb, Alicia wiped away Gina's tears. In Grandpa's flashlight beam, dark, unfamiliar, frightening shapes became her family, and her fear melted, except for a small ice-cold center somewhere inside that she could neither identify nor wipe away: a sense of something awful, worse than the tornado.

Slick returned, lifted Gina into his arms, carried her, came back for Alicia, and guided her to the bottom cellar step, close to Gina and Momma.

The light from the flashlight illuminated Shadow's black coat.

"Am I seeing things?" Momma asked. "Is that a dog? I thought I heard a bark before, but …"

"Well, I'll be darned if it isn't," Grandpa said. He lit the dog from nose to tail. Shadow went to Momma, placed her head in Momma's lap, and wedged her nose under Momma's hand. The dog whimpered, a cry that came from deep inside her, as if she were talking to Momma.

"Is she female? I think she knows what's going on. Oh, no, Ed." Panic filled her voice. "My water just broke."

"Oh my God, not now. Slick, what's it like out there?"

"A big elm in front is down, but it missed the house and your car. Trees are down all over Fullerton, debris tossed everywhere. I don't know …"

"Ed," Momma insisted, "We don't have a choice. They're coming more often now, and Donna's not home to help. We'll chance the highway is clear. If we can get out of town, there aren't any trees along the highway." Momma cried out in pain. "I need to go. Now!" She struggled to stand.

Gina whimpered. Alicia drew her closer.

"Alicia, you and Slick go upstairs, find my suitcase—it's in the front hall closet—and meet us at the car. Gina, slide over here and listen to me. The storm is over, and I need you to be a big, brave girl. I'm going to get the baby, and Grandpa and Alicia will stay here and take care of you." She wrapped Gina in her arms and bent to touch her cheek on Gina's head. "That's my big girl."

Alicia shivered not from cold, rain-soaked clothing, but worry.

"Come on. They'll be all right," Slick said. His flashlight guided her up the steps and through the dark house to the hall closet. She handed the suitcase to Slick, removed Momma's spring coat from its hanger, and carried it over her arm to Poppa's car. The sky had cleared, and a full moon illuminated tree branches piled like a game of Pick-Up Sticks. Momma hugged Grandpa and the girls before Poppa helped her into the car, and like that, Momma and Poppa disappeared into the storm-ravaged night.

Gina held Alicia's hand tightly as if Alicia, too, might also disappear into the night.

"Might as well go inside," Grandpa said.

Slick handed the flashlight to Alicia and took Grandpa's arm. "Don't know how long the power will be out. Sure could go for a cup of hot coffee." The fallen elm branch scraped the dining room window with an eerie sound. Gina shifted closer to Alicia in the big wingback chair. Grandpa lit an oil lamp. "Seeing as we missed supper, I'll round up some food. Then you girls better go to bed. Tomorrow's going to be a busy day. Slick, why don't you bunk on the sofa?"

In bed, fed and exhausted, with Gina and Raggedy Ann snuggled next to her, Alicia fell asleep to the lull of Slick and Grandpa's voices drifting upstairs.

Gina tossed and turned most of the night, sometimes grabbing Alicia in a frantic clawing motion until reassured, time and time again, that the storm was over.

***

Alicia eased out of sleep; the sound of Clara's voice brought her fully awake. She threw on her dungarees and buttoned the blouse on the steps. Grandpa and Clara were at the kitchen table drinking coffee. Grandpa's hand dangled at his side, scratching Shadow's ears. "Get yourself a cup, Alicia. It's the only hot thing in the house. From Bill's gas stove. He said Donna stayed at the hospital, helping with the twister injuries. Some were pretty bad. You'd think by now people would have the sense to take cover." He sipped his coffee. "Ed called when they got to the hospital."

Relieved that Momma and Poppa had arrived safely, she nodded and poured milk into the coffee.

"No baby yet." Grandpa said. He and Clara exchanged worried glances.

Finally fully awake, Alicia asked, "Clara, how did you get here? Does Poppa know?"

"The tornado hit just as Graffie and I were closing the Trading Post. That old hanging sign smashed Graffie's truck. I stayed all night huddled in a booth with an old horsehair blanket. As soon as it was light, I came to see if you were all right. You, Gina, and me are going downtown to help the Ladies Aid. Wake up Gina for some cereal, and we'll be gone before Ed knows I was here."

"Slick went on ahead to get things rolling. The menfolk will clean up the debris," Grandpa said. "Time's a wasting. And put on a sweater. Cold winds are trailing the storm."

Beyond the porch, lightening had stripped an old elm raw of its bark. The girls, led by Shadow, detoured past a downed wild plum tree through the garden. Grandpa's scarecrow—blown off his broomstick handle onto bent knees, straw hat tilted on bowed head—appeared to be praying. Bill's garage was completely gone, the cement floor wiped clean. Downed trees along Center Street looked like oversized toothpicks blocking the road. In the midst of one of the rubble-dotted yards, a bicycle stood erect on its kickstand, untouched. The Quaker State Oil sign at Poppa's shop was gone, and shingles littered the streets. At the corner of Main, the banker and two of his tellers boarded up the big front bank window. The barber pole had stopped its spin. A group of railroad men milled around on the sidewalk in front of the Cozy Café next to Bill's store with steaming cups of coffee in hand. They parted to let the girls enter.

Sarah paused, set a donation basket beside the cash register, and approached Alicia. "Slick said you hadn't heard any news from the hospital, and from the look on your face, I'd guess you still haven't. Don't you worry. Sometimes it takes a while." She waved Clara towards the restaurant kitchen. "Clara, grab an apron and help cook breakfast. Gina, bring the dirty dishes to the back. We're sure lucky to have the propane stove here. Alicia, Slick's waiting out back. We set up calls on the party line. We don't know how long it's going to take to get power, so most people are donating food from their refrigerators before it spoils. You and Slick drive around and pick it up. Make sure you tell everyone they are welcome to eat here until the power comes back on or the food is gone."

"Where do you want this hamburger?" Graffie asked. He and Joe each carried an armload of bulging brown paper bags.

"Where does Graffie come up with all this stuff?" Sarah asked.

Alicia found Slick leaning against his car. She shook her head, climbed in, and focused on the debris and fallen trees. Even with windows closed against the raw north wind, the smell of cut wood seeped in. The park across from the café was empty, and the streets were void of bicycles and shouts of children.

"As soon as daylight came," Slick said, "we got the railroad tracks cleared. Mr. Oldenburg telegraphed the other depot agents last night, both north and south, that our tracks were blocked. He tripped in the dark and got a bad cut above his forehead, but he's still at the depot."

They made several trips to homes and back to the restaurant with only a few people not answering the door. A silence filled Alicia, too.

When they drove up with the last of the food, she spotted Poppa's car parked sideways in front of Bill's store. He wildly waved his arms and stuffed cigars into every man's shirt pocket lined up in front of the café. Gina stood beside him, beaming. Alicia jumped from the car before it completely stopped. "Poppa!"

Poppa lifted her up and twirled her around. She felt fear for just a moment until she saw his face. "It's a boy!" he shouted again and again. "William ... William the conqueror!" He drew his face close to hers and whispered. "Everything is going to be all right now."

His smile faded, his eyes blinked and hardened, his face turned white as if he'd seen a ghost.

Alicia turned around. Clara stood on the top step of the restaurant. Poppa lost his hold on Alicia. She slipped to the sidewalk.

"Keep her away." He pointed at Clara. "Stop her before she puts a curse on my baby!"

The blustery wind ceased; a steel gray cloud crossed the sun. Slick appeared and ushered Clara inside.

Poppa trembled, stumbled backwards. "Can't you see it?" His eyes moved from man to man in the crowd. They looked down, away. He grabbed Alicia by the shoulders, imploring. "You must see it, you must help save my baby."

Grandpa's arm circled Poppa. "We're going to the hospital," he said. The two of them climbed into Poppa's car, Grandpa behind the wheel.

Slick came out of the cafe. "Show's over," he said.

14

After a week of cleanup, Fullerton emerged from piles of rubble and debris. Broken glass, shingles, and tree branches filled the town dump. Sarah's cat and kittens returned after a four-day absence. Gina added two new license plates from cars of newspaper reporters from North Dakota and Nebraska. Stories filtered into town of lives lost, their tales answered with whispers of how lucky Fullerton had been.

Outside, Grandpa, Gina, Alicia, and Shadow waited. A gentle breeze sifted through the leaves. Gina sprawled out on the grass. Drowsy clouds shaped like elephants, rabbits, and monster donuts drifted across the blue sky like giant balloons without strings. Alicia sat in the dappled shade of the apple tree.

A beautiful day for our baby.

"Aren't they ever going to get here?" Gina rolled onto her stomach.

Shadow fetched a well-chewed stick, dropped it onto Gina's back, and flopped down beside her with anticipation. Shadow suddenly cocked her ears, whipped blades of grass with her tail, and barked her goofy bark reserved for Slick.

Slick's jalopy roared into the driveway and stopped in front of the car shed. Clara sat in front with Slick, while, in the back, Alphie slithered down. Shadow trotted to meet Slick and Clara. Slick gave Grandpa a white package tied with a blue ribbon. "Diapers from me and Clara. "Hi, Alicia. Hi, Squirt."

Clara sat beside Grandpa and covered his hand with hers. "Slick said Ilse and Ed named the baby William Johan Drake. Johan would've been so happy! And proud."

Grandpa placed his other hand on Clara's. Alicia was aware of the sadness she sometimes saw exchanged in the eyes of Clara and Grandpa, and this was one of those times.

"I wish I could stay to see the baby." Clara stood, still grasping Grandpa's hand. "Ed will be here soon and I don't want to spoil this special day for him."

It made no sense that Poppa could still be mad at Clara for what happened last Thanksgiving.

The horn on Slick's car honked repeatedly. Shadow ran to the car, put her paws on the open window, and growled at Alphie as he leaned over the driver's seat. Shadow loved everybody, it seemed, but Alphie. "I wish that brother of mine would grow up," Clara said.

When Clara and Slick were back inside the car, Grandpa spoke. "Not likely."

The road dust from Slick's car had barely settled before Poppa pulled in.

"Momma." Shadow at her heels, Gina ran to the car. Poppa guided her around to Momma's door. He reached inside and took a blue-blanketed bundle from Momma's arms.

"Let me see him! Let me see him," Gina pleaded.

"Wait until we get inside." Poppa's whole face smiled. Alicia couldn't remember seeing Poppa this happy.

Shadow trailed them, but when she reached the screen door on the porch, it was already shut. She walked down the cement steps, stood there, tail down, whimpering, until Momma, joined by Alicia and Grandpa, held the door open. Shadow trotted into the living room where Poppa sat on the sofa with Gina and William. She sniffed the baby's head and fingers. Apparently satisfied, she lay down beside the lace-draped bassinet—a gift from Donna and Bill, and unknown to Poppa, also from Sarah and Joe.

"Alicia, come and see your new baby brother." Poppa patted the sofa next to him.

Poppa gently unfolded the blanket. William's fair skin was the color of Momma's string of pearls, his head crowned with wispy red hair.

"He's perfect, Poppa. As small as Gina's china doll."

Poppa nodded, still smiling.

Alicia returned a smile of hope.

On the other side of Poppa, Gina leaned forward on her knees, her nose touching baby William's forehead. She took a deep breath. "Grandpa says babies come from heaven. Is this what heaven smells like?"

Excited whispers followed the creaking of the porch door. Sarah and Donna peeked around the jamb. Sarah's hand rested on the shorter Donna's arm.

"Is William awake?" Sarah asked. "I can't wait to see him without the hospital nursery glass between us."

She walked straight to Poppa and sat on the arm of the sofa beside him and William. "Just look at that beautiful boy, would you?" Her face beamed in the low light of the shade-covered, south windows. "He has red hair just like Gina."

At the sound of her voice, William opened his eyes. They were the color blue of the sky on a day when it seemed to touch the heavens. Alicia's arms ached to hold him. "Those are your eyes, Alicia," Sarah said. "Just like your Momma and Johan's." Her hand trembled as she reached to touch the baby.

Poppa, recoiling, turned William away from Sarah. Happiness drained from her pale face.

"So, my son looks nothing like me." Poppa spoke in a low voice tinged with anger, and his smile disappeared as if Alicia had imagined it. Gina's mouth opened, but Alicia quieted her with a quick shake of her head. Sarah rose and slowly walked into the dining room to sit between Momma and Donna. Momma patted her hand.

"Donna, come have a look," Poppa called to Sarah's back.

"Ed," Donna said, "you forget. I saw him in the delivery room before you did. All six pounds and nineteen inches of him." The women bent their heads together as if in prayer. Momma's cigarette burned untouched in the ashtray. Donna snubbed it out.

Alicia stared back and forth between Poppa and Momma. A feeling, unfamiliar, urged her to join the women. She belonged there. She started to rise, but Poppa tugged at her arm, forcing her to pay attention to him.

"Everything is going to be all right now that we have baby William. You know that, don't you?"

Alicia nodded, but she didn't know what he was talking about.

"What was lost has been found."

Is he quoting the Bible or Pastor Anderson?

Snippets of conversation floated away from the three women. Alicia tilted her ear towards them to better hear, but Poppa's words rolled over the top, smothering theirs.

"… such a long labor," Donna said.

"… and you can hold him, Alicia," Poppa said.

"… look so tired," Sarah said.

" … William … rebirth for all of us," Poppa said.

"… I'm worried," Momma said.

Poppa stood, clasping William to his chest. His eyes were moist and shining. "It will be just like before the War. My family will be safe. I'll be safe." He put William in Alicia's arms and passed by the women.

It felt so good to hold a tiny baby. "Welcome home, baby brother." His little fingers grasped Alicia's finger. She had never touched anything so soft. Joy overwhelmed her. William was locked in her heart—forever.

Alicia cupped William's head in the palm of her hand. She looked across the living and dining rooms at Grandpa, hoping for an explanation for Poppa's strange words.

Grandpa was bent forward as if a heavy weight were strapped to his back. He shook his head, walked to the sofa, and sat down. "Uff da. Alicia, your job is to grow up. Not to save the world."

Alicia shifted the baby into Grandpa's arms.

"He sure does favor Johan," Grandpa said. William opened his eyes. "Ever notice Slick has darker flecks of blue in his eyes, too?"

William smiled.

"Gas," Grandpa said, matching William's smile with his own.

"But he'll be smiling soon." Alicia made a cradle of Gina's small arms, and Grandpa nestled William on them.

"Oh my," Gina said.

The sun continued its long trek towards nightfall. An unfamiliar calm, disturbed only by the black fan moving hot air, surrounded Alicia. She read another *Bobbsey Twins* adventure. William slept in his bassinet with Shadow napping on the multicolor braid rug below. Her snout hung over the edge and gave an occasional snort.

Poppa's footsteps pulled Alicia's eyes away from her book. He walked into the living room wearing his coveralls and carrying a large wooden board. "Where's your Momma? Where's everybody?"

"Momma went upstairs to rest as soon as Donna left. Gina is at Sarah's house, and Grandpa is playing whist at the Cozy Café."

His breath went out like a deflating balloon. "I wanted to show her this." Poppa reversed the board, revealing a white painted sign with black lettering:

EDWARD DRAKE AND SON
TIRE & AUTO REPAIR

He propped the three-by-five-foot sign against the sofa and left.

Momma came down the stairs an hour later. Alicia had a few pages left to read.

Momma yawned and walked by Poppa's sign without comment. "I'm going to take William upstairs and feed him. Grandpa's home. Go help him with supper."

"Uhhuh. Grandpa will call me when he needs me."

"Now, young lady." Momma picked William from his bassinet and carried him towards the stairs.

Shadow followed as far as Alicia and sat down beside her chair. She reached an arm over to scratch the dog's floppy ears, waited until Momma was out of sight, and then reopened her book.

The telephone in the kitchen rang. Two short and one long ring. "Alicia, come answer that," Grandpa called. "I got grease splattering."

Followed by Shadow, she carried the book with her finger marking the page, picked up the receiver on the wooden telephone, and leaned into the mouthpiece.

"Hello?" The dog sniffed her empty food bowl, went to Alicia, and nudged her leg with a wet nose.

"Hello?" she said again.

A deep voice answered. "Hello? Hello? Can you hear me? I'd like to speak with Sergeant Edward Drake, please. This is Lieutenant Calvin Meyer."

"Just a minute. Grandpa, where's Poppa? A lieutenant wants to talk to him."

"He's in the car shed. Run and get him."

Alicia and Shadow ran to the car shed.

"Poppa?" She turned the handle. Locked. "Poppa?" She knocked. Shadow barked. The door cracked open, but Poppa stayed back in the dim light, holding something behind his back.

"A soldier wants you on the telephone."

Poppa came out, locked the car shed door, put the key in his pants pocket, and ran. Shadow paced Poppa to the porch door but waited for Alicia who hung back a few feet. She let the dog in but waited outside the open kitchen door.

Poppa's hand shook as he lifted the dangling receiver. "Yes, sir, it is. If you don't mind my asking, sir, how did you get this number?" Fingers tapped an unknown cadence on his leg. "Oh, that's right. Ilse did give it to you, sir." He seemed to stand straighter with each word. "You're coming here? To Fullerton? Tomorrow?" He patted his coverall pocket, took out a pack of cigarettes, and shook one nearly out of the package. "Someone wants to talk to me, but who, sir? I mean Cal." Poppa's hand froze mid-way to his mouth. "Can't say? Yes, of course. So long, ah, Cal." Poppa let the earpiece slip from his hand, his eyes fixed on the mouthpiece. He looked around the kitchen the way a stranger might. Without a word, he disappeared past Alicia as if she were invisible. Grandpa replaced the earpiece.

"Poppa didn't even stop when I asked him to see my wagon," Gina whined. "And I've been calling you, and you're standing there and not answering me." Gina's face was pressed against the screen door. "Come see what Joe and Sarah did to Uncle Johan's old red wagon. I'm going to pull my dolls in the Fourth of July parade tomorrow."

Once outside, Alicia ignored Gina and searched for Poppa or his car. Both were gone.

"Look!" Gina put her hands on her hips and stamped her foot. "Grandpa said I could … and he said Johan would be happy to have his wagon in the Fourth of July parade."

"What?" Alicia slowly focused on her sister. "Show me the wagon." In the late afternoon sun, Johan's old rusted wagon now glistened with a new coat of red paint. A piece of black garden hose covered the bent metal handle, and red, white, and blue crepe paper streamers lay in the bed ready to be unfurled the next day. "Johan would be very happy for you. And next summer you can give William rides in the beautiful wagon."

"Well, we can go inside now." Gina walked taller, prouder.

A pang of guilt lodged itself in Alicia's stomach for hiding away, her nose in a book, instead of taking care of Gina.

***

Long past supper, long past the last page of Alicia's book, long past Gina's bedtime excitement, and long past the time Alicia should've been asleep, she heard Poppa come home. He paced the kitchen floor, his cigarette smoke filtering upstairs. Unusual noises—a rustling, a dull thud, the opening and closing of a window—not the same as those noises he made most nights when he wandered the house. She crawled out of bed and crept down the stairs, making certain to walk along the step sides to prevent them from creaking. At the bottom, she let her eyes adjust to the light of the crescent moon hanging in the sky. In the kitchen doorway, she hung back in the shadow.

A stack of newspapers were spread in front of Poppa, barricaded by Momma's sewing scissors, a jar of white paste, and a dark green photograph album held together by black ties. He paged through the newspapers, cut something out, crumpled it, and heaved it onto a pile beside his bare feet. When all of the pages lay in a heap, he stared at the darkened north window as if seeing something besides his reflection. With the sweep of one hand, everything flew from the table and scattered across the floor. Poppa bent his head onto crossed arms and sobbed.

Alicia cemented her feet to the rug. She was unable to go to him or to leave him. The ticking of the clock marked each second of her indecision. Finally, when Poppa went outside, she returned to bed.

15

Another holiday: Fourth of July, just five weeks after Decoration Day. Alicia was struck with the similarity—except for her new baby brother. Grandpa read the newspaper. Momma cuddled a sleeping William and ate oatmeal with her free hand. Poppa faced the stove with a coffee cup in one hand and the pot in the other, poised to pour. The scene appeared normal—if that word still had meaning in her family.

Three firecrackers exploded in rapid succession.

Poppa's cup crashed to the stove, and coffee sizzled on a hot burner. His face reddened as if the coffee had splattered and burned his face. "Damn kids and their firecrackers. I could've been holding Baby William."

Momma motioned for Alicia to take her brother. He stirred but stayed asleep. Momma turned the stove off, poured Poppa another cup, and urged him to sit down. He strode to the north window overlooking the backyard and highway. His head swiveled. The bitter smell of burned coffee lingered.

"Ed," Momma asked, "did Cal say what time he'd be here?"

Perhaps he hadn't heard her.

"I wonder if he ever got engaged to Mary Lou," Momma continued. "They made such a cute couple. Remember you told him he was way too ugly for her? Him being your lieutenant." Her smile was in her eyes, too. "I almost crawled under the table until he laughed and said you weren't no pretty boy, either."

A single boom, louder than the first three firecrackers, echoed through the room. Poppa jumped backwards away from the window. "A cherry bomb," he said. "That damn Alphie's at it again. That's it. I warned him to stay away." The slammed screen door punctuated his departure.

Momma shook her head and reached her arms out to take the still sleeping baby from Alicia. "I hate to wake him, but it's time for his feeding." The jar of paste rolled in front of Shadow as she belly-crawled out from underneath the table. Last night's journey to the kitchen had not been part of a nightmare. Shadow trailed Momma and William into the dining room.

"Ed's going to have a busy day if he thinks he can stop the firecrackers." Grandpa picked up the jar of paste, set it on the countertop, and glanced out the same window as Poppa had stared. "Alicia, round up Gina, and we'll head to the park. Sarah roped me into helping with the shindig—as usual."

"I'm already rounded up, Grandpa." Gina stood in the dining room doorway. She wore a blue, sailor-like pinafore dress that Momma had sewn from Alicia's ripped birthday dress. A big white bow tied back her red curls. "Why was Shadow there?" She peered under the table and nearly dropped her armload of dolls.

"I think the firecrackers scared her." Alicia turned to help Gina with the dolls and stopped suddenly. "You found Snirpa? How?" Memories caught her by surprise, grabbed at her stomach. She'd stuffed Snirpa, the doll Poppa had given her when he'd left for the War, in an old hat box and hidden it in the back corner of her closet. It had been there since last Thanksgiving Day.

The day everything changed: Clara was forbidden to come near Poppa's family. Blame rushed over Alicia.

Me and my dumb idea.

Thanksgiving dinner should have been a milestone for Alicia: She was allowed, for the first time, to sit at the grown-up table between Clara and Julie, Poppa's sister—away from Gina; away from her two cousins, Roger and Wally; away from their kicks under the kid's table. Alicia let words and laughter from the table surround her like a cocoon, her mind on the idea that, finally, Momma and Poppa realized she was growing up. Thanksgiving food, most from Grandpa's garden or bartered for, was passed around: roasted turkey, candied winter squash, green beans, mashed potatoes, and giblet gravy.

Clara handed Alicia the gravy boat, and it slid off its plate, covering Momma's good white linen tablecloth and splattering Julie's dress. All conversation stopped.

Poppa pushed back his chair, but Julie laid a hand on his arm, assuring him that everything was fine. Poppa disagreed. His low rumbling voice banished Alicia to the kid's table. Alicia carried her kitchen chair to the empty place where Momma had set her plate. The boys stifled their laughter by kicking her under the table; only Gina looked sympathetic. With each bite, she was forced to swallow her embarrassment and anger. Afraid of choking or throwing up, she quit eating and waited for the meal to end.

After dinner, Alicia and Momma went upstairs to the girls' bedroom. Momma covered Alicia with a blanket and perched on the bed's edge. "I know it was an accident, Alicia. About Poppa." Momma's eyes seemed to rest just above Alicia's head. "He needs more time to get used to everything." She lowered her eyes to meet Alicia's. "Could you give him more time?"

Alicia had a question of her own—*get used to what*? Instead of asking, she nodded.

Momma left when Clara came into the girls' bedroom. Clara placed a plate of food on the dresser, sat beside Alicia, and leaned against the white metal headboard. She tucked her feet under the blanket.

"Remember when Ed came home three weeks ago, right before Halloween, when I explained how Johan had asked me to take care of you? Now I know why."

Her words sent a shiver down Alicia's back.

How the idea came to Alicia, she was never quite certain, even after the fact. "Clara, can we be blood-sisters?"

Clara seemed surprised, but she only smiled and nodded. "Sure."

Alicia ran to the bathroom and came back with Grandpa's straight edge razor. She and Clara made tiny slits on their thumbs and squeezed until small drops of blood appeared. They joined thumbs, and a high pitch wail shattered the silence. Alicia turned her head towards the open door where Gina stood, her face white as the snow outside and her scream like the howling wind. Alicia grabbed her Snirpa doll from her pillow and quickly dotted blood droplets on the doll's dress. Gina flung herself into Clara's arms.

Behind Gina, a plate of food crashed to the floor.

"What the hell is going on?" Poppa rushed into the room and grabbed Clara's elbow.

She winced.

"You! Goddamn. I knew it. Hasn't there been enough bloodshed?" With his free hand, he jabbed a finger at her face. "What kind of revenge are you after? If you so much as come near my family, I swear to God, you'll be sorry. Now get out! Get the hell out of my house and away from my family."

Clara jerked her elbow from his grasp and made no move to leave the room. The air became impossible to breathe. Several long minutes passed and Clara came close to Alicia and whispered, "Remember my promise to Johan." She left and shut the door behind her.

Poppa had stared blankly at his daughters—as if they were strangers.

A call from Sarah jolted Alicia from the memory. She stared down at the once treasured doll, her hands burning. "Take it, Gina. I don't want it anymore."

Poppa's car was gone. Probably still hunting for Alphie and his cherry bombs. Gina and Sarah propped Snirpa in the back of the wagon filled with dolls. They had so many broken or missing limbs it looked like a doll ambulance. Alicia suspected Gina had canvassed the neighborhood in search of these dolls so they wouldn't miss the parade. Sarah and Gina pulled the wagon, and some of the red, white, and blue crepe paper ribbons trailed like colorful puppy tails. The real dog, Shadow, was nowhere in sight—hiding under the porch, away from the firecrackers. "See you in the parade, Gina," Alicia called and went back inside.

"Ready, Alicia?" Grandpa asked. "Ilse, I'll be back to get you, William, and the hot dishes for the pot luck."

***

Downtown, American flags on every building unfurled and snapped in the wind, appearing for a moment, as if painted on the blue cloudless sky. City Park teemed with activity. Cars lined the perimeter like a metal fence. Men leaned against their fenders, smoking. Ladies carried picnic baskets and food bowls wrapped in white dish towels knotted at the top to a row of redwood picnic tables. Excitement tinged the air.

Younger men, also back home from the War, gathered in small groups, tugging at shirt collars open in the heat. They pointed towards the neglected baseball field: weed-crowded base paths, a flat pitcher's mound, a teetering backstop, and the missing team benches. They'd been readied for the War's end only to be shredded into splinters by the June tornado. High school boys tossed baseballs back and forth in front of high school girls who sat on metal swings. Children ran in and out of shadows. Boys in cowboy shirts and hats galloped on stick horses and shot cap pistols in the air. "I'm John Wayne," one yelled.

To the left of the picnic tables, in the shade of tall evergreen trees, Donna and Clara squeezed lemons for lemonade. A step behind, Joe hosed off watermelons, and Slick placed them in an ice-filled, corrugated metal trough.

Finished, Slick left Joe, meeting Alicia halfway to the bandstand. "Will you put those white crepe paper roses on the first six rows in front of the band shell? They're reserved for veterans, their families, and Gold Star mothers."

Slick returned with a folding chair in each hand. "I'm taking these across the street to Bill's store. Those marble steps and overhang will make it cooler for your Momma and William. Have you seen Ed?"

Alicia shook her head.

"Tell him his Army buddy and wife are looking for him. And come over when you finish."

Alicia shaded her eyes. She looked to see if Poppa was with Gina in the lumber yard parking lot, waiting for the kiddie parade to begin. He wasn't.

Why isn't he here?

When she was satisfied with the position of the roses, she headed across the street. A tall, sandy-haired man came away from the awning over the Cozy Café window.

"Hi. You're Alicia. I'm Cal. I recognize you from the picture Ed carried. Did I talk to you yesterday on the telephone?"

She nodded.

Cal looked around. "Where is Ed, anyway? I told him I had someone that wanted to talk to him. This is my new wife—Mary Lou." He had his arm around a petite, dark-haired woman not much older than Clara. "We're on our honeymoon, and we wanted to surprise Ed and Ilse."

"You look like your Momma," Mary Lou said. "I can't wait to see her. We had such a good time last October down in Iowa when the boys came home."

Slick extended his hand. "I'm Slick. I'm a mechanic in Ed's shop. Come next door. There's some shade, and we can wait for Ilse. I'll get a couple more chairs."

"So Ed got his shop," Cal said. "That's all he ever talked about besides his girls back home. Of course that was before he …"

Grandpa's car stopped in front of them. Cal rushed to open Momma's door. "Look at that—a baby! I guess Ed had a surprise for us, too." He took William from Momma's outstretched hands. "Hey there, little guy." Momma ran into Mary Lou's open arms.

"Hey, don't squeeze the life out of my wife."

"Wife?" Momma lifted Mary Lou's left hand and examined the shining gold band. "So you're the surprise person for Ed. He'll be so glad. When was the big day?"

"Saturday. Where's Ed?" Mary Lou held out her arms to take William from Cal. "Oh, he's the prettiest baby I've ever seen. How old is he? What's his name? Why didn't Ed let us know?"

Momma smiled at the rapid-fire questions. "His name is William Johan, born eight days ago. I'm sure Ed'll be here soon." Alicia heard an undertone of uncertainty in Momma's voice.

Grandpa returned, shaking his head. "No sign of Ed."

In the silence, Cal and Mary Lou exchanged glances.

"I met Cal and Mary Lou a while ago," he said. "Have a seat. Parade's starting." Grandpa bent his head in the direction of the families lining the street. "Looks like Bill better make sure he has a lot of diapers for sale, judging by all those girls over there in a family way. Must be an epidemic."

Cal winked at Grandpa.

Sarah and Joe had marshaled the kids, more or less, into a line stretching the length of the parking lot from the lumber yard to Main Street.

"The first girl with the red wagon, leading the doll buggies, is Gina, my other granddaughter," Grandpa said.

As Gina passed by, she stared straight ahead, a serious look on her face until she was directly in front of Momma. Discreetly, using her free hand, she gave a small finger wave from her side. Toddlers on tricycles, decorated in red, white, and blue, followed the doll buggies. Older kids on bicycles with playing cards clothes-pinned to wheel spokes, waved small forty-eight star flags and rode in tight figure eights to avoid bumping into the herky-jerky parade. Children's laughter and squeals rode the summer breeze. The parade ended at the intersection of Main Street and Depot Road where Bill stood in the shade of the Railroad Hotel. He draped a "gold" medal suspended on red, white, and blue ribbon around each child's neck.

Gina pulled the doll wagon back to her family. Her medal bounced on her chest. "Where's Poppa? I get my own medal, and Poppa's not even here to see it."

Gina's disappointment saddened Alicia.

Gina stared at Cal and Mary Lou. "Who are they?" she asked in a loud whisper.

"They're Poppa's friends," Alicia said.

"Then he should be here."

"Out of the mouth of babes ..." Grandpa said.

"Come on, Squirt," Slick said. "Hop in with your dolls. We'll go to the park swings, and I'll push you until the ceremony starts. Alicia, save a chair for Gina. I made room for Cal and Mary Lou with your family in the veteran's rows.

Children in tow, the milling crowd moved to the newly painted concrete band shell and rows of mismatched folding chairs. Donna climbed the three steps leading to a podium flanked by the American flag and the Minnesota State flag. She asked all to rise and join in the singing of the national anthem. Her voice seemed to flow from the band shell and land on leaves quieted for just that moment. After Pastor Anderson gave the invocation, Alicia looked for Poppa. The chair beside Momma remained empty, and he was nowhere in sight.

A cherry bomb snapped the silence.

An Army officer climbed the steps, and one by one, he asked the WWI veterans, the Gold Star Mothers, the WWII veterans, and their families to stand and be recognized when he called their names.

Alicia's cheeks burned as they stood without Poppa. She thought she heard people whispering about Poppa's absence, but she couldn't be certain.

The soldier returned to his seat, and Bill addressed the quiet audience. "Thanks to the American Legion for sponsoring this celebration to honor all our veterans. And a heart-felt thanks to all of you for your service and sacrifice. Now let's celebrate the freedom they fought so hard for."

Momma's eyes searched for Poppa. "Let's get in line for food," she said. "Before you go fussing, Mary Lou, Pa always brings extra food. Times are still hard, what with the food shortages and all, but his garden is producing so much it seems like a miracle. And it's his way of thanking all the townsfolk who donated food and labor after the tornado."

"We heard about the tornado up in Brainerd," Mary Lou said. "It was another reason why Cal wanted to see how Ed was doing." She lowered her voice. "Has Cal talked to you yet?"

Concern on Momma's face mirrored Mary Lou's.

After the pot luck dinner, still no sign of Poppa.

Grandpa played horseshoes, Gina played games with the younger kids, and Cal and Momma huddled away from everyone else. Alicia held a sleeping William and talked to Mary Lou. When Clara approached, she handed her baby brother to her and introduced the two women. Clara's eyes glistened as she rocked William in her arms.

Out of sorts—too young, too old at the same time and feeling excluded—Alicia glanced around the park, hoping to see Slick, but she guessed he was searching for Poppa. Her eyes were drawn to a treeless spot where a dark truck shaped like a milk van was parked. It had United States Army painted on the side. Rifles leaned against a nearby table. Alphie's back was to the park, but Alicia was certain one of the uniformed soldiers was talking to him.

Cal noticed her stare. "That soldier is a recruiter. I thought only the Navy drove those trucks around, but I guess maybe with all the boys leaving the service, the Army is doing the same—at least around here. That boy seems pretty interested in those weapons."

Alphie picked up a rifle and pointed it in Alicia's direction. She shuddered. The soldier put a hand on the rifle and pointed it down.

William cried softly. "It's time to go home," Momma said.

Clara gave William to Momma and placed a comforting hand on Alicia's shoulder.

"Looks like we'd better get going, too." Cal picked up his box camera from the table. "Get in there girls."

Alicia and Gina leaned against Momma and waited for Cal to snap the pictures.

"Tell Ed sorry we missed him." Cal looked as if he might say more, but hand in hand, he and Mary Lou walked to their car and waved as they drove away.

Flags that had swirled and snapped in the Fourth of July wind lay languid against the afternoon sun.

***

Three hours later, nearly nine o'clock, Poppa drove into the yard. When she heard the car door shut, Alicia scrambled across the bed to the open window. On the sidewalk beneath her, Momma stood like a sentinel. "Where in heaven's name have you been? Cal waited as long as he could. Why would you disappoint a friend like that? He married Mary Lou, and they wanted to surprise us."

"Ah, hell," Poppa said. "If I'd only known he was bringing Mary Lou and not those soldiers I saw at the park."

16

William was a tiny white bundle in Poppa's big, bear-like arms. The baby's eyes seemed fixed on the ceiling light, ignoring Poppa's new shop sign.

"The world is balanced now," Poppa said.

As usual, Alicia tuned him out when he used words in strange ways. She could hardly wait to hold William again. Momma teasingly accused her of spoiling her baby brother. William fascinated Alicia—the way he wrapped his fingers around hers, the way he kicked his legs in the air and waved his tiny arms, the way he quieted when she held him close. She didn't know it was possible to love anyone that much.

"Balanced world? How so?" Grandpa asked from across the table.

"Men going back to work; women giving back their jobs." Poppa put William into Alicia's arms and paced the kitchen linoleum, the familiar sound—heard night after night before William was born. Poppa shifted his gaze away from Grandpa, a faraway look in his eyes. "Women working, holding down a job, keeping it from a man. Like Clara. It was you," he pointed at Grandpa, "did that when we were gone—putting silly, dangerous notions in their heads."

Grandpa snorted. "Feeding their families … dangerous?"

"I'm going to put William in his bassinet," Alicia said.

Neither of the two men paid attention. They were too busy locking verbal horns. She kissed the top of William's head and set him down. Shadow lifted her head, laid it down, and went to sleep. All week, since Alphie had pointed the rifle at her, her anger sizzled, mixed with fear. Not for herself, but if he did something, again, like the rat to scare Momma or Gina … She had decided on a plan, but for that, she needed money. "Momma," she called.

"Shhh. Don't wake William. I'm right here." Behind her, Momma struggled to carry William's water-filled diaper pail. "What do you want?" She sounded exasperated.

"Let me help." Alicia wrapped her hand around the metal handle of the heavy pail, and together they carried it down the cellar steps. "I was wondering … could I have a nickel to buy a new pencil sharpener? I … uh … lost mine."

One lie a day.

Momma bent to rinse the diapers in clear water and then put them into the washing machine. She straightened and blew away a hair that had fallen across her face. "My pocketbook's on the buffet."

***

She had completed the first part of her plan. The money was necessary to complete the second part. She took a deep breath and opened the door to Bill's store. He was stacking cans of peas and talking to Sarah. "I didn't get any coffee shipped," he said. "I guess I'll have to raise my prices just like I had to with the butter shortage. I don't understand how this country can win a war and not be able to feed its people afterwards—unless the shortages aren't real."

Apparently unnoticed, Alicia crept to the far store corner where Bill stored school supplies during the summer. With her face to the shelves, she picked up a dusty red and yellow pencil sharpener and waited until the tinkle of the bell on the door signaled Sarah's departure.

Bill looked surprised when Alicia emerged from behind the notions aisle. "Guess I didn't hear you come in. What can I do for one of my favorite Drake girls?"

Alicia put the sharpener on the glass counter top. "Do you have any more Rainbow Tablets? Gina needs another one." The dime she had taken from Momma's pocketbook burned her palm. Bill nodded and left for the back storeroom. Alicia darted behind the counter, grabbed a package of Lucky Strike cigarettes, stuffed it into her dungaree pocket, and laid the dime down as the storeroom door creaked open. Her cheeks warmed with shame.

"Get a little too much sun? Your cheeks look sunburned." Bill put the sharpener and tablet in a small brown paper sack and handed her back the dime. "Today's your lucky day," he said.

Alicia noticed the list for funeral flowers for someone she didn't know. She signed Mr. and Mrs. Ed Drake and dropped the dime in the jar.

The third part of her plan: find Alphie.

He was next door on the steps of the Cozy Café, getting in the way of customers. He pointed his finger pistol-like as she approached. Alicia could barely look him in the face, but there was no backing down. "If you leave Gina alone, you can have these." The cigarette package lay in her outstretched palm.

The smile on his face failed to reach his beady eyes. "I'll be damned. Look here what miss goody two-shoes went and done! Nah, won't stop me. But if these don't keep coming …" He jerked the package from her hand, smirked, and waved it in her face before heading into the café.

Digging myself a deeper hole.

Alicia raced home as if speed could create an invisible shield around her. She gasped for breath inside the porch. On top of one of Poppa's newspaper storage boxes, dated July 3, a once crumpled newspaper page had been smoothed flat.

She scanned the large black headline:

MEAT SHORTAGES CONTINUE
PRICES SKYROCKET

That wasn't news; all summer long everybody had talked about that. Alicia attempted to make sense of Poppa's actions. The other night in the kitchen, she'd seen him cry for the first time; the next day he'd run away from the celebration and his friend. Poppa who was afraid of nothing. It was something else, and maybe, an opened green album, a jar of paste, and a scissors held answers.

Grandpa was dipping his morning catch of bullheads in batter, and Momma was snapping the ends off string beans. Before either of them spoke, Alicia put the pencil sharpener and Rainbow Tablet on the table.

"Bill gave me the sharpener for free, and he gave me a Rainbow Tablet for Gina. I gave the dime, ah nickel, for flowers for the funeral and signed your name."

Lie number two for today.

"That was nice of you," Momma said.

Momma's compliment served to make Alicia feel worse, but with just ten minutes before Poppa came home from the shop, she hurried out of the kitchen, ran to the stairs, and climbed two steps at a time to Poppa's bedroom. She searched his bureau drawers and closet. Nothing but clothing. She lifted the bedspread corner. Dust and a dog bone. At the sound of Poppa's car in the driveway, she halted her search and scurried into her bedroom. There she hid behind an open *Bobbsey Twins* book until he passed her door.

17

The unending heat of August days stretched far into nightfall; leaves drooped as if waiting for a cooling breeze that never materialized. Grandpa promised to take the girls swimming at Dead Coon Lake, but only after Alicia told him Clara would be there. He wanted to show her photographs of William.

"You girls about ready?" he asked after his nap that seemed to last all afternoon.

Worried that Slick and Clara might leave before they reached the lake, Alicia urged Grandpa and Gina to hurry. Shadow, catching the excitement, raced in circles.

Grandpa seemed to be racing the cloud of dust behind his car. It was certainly the last chance for the girls to swim before the dog days of summer turned the lake water a murky green, and black slimy bloodsuckers haunted the shallows.

Alicia braced herself on the glove box when the car swung wide into Dead Coon Lake parking lot. Shadow stuck her head out Alicia's window, sniffed the lake air, and barked. Grandpa killed the engine and leaned back in his seat.

Gina scrambled into the front seat and bounced across Alicia's lap. "Clara's here!"

With his still unfinished Steinbeck book in hand, Grandpa ambled across the grassy strip to an ancient stone picnic table and Clara.

Gina tugged Alicia's hand, trying to pull her along towards the concrete block bath house to the left of the lifeguard's stand, but Alicia hesitated and slowed to a walk near the roped-off swimming area. The lifeguard blew his whistle and waved at boys shoving each other off the wooden raft. Shadow raced ahead, plunged into the lake, swam towards Slick, and together they swam back to shore in Grandpa's direction.

Gina sniffed the air like Shadow. "What's that stink?"

"Fish," Alicia said. Dead fish littered the sand between the picnic area and the swimming beach. One still had a hook in his mouth. "Careful."

Inside the cool, concrete bath house, Alicia drew the faded, coarse canvas curtain across the cramped changing stall opening. Candy wrappers littered the floor. The smell of concession stand popcorn lingered in the damp air. Gina climbed onto the wet, sand-covered bench and struggled out of her clothes and into Alicia's hand-me-down pink polka dot bathing suit. Alicia slipped out of her shirt and tugged at the bottom and top of her soon-to-be-too-small bathing suit.

"Alicia, you shaved under your arms. Momma told you not to."

Alicia rolled her eyes. She draped towels around their necks, folded clothes, stacked their shoes on top, and set them on the sandy bench. Then she faced her sister. "If you don't tell her, she'll never notice. Or care." Alicia adjusted the twisted strap on Gina's bathing suit. "And you won't tell because we have our sister secrets like the lumber yard and your license plate list. Right?" Alicia spoke harshly.

Gina stared at the floor and nodded, her chin nearly touching her chest.

Alicia wished she had bitten her tongue and kept silent. "Let's get Clara and swim."

A westerly breeze had cooled the stifling afternoon heat. Grandpa sat across from Clara with the photographs of William and the envelope of negatives between them on the picnic table. He had a smile on his face, but he still looked tired.

Gina ran ahead. "Clara, will you teach me the dead man's float?"

Grandpa waved them away and opened his book. Clara and Alicia each took one of Gina's hands and swung her back and forth over grass and rough sand to the water. Shadow loped along the shore in and out of the small choppy waves, tilting her head as if to say, *follow me.*

They set Gina down in waist-deep waters. Alicia turned to wave to Grandpa, but the sun caught her eye, and lost in the glare, he disappeared. She plunged into the lake and swam a few strokes, but something pulled at her legs. Upended and spewing water, she broke the surface to find Slick laughing at her. She dove, swam around him, came up, jumped on his back, and pushed his head under. He sputtered.

She splashed more water in his face. "Who's laughing now?"

"Nice dunk." He rolled over and swam on his back next to her. "I'm glad Anton brought those photographs. Clara asks about William every time I see her." He shaded his eyes and stared at the shore. "Looks like swimming lessons are over. Crowd's thinning out. I'm going to talk to Anton. Uh, Alphie came with, so he's around here some place."

Alphie stood near the shoreline talking to a girl who backed away from him. He picked up a stick and tossed it beside a dead fish for Shadow to fetch. The dog ignored it. Alphie thumbed his nose at Alicia, sauntered into the lake, swam to the wooden raft, and hoisted himself up. One of the boys came up behind him and pushed. Alphie belly-flopped like a hooked bullhead and swam to shore.

Alicia desperately wanted some time alone with Clara, to talk, to ask her advice. But with Alphie nearby and Gina so scared of him, that was impossible. Since the Fourth of July, Momma had gone quiet, as if her mind was always elsewhere. Gina hadn't said anything, yet Alicia knew it bothered her, too. Worse yet, Gina was becoming a quiet imitation of Momma.

Clouds passed over the sun, and a chilly breeze crossed the lake. Gina shivered, and goose bumps dotted her skinny arms. "You need to warm up, Gina." Clara scooped Gina into her arms. "I have a blanket at the picnic table."

The lifeguard's shrill whistle pierced the silence. He whistled again and motioned for the boys to come to shore. Except for Alphie, they piled into an old jalopy and drove away. The lifeguard climbed down from his perch and announced he was closing the beach. A steady procession of cars left the parking lot.

Slick picked up Clara's towel and blanket from the picnic table and handed them to her. "Time to leave."

Grandpa pointed at the sky on the western edge of the lake. It had darkened with steel gray rain clouds. He looked up at Clara and Slick. "It's coming fast, Johan."

Slick motioned Clara and Alphie to his car. They drove away, and except for Grandpa and the girls, the beach was deserted.

Grandpa gathered his book and photographs. "You girls get your clothes and hurry up about it."

"All right, Grandpa." Alicia tugged her sister's arm, and pulled her towards the bath house. "C'mon. You heard Grandpa."

"Please, please," Gina said. "I'm warm now and I can do the dead man's float now. Let me show you, please?"

Unsure, Alicia hesitated at the water's edge. She glanced back at Grandpa who sat and stared across the lake at a sky stained blue-black with gathering clouds. Even though the wind blew stronger and colder, he didn't call them to shore. Memory of the June tornado tormented her.

"Make it quick."

Gina put her face in the water, spread her arms and floated. Forked lightning danced across the sky. Alicia grabbed the back of Gina's bathing suit and pulled her upright. "Now we gotta go!"

Thunder rumbled closer and closer as if chasing them into the bath house.

Alicia struggled to put her clothes on over the wet bathing suit. She shoved her feet into her shoes. A lightning flash lit the bath house. "Never mind, Gina. Just grab your stuff."

A sound, half whine, half bark, echoed through the small building.

"We're in here, Shadow," Alicia called.

The dog charged through the curtained door; she nudged Alicia's leg with her nose and pushed the curtain partway open. Shadow barked louder.

"Something's wrong," Alicia said. "We have to get to Grandpa."

Outside, it was dark as night, and sheets of rain poured from the sky. Again, Shadow nudged Alicia's leg with her nose and then galloped to the picnic table and stood over Grandpa who lay crumpled on the rain-soaked grass like a motionless marionette loosened from its strings.

Alicia dropped everything, ran to him, and knelt. Rain, like tears, drenched his face. "Grandpa, what's the matter?"

The parking lot was empty and the concessions shuttered and locked. The door to the bath house slammed back and forth against the concrete block. Howling wind lashed the trees, and trashcans tumbled along the beach. Whitecaps smashed into the shore.

"Gina, help me get Grandpa to the car. We gotta get out of this storm."

Gina seemed not to hear. Alicia shook her sister. Desperation crept into the words she screamed. "You've got to help! Do you understand? There's nobody but us here."

"I cant … I can't move," she whispered.

Wearing just her drenched dungarees over her bathing suit, Gina had a look of horror pasted on her face. Alicia got up and wrapped her arms around Gina and surrounded her with soft assurances that everything was going to be all right. Still Gina clung to Alicia as if she wanted to crawl inside of her sister's skin.

"We can get Grandpa into his car. We have to."

Shadow barked and ran back and forth between the car and Grandpa's inert body.

Together the girls wedged their arms underneath Grandpa's back and raised him to a sitting position. His head lobbed sideways, and he slid out of their grasp. Shadow whimpered. Lightening slashed the midnight blue-black sky over the lake.

"This isn't going to work," Alicia said.

Gina trembled.

"I think I know what to do." Remembering how Grandpa moved heavy furniture by sliding a rug underneath and pulling, she ran to the dropped towels, shook everything from them, and stretched one beside Grandpa.

"Help me roll him, Gina."

Alicia locked her fingers around Grandpa's belt between the loops and pulled him on his side. "Gina, tuck the towels under him." He moaned when Alicia let go. She ran to his other side to lift, and Gina slipped a second towel beneath him. "Now we can pull him to the car."

They pulled the towels by their top edges and inched Grandpa across the grassy strip to the parking lot. Once there, they paused to catch their breaths before continuing over pebbles and gravel to the passenger door where Shadow waited. Alicia opened the door. She and Gina raised him to a sitting position on the gravel and let his body slump inward to the passenger seat. Alicia scrambled onto the driver's seat, pulling Grandpa as Gina pushed until he lay halfway across the bench seat.

"Don't let him slip," Alicia pleaded. She ran around the car, and with Gina's help, shoved his legs to the floor and shut the door.

"Come on, Gina, get in the car—you and Shadow—back seat."

Inside, she lifted Grandpa into a sitting position away from the shift lever, and he fell against the window.

Alicia put her shaking hands on the steering wheel and whispered a mantra: "I can do it. I can drive us home." She reached into Grandpa's pocket for the key, inserted it into the ignition, and pulled out the choke as far as it would go. She put one foot on the clutch and the other on the starter beneath the accelerator pedal and pressed until a gasoline smell filled the car: the engine had flooded.

Gina whimpered in the back seat.

"Shh, Gina, please."

Shadow leaned forward with her head hanging over Grandpa's shoulder.

In an eternity's worth of time, the smell faded. This time, she pulled the choke just halfway out, her feet on clutch and starter. The engine coughed to a start. She released the clutch too fast, the car lurched forward, and Grandpa's head rammed the glove box knob. The engine died. She pulled Grandpa upright. Blood trickled down his forehead.

"Blood. Is he going to die?" Gina's whimpers turned into sobs.

"Shut up! You're scaring Grandpa—and me."

She remembered Grandpa's instructions from the times he'd let her drive back and forth on the driveway.

Choke partway out, clutch in, press starter, shift, ease out the clutch, and step on the gas pedal.

They were moving.

The car hurled itself across the parking lot. Alicia barely managed the right turn onto the graveled county road. She scraped the fender on the fencepost that marked the lake entrance.

"Five miles and we'll be home. Five long miles."

Lightening ripped the sky, and rain fell in torrential sheets. Alicia finally found the windshield wiper knob, but it failed to clear the glass. It was like trying to see through a thick, white curtain. She glanced in the rearview mirror: no cars. They were utterly alone. Afraid to shift to a higher gear because the engine might quit, Alicia drove at a snail's pace: ten miles per hour. They were trapped in a rain-hammered thunder tunnel. Alicia steered more by feel than sight. When the wheels edged the left shoulder, she steered sharply to the right and Grandpa fell back against the door.

"Alicia! Grandpa is trying to get out of the car."

"No, he's not. He's just resting from his fall. Now be quiet, okay?"

To be sure, Alicia glanced sideways. Grandpa was slumped against the car door, his face blue in the lightening flash. Fear churned in her stomach like the wheels on the gravel road.

The rain seemed never-ending. At Graffie's, Alicia rushed through the stop sign onto the rain-slickened highway and through the flooded railroad underpass. Grandpa's car was a submarine. Hoping that the sputtering engine didn't mean the car would quit, she drove the last mile to Depot Road, up the hill into her driveway, and across the lawn. She slammed on the brakes inches from the concrete porch steps. She laid her head on the horn button; its blaring sound reassured her that she was still alive.

18

Shadow barked. Rain steamed off the car hood like otherworldly fog. Momma's blurred, body-less face appeared in the window. She jerked the driver's side door open.

"I was so worried. Alicia? What's going on here? Pa, what were you thinking? Letting a child drive in this weather." She leaned into the car and pried Alicia's hands from the steering wheel.

Grandpa made mewing sounds. Gina wailed from the back seat with her arms outstretched like a baby waiting to be picked up.

"My God, Alicia. What happened?"

Alicia's tears flowed for the first time since she'd seen Grandpa on the rain-soaked grass. "Momma … he can't talk."

Momma circled the car to the passenger door and opened it. She put her hands on Grandpa's shoulders and gently shook him. "Wake up, Pa. Please."

He remained silent and motionless. She licked her thumb and wiped the blood from his forehead. Her arms stretched around him, and she tried to lift. He fell forward against the glove box knob and re-opened the gash on his forehead.

Blood poured like tears.

"Oh my God. He's dead weight." Momma sat him upright and blotted his head with her handkerchief. "I can't do this alone. I'm going to call Ed and Doc Swenson. Come inside, girls."

Alicia shook her head. "Me and Shadow will stay with Grandpa until Poppa gets here."

"Okay. Gina, you come with me. Baby William and I need you to be a big, brave girl. Can you do it?"

Gina nodded, still whimpering.

Momma eased her out of the back seat and guided her inside.

Shadow climbed over the seat, wedged under the floor shift, and nudged her head under Grandpa's limp arm. Alicia petted the dog, seeking her own comfort from guilt.

Why did I beg to go to the lake?

Momma returned with Poppa's jacket and covered Grandpa's soaked clothing. "Your Poppa isn't answering the telephone. I need you to ride to the shop and get him. If he isn't there, go by the station and bring Joe. I'll stay with Grandpa. It's going to be all right." Momma's smile reached neither the corners of her mouth nor her sad eyes.

Alicia's drenched bicycle leaned against the porch siding, handlebars and seat slippery as she climbed on the pedals. The bicycle swerved on the wet grass, but steadied when the wheels touched the graveled driveway. Shadow matched her hurried pace along the empty streets. To the east, the storm clouds still raged with explosions of lightning and thunder. Back to the west, the sky cleared, and above Fullerton, a cold steady rain fell. Alicia's teeth chattered, and goose bumps prickled her arms. Her stomach churned in rhythm with the pedals. Shadow raced ahead around the corner of Poppa's shop and through the open bay door.

Alicia jumped from her bicycle and followed. She bent to catch her breath. "Poppa, hurry! Momma needs you home right away."

Slick stopped stacking motor oil cans and ran to her. "Alicia, what's wrong?"

Poppa slid out from under a raised car. His wrench slipped to the concrete. "William?"

Poppa's worried look tore at Alicia. "No, it's Grandpa. Something bad happened. Momma can't get him out of the car by herself."

"Anton? In his car?" Slick's voice was worry-laden. "You take off, Ed. I'll lock up and be right behind you."

Poppa wiped his hands on his coveralls and headed for the door. "Come on, Shadow."

"We'd better hurry. Leave your bicycle." Slick guided Alicia outside and pulled down the bay door. His hands shook as he inserted the key in the lock, opened his car door for her, and set the heater on high.

"What happened to Anton? How did you get home? When I left, Anton's car was the only one left in the parking lot." Slick seemed to hold his breath, waiting for an answer.

She leaned forward to capture the heat for an inside cold—one that wouldn't warm up. Detail by detail, she told him. Alicia felt like she was watching herself in a picture show, but when she spoke, it became real, too real, and self-blame underlined her words. "It was my fault. Grandpa looked tired. I shouldn't have asked him to take us to the lake."

"It's not your fault. Things don't work that way." Slick sped to Alicia's house and bolted from his car.

"Over here. We need your help," Poppa said.

Inside Grandpa's car, Momma sat sideways on her knees, her hand on Grandpa's immobile arm, trying to hold him upright. He kept slumping forward. On the passenger side, Poppa and Slick worked together to get ahold of Grandpa.

"On three," Poppa said. "One, two, three."

Together they hoisted him out of the car and carried him up the porch steps and through the porch door that Alicia held open. Grandpa's head jerked backwards as one foot of his tall body caught on the kitchen threshold.

Alicia returned to the car and Momma, who held the car key in her hand and stared as if it was unrecognizable. Finally, she slammed the car door with a fierceness that startled Alicia. Her next words, directed at Alicia, were hushed. "Go change your clothes before you catch your death." Momma clapped her hand to her mouth as if to retrieve the word: death.

Alicia was caught in a whirlwind of feelings: blame, fear, and sadness because she was certain that the light in Grandpa's eyes had gone out. She clasped Johan's cross.

What will I do without him?

Shadow lay on her rug beside William's bassinet. The room smelled of wet dog. Gina's head and arm were draped over the bassinet, and she held William's tiny fingers around his pink and blue rattle.

Alicia kissed Gina and the baby. "That's for being so brave on the way home."

Tears rimmed Gina's eyes. "I cried 'cause I was scared and … and I forgot my new shoes at the lake. And Poppa's really going to yell at me." The tears slid down her cheeks.

Alicia sighed inwardly.

Not you—me. I'm in for it now.

"I was scared, too, Gina. Don't worry about the shoes. I'll tell Poppa that I left them because he's already going to be mad at me for driving the car."

Alicia's thumb wiped away Gina's tears. "You should stop crying before your tears drip on William."

Gina wiped her eyes and nose on her clean, dry blouse sleeve. Alicia shivered in spite of the warm room. "I'm going upstairs and change into dry clothes." Gina jumped up and followed her sister, seemingly afraid of being separated.

After changing, Alicia let Gina send their wet clothes down the clothes chute, mostly as an excuse to be in the hallway outside of Grandpa's bedroom. Both girls peeked around the door frame. Grandpa's wet clothes were in a heap near his bed. Dr. Swenson held a stethoscope to Grandpa's chest, listened for a moment, and then returned it to the worn black medical bag sitting open on the foot of the bed. The snap of his bag closing echoed through the upstairs. He took off his glasses, polished them on a handkerchief, and put them into his breast pocket.

"I'm sorry, Ilse. Anton's had a severe stroke. Only time will tell if he will be able to talk or walk again."

Momma sobbed quietly with Poppa's arm around her.

"I'll get ahold of Donna at the hospital tonight and have her drop by in the morning after her shift to check on Anton. Try to get some rest. You know you can call me anytime," he said. "I'll see myself out."

Not wanting to be seen, Alicia tugged at Gina's hand, and they went back into their bedroom. She heard Doc Swenson's car leave, followed by Slick's. Hushed words from Momma and Poppa floated on cigarette smoke filtering up from the kitchen.

"I'll be right back," Alicia whispered. She slipped into Grandpa's bedroom. A golden shaft of light from the setting sun shone through a hole in the shade and reflected off the mirror, casting a glow on the picture of Johan in his white Navy uniform. A cold wind that didn't belong in mid-August haunted the room. Shadow rested her long nose on the wedding ring quilt that covered the foot of the bed. Grandpa lay on the bed with a sheet and blanket pulled up to his neck. His right hand was on top of the covers, his left hand nowhere in sight. The blank look on his face frightened Alicia.

"Alicia, are you in here?" Gina whispered. She approached cautiously, and clung to the back of Alicia's shirt. "Is he dead?"

"No."

But that is what he will look like in his casket.

"He's going to be sick for a while. You know what? Me and you can be nurses like Donna and take care of him. Maybe Donna has an extra nurse's cap we can use. Why don't you get Raggedy Ann and I'll come into the bedroom and you can read your license plate list to me."

Gina backed out of the room.

Alicia sat on the edge of the bed and covered Grandpa's hand with hers. "I'm so sorry, Grandpa."

Shadow came round the bed and nuzzled her nose into Alicia's lap.

"Come, Shadow," she said at last. "We need to take care of Gina, too."

19

Alicia tossed and turned, unable to sleep, except for brief snatches. Images—of Grandpa lying motionless on the grass, of Gina's rained-soaked new shoes, and of Poppa's anger certain to come—plagued her.

By morning, Alicia had twisted the sheet mummy-like around her. Gina was still asleep on her side of the bed. Alicia's only plan was no plan, so she untangled herself and pulled the sheet over her head to wait for Poppa to leave for work. But, as usual, anything involving Poppa never happened as planned.

His yell penetrated the sheet. "Alicia, get down here, and I mean now." She scrambled out of bed in her nightgown and hurried downstairs, knowing a delay would only make Poppa angrier.

How did he find out so quick?

Poppa stood in front of the open porch door, his face darkened in shadow. In his hands were Gina's shoes dripping water on the linoleum.

"Look what I found outside this morning." He waved the shoes in her face as if he were determined to hit her with them. A lone shoestring struck her left cheek.

Alicia back-pedaled.

Poppa followed. "Do you think money grows on trees? I hardly make a living. The whole damned town is turning against me—taking their cars all the way to Marshall for repairs. Hell, even old Mr. Oldenburg." He squatted, eye to eye. "Who put you up to this?"

His question made no sense. "What, Poppa? Who? Nobody."

Don't you sass me, girl." Poppa grabbed her arm. His fingers squeezed hard, bringing up bruises where the old ones had faded. She winced, but didn't call out. "From now on, you take over Anton's garden—hoeing, weeding, picking. No bicycle riding. No playing with friends. And don't go thinking you're something special because you drove the car home." Poppa shoved her and stomped out the door.

"What friends?" she said to his back. "I haven't got any friends anymore 'cause of you." She stared at the box of Shredded Wheat cereal on the table. Poppa's anger had chased away her hunger. She went upstairs to get dressed but stopped at Grandpa's bedroom door. Momma and Gina were hovering over the mound that was Grandpa in his bed. Shadow lay on the floor, her nose resting on her front paws.

"Is he any better?" Hope surrounded the question.

Momma shook her head.

Guilt-ridden, unable to face Grandpa, Alicia left the house. Outside, the heat slapped her in the face. Things were never going to be the same again. A helpless feeling swept over her. She put on Grandpa's straw hat, picked up his hoe, and hesitated at the garden's edge. Memories buzzed in her head like mosquitoes she swatted away.

Just three years ago, when she was eight, Grandpa had stood beside her in the garden, stretched his back, and wiped a smudge of warm black dirt from Alicia's cheek. She had imitated his backward stretch.

"Is this a Victory Garden like I read in the newspaper?" Alicia had asked.

Grandpa nodded, his straw hat bobbing an affirmation.

"Then I'm helping win the War so Poppa can come home aren't I, Grandpa?"

He had leaned over a pile of weeds between them and had hugged her.

Today, anger replaced that pride. "I wish I hadn't worked so hard to bring Poppa home." A lie. Nevertheless, it felt good to say. She picked up the hoe and stared at the garden that seemed to have stretched overnight. "It's as big as the school softball field," she told the scarecrow. Weeds seemed to spring up between rows of potatoes as she watched. A crow perched on the silent scarecrow's tattered straw hat and cawed.

"I only know how to weed and pick vegetables. What if we get bugs? Gina will cry if I have to squash the squash bugs. Squash the squash bugs … Grandpa would laugh at that. What am I going to do, Mr. Scarecrow?"

"I'm here to help." Alicia dropped the hoe.

"Slick?"

"I didn't mean to scare you. Is Anton any better?"

Alicia shook her head.

"Ed took off for someplace, so I locked up and came to help. He held up a swollen lump of paper. "And to return Anton's book, even if it isn't much good anymore." The rain-soaked pages of *Cannery Row* had split the binding, and the cover was stained with mud.

"Did you find the photographs Grandpa brought to the lake? The ones of William."

"No. They must've blown away in the storm. Sorry. He surveyed the garden. "Looks like you need my help." He reached for the hoe.

Alicia held firm. "You can't. This is my punishment because I left Gina's shoes at Dead Coon Lake, and now they're ruined—her good school shoes." She rubbed her arm.

I can't let Poppa get any madder at me.

"We need the food; Momma worries all the time about the food shortages and how much food costs. And I'm strong and I'm not going to let Grandpa's garden die." Tears welled up in Alicia's eyes. She grabbed the hoe from Slick and furiously worked at a weed clump, but she sheared off a small green acorn squash.

"Now look what I've done!"

Slick eased the hoe away from her and struck at the base of the weed, reached down, and came up with the invader in his hand.

"I drove out to Dead Coon and brought the shoes home. I heard you tell Gina you'd take the blame for the shoes. Instead, you should be getting credit for driving Anton home; who knows how long before someone came looking for you. He could've …" Slick put his hands on her shoulders and locked eyes with her. "Alicia, I know you're strong, but you're also stubborn. I'm going to keep an eye on the garden, and if it needs work, I'll do it. Ed won't find out either. You make sure to pick the vegetables when they're ready. Now let's fill that basket with tomatoes, take them inside, and see how I can help."

Alicia set the basket of tomatoes in the sink. The hands on the kitchen clock pointed straight up. The stove burners were cold and empty. Dirty dishes were stacked high. Donna and Momma sat at the kitchen table with empty coffee cups, a full ashtray, and an open aspirin tin between them.

"Slick," Donna said. "Just the guy I want to see. Go upstairs and see if Anton can use this bedpan. Alicia, when Gina comes back, give her my nurse cap. Ilse told me your idea to get her involved. It's a good one; she looked overwhelmed when she left with Sarah."

The porch screen door shut quietly as Sarah and Gina entered the kitchen. "Chow's on," Sarah said.

Alicia put Donna's nurse cap on Gina and tilted it slightly so it wouldn't slide down her nose. The smell of roasted ham made Alicia's stomach rumble, reminding her of a morning without breakfast.

"I made a clear chicken broth for Anton," Sarah said. "Alicia, wash and slice up some tomatoes. Those beauties have my mouth watering."

Momma shoved her chair back, grabbed at her stomach, and rushed out of the kitchen. Donna raised an eyebrow. "That happen often?"

The answer was yes, but Alicia kept quiet.

"Yes," Gina said. She glanced at Alicia. "Did I say something wrong? Was it a secret?"

"No, you didn't. We nurses need to know things, don't we?" Donna removed two bobby pins from her pocket and pinned the white cap to Gina's hair.

"Time to eat. There's plenty," Sarah said. "Graffie brought the ham over last night. Where that man finds things with all the shortages is beyond me. Slick, how 'bout you take some of this food, and you, Gina, and Shadow get yourselves a picnic?"

Sarah poured two glasses of milk and fixed two plates of sliced ham and corn on the cob—first of the season—also from Graffie. She handed a tray to Slick and gave him a not-so-subtle hint to take Gina for an ice cream cone afterwards.

"But…" Gina said. Then she looked at Donna and Slick who nodded in apparent agreement. With a sigh, she picked up the silverware and carried it out the door.

Alicia wondered why she hadn't been exiled along with Gina.

A pale Momma came back and sat next to Donna. She shook her head at the plate of food and lit a cigarette instead. Alicia cleared the table, refilled the coffee cups, and emptied the ashtray. Feeling proud, Alicia realized why she had been included when the table discussions ebbed and flowed around caring for Grandpa. Donna said she and Slick had talked upstairs and he would gladly help with Grandpa and anything else the family might need.

"For the next week or so," Sarah said, "someone from the Ladies Aid at church will bring the noon meal to give you some breathing room." She held up her hand. "No, Ilse, don't say a word. Everyone at church and the whole town knows how much Anton helped during the Depression—the way he shared his garden, way he extended credit at his general store for years. You did his books. You know. Even the Baptists and Catholics have volunteered food."

"Slick also said he'd mind the garden, and no one needs tell Ed," Donna said. "I'll teach Slick basic care for Anton, and I'll be over every morning after work to check on him."

Alicia began to wonder why they had let her stay. "What can I do?"

"I'll take some more coffee. Half cup," Sarah said. "Alicia, you can watch Gina when she's not at my house."

I'm doing that now—Poppa's orders.

Sarah's words crushed Alicia.

Treat me like a baby—as usual.

"Joe will come afternoons when Ed isn't around," Sarah continued. "I don't like going around Ed like this, but you never know about him." She touched Momma's arm. "He seemed back to his old self for a while after William was born, but lately …"

Momma rubbed her temples and reached for the aspirin tin.

20

Angry and unappreciated, Alicia walked away from the women and went outside through the living room door. A solitary robin scavenged for worms as if it were any normal day. He squawked when another red-breasted male flew too close to the ground. Gray clouds hid the sun and sky.

Despite Poppa's warning not to ride, Alicia mounted her bicycle. She rode aimlessly around Fullerton, streets deserted in the heat—a ghost town. Driven by an inner compulsion, she raced across the highway onto the road alongside the town dump and gravel pile. Pedaling faster and faster, she searched for escape from the guilt and worry that rode her shoulders. She paused for a second on the hill's crest above Cutters Creek and then plunged down the graveled road towards the bridge at break-neck speed.

I deserve to die.

Another voice spoke of the impossibility of abandoning Momma, Gina, Grandpa, and William. With that small kernel of determination, she coasted to a stop on the bridge.

Alicia sought strength outside herself, and maybe that had been her intention from the first moment of the ride. She hid her bicycle in a stand of cottonwood trees, away from Poppa's eyes should he drive by. She slid down the embankment, grasping branches of berry-laden chokecherry trees. The creek led her through the glade, past the thundering waterfall. She paused in the shade between tall, gray rocks. Summer songbirds were silent. Like Grandpa. She climbed the seven steps to the tunnel covered by flowering vines that now were intent on strangling each other. A cool breeze flowed from the tunnel's mouth when she parted the foxtail and bluestem.

It was narrower, rock walls sharper than before. With only a hand held to the wall to guide her, she reached the rock cavern. Lights from the domed ceiling no longer dazzled, but were gray, fog-like. The wind choir was silent, replaced by a deafening drip, drip, drip of water. She faced the stone alter, crumbled as if destroyed by the June tornado. Yet, she begged, "Make me stronger." One by one, the twinkling stars embedded in the rock walls dimmed until, at last, total blinding darkness.

Devastated, overwhelmed by her own hollowness and stripped of answers, Alicia backed out of the cavern, paused at the tunnel entrance, and shivered. A cold, slow, steady drizzle fell, blurring the world. Purple milkweed blossoms lay crushed in the mud. A faint smell of skunk lingered. She traced her steps back to the bridge, but before she could begin to comprehend the meaning and the consequences, she heard Alphie yell.

"Hey, Brat. Over here." Underneath the bridge, he leaned against a metal support on the creek's bank. "Got any more cigarettes for me? I could use some. That asshole Graffie kicked me out again." He pitched his cigarette butt at her, but it landed in the creek a few feet away. "I've been wanting to get you alone for a little talk. I'm thinking now that it was Gina who drew that rat picture of me." He posed with his nose in the air, finger on his chin. "Hmmm. How can I get even?"

"You stay away from her!"

"Who's going to make me? You? Ha!" He came towards her in long purposeful strides.

"What have I ever done to you, Alphie?"

"You're stealing Slick away from me. You've tricked him into helping take care of that crippled old bastard grandfather of yours, and now Slick says he's too busy with that and work to hang out with me. Slick's my only friend." As if he'd said too much, he closed in: six feet, five feet, four. A menacing leer lit his face.

Grasses trembled and quivered as Alicia stepped backwards on the mud-lined bank, almost slipping into an angry and swollen creek. She caught a branch of a chokecherry tree to steady herself. She stepped sideways, looking left and right for an escape. If she'd learned one thing when dealing with Poppa, it was to stay calm. "What do you mean? Slick's your friend."

Alphie narrowed the distance: three feet, then two. The smell of his aftershave failed to mask the stink of his body odor. He grabbed for her. Alicia sunk to her knees, picked up a fist-sized rock, stood, and hurled it at him. It ricocheted off his chest. She turned and ran, but she wasn't fast enough.

"Damn you." With one arm, he grabbed her around the waist and pulled her to his chest. "See? I can do whatever the hell I want, and you're going to keep your mouth shut or Gina suffers."

She kicked backwards at him and flailed her arms.

He wrapped his other arm around her neck, pinning her to his body. "Going somewhere?"

Alicia bent her head and bit down on his forearm. Hard.

Shouting curses, Alphie shoved her to the ground, slipped on the green mossy rocks, and fell backwards into the creek beside tall grasses laid flat by the swift current. He came up spewing water and hate. "You're really going to be sorry now." His eyes were colorless in shadows. "Watch that brat sister of yours. Slick can't always protect both of you." He climbed the creek bank, shook off water like an old dog, got into his pa's car, and drove away.

Instead of finding the solace she had sought in the cavern, Alicia's burden became heavier, like a boulder chained around her neck, swinging at her heart. She pushed her bicycle to the road. Off in the distance, past the town dump, Gina and Shadow were walking in the middle of the graveled road. She clapped her hand to her eyes, as if she could shut out the image, and then climbed on her bicycle and rode hard to them. Shadow wagged her tail at the sight of Alicia, but she stayed beside Gina. Alicia tried to keep the anger from her voice, but the idea of what Poppa might say or do to her, prevented it. "Gina! What are you doing here? You shouldn't have crossed the highway."

Foxtail grass hissed in the wind beside the road while Alicia waited for an answer. Gina's face wrinkled like she was about to cry. Shadow's head was under Gina's hand. "You left me … And Poppa was really mad 'bout something."

What else can happen?

"Poppa? Gina, I gotta get you home—right now!" Alicia steadied the bicycle by its handlebars. "Step on the bar between the pedals and climb into the basket." Gina maneuvered herself into the basket, but her added weight made every push of the pedals more difficult. The drizzle had passed, but mottled clouds scudded across the sky, urging them to hurry. Shadow raced in and out of the ditch, leading the way home.

"Gina, don't wiggle. You'll tip us over."

Alicia paused at the entrance to the gravel pile to catch her breath. Out of the corner of her eye, she saw Poppa's black car turn from Depot Road into their driveway.

"We'll hide until Poppa leaves, all right?"

Gina nodded and wrapped her arms around Alicia as she was lifted down from the basket.

Alicia dropped the bicycle and ran with Gina to hide behind the twenty-foot mound of gravel shaped like a kneeling camel.

Shadow sniffed along the grassy edge of the gravel pile between a dump truck and a snowplow until she flushed a cottontail. The chase was on.

"Shadow!" Alicia yelled. "Come here." She peered around the mound. Shadow abandoned her chase, ran past the dump, crossed the highway, and headed into Grandpa's yard.

Poppa came to the edge of the driveway, petted the dog, and shielded his hands over his eyes in their direction. Alicia pulled back and flattened herself against the gravel mound.

Too late. He knew where she was. If only she could think of a reason, an explanation to keep her and Gina from Poppa's anger. Her mind was blank. She took Gina's hand and led her out from behind the mound. They were visible and vulnerable—each step felt as heavy as a rock-filled boot.

Poppa headed for them in his car.

Alicia stood in front of Gina as pebbles flew from his tires. A fury of red-faced anger bolted from the door.

"Give me the girl." Poppa jerked Gina from Alicia's grasp, opened the passenger door, and pushed Gina into the back seat. "Now for you." He shoved Alicia backwards. "I said no riding. I said work in the garden. I said take care of your sister. You disobeyed direct orders." Spit flew from his mouth. "It's Clara, isn't it? She wants her revenge, and she's turning you against me. And now Gina, too."

"No, Poppa. Nothing like that. I didn't see Clara, and it's not Gina's fault."

He kept shoving Alicia back over stony dirt and thick clumps of grass until she was forced down on her heels, her back pinned against the wheel of the dump truck. He swung his open palm against her cheek so hard her head slammed into the tire's lug nuts. She wanted to feel for blood, but instead she clenched her hands into a fist so tight her fingernails dug into skin. A monarch butterfly flitted in slow motion over a purple milkweed pod.

Poppa lumbered to his car, stumbled into the driver's seat, and gunned the car in reverse towards his daughter.

Alicia screamed soundlessly.

He drove over her bicycle again and again, in what seemed like an endless nightmare, coming closer and closer.

He's gonna kill me.

A deafening shriek of metal against metal.

Tires exploded. Gina stared out the back window, tears streaming down her cheeks, her hand spread on the glass, reaching out to her sister. Finally, Poppa drove away in a hail of gravel and mud clumps. The bicycle was a heap of unrecognizable metal.

Certain he could no longer see her, Alicia crumpled to the ground. Her slapped cheek radiated heat. Blood from the back of her head covered her palm. She struggled to pull the ravaged, mangled bicycle to the town dump and kicked it into the debris- and garbage-filled trench. It landed near branches torn loose by the tornado. A rat fled from an old rusted washing machine. Two crows mocked her from fence posts.

With her bicycle gone, she had no escape; she was trapped. She walked home and up the hill behind the house, between gooseberry bushes, through the cellar door, and silently up the stairs. In the bathroom, she used a washrag to blot blood from the tender lump on the back of her head. When she finished, she rinsed the blood down the drain and hid the washrag behind the toilet.

Tears threatened her lower lids, but Alicia held them back.

I'll never cry for him again.

Gina sat on their bed, clutching Raggedy Ann. Tears streamed down her cheeks when Alicia entered the bedroom. Sadness outlined her face.

Alicia sat down, and Gina lunged into her arms.

"Poppa pushed me. Why?" Gina's cries became sobs.

Gina felt so small, so helpless in Alicia's arms. Alphie's threat—a very real threat—against Gina, and now Poppa's brutal treatment loomed large.

I can take care of myself. But Gina ...

Anger twisted like a knife in Alicia's heart. Just like the lightning rod attached to the house, Poppa's anger and Alphie's hate would go through Alicia first.

"Shh, Gina. I'll take care of you. No matter what."

***

By the time Alicia dared venture downstairs the next morning, Poppa was gone. Slick had already fed, shaved, and carried Grandpa to the wheelchair Graffie had bought at an auction when the government had shut down another POW camp up north. In spite of the heat, a small blanket was draped over his knees. He no longer looked like Grandpa. Skin sagged from his face, and eyes that always smiled at Alicia were flat, dull, and often filled with tears. Sadness overwhelmed Alicia.

Wake me up from this nightmare.

She chided herself for being so foolish.

***

Alicia wandered down Center Street, absorbed with the thought of protecting Gina from Poppa and Alphie. That had seemed like a good idea last night, and still was, if only she had a clue of how to do it. Until she had a plan, she was going to keep as much distance between Gina and Alphie as possible. Poppa was another matter. She approached the shop, avoiding the open door.

"Alicia, stop," he shouted.

She pretended not to hear him. He must have been standing back, hidden in the shadows.

"Are you deaf?"

She touched the lump on the back of her head and turned around. Poppa wheeled the shiny new red bicycle from the Gambles Store window towards her. "My birthday wish," she whispered. There it was—escape. Ride away; leave problems behind. Tempting …

Poppa wheeled it closer. "I made a special trip to Marshall this morning to buy this for you. Come on … take it." He pushed the front tire up against her leg. "I'm sorry for yesterday, but if you hadn't disobeyed me and taken Gina across the highway to Clara, I never would've hurt you or your bicycle."

Her hand was reaching for the handlebars when Poppa said, "I'll never hurt you again. Now take it." The smile was on his face and not in his eyes.

"Liar." She dropped her hand and walked away.

His angry threats slid over her and collected like puddles in her wake.

21

Grandpa sat in his wheelchair, Poppa paced the kitchen, and Alicia and Gina sat quietly in their chairs. Eyes downcast, Gina spooned sugar into her bowl of lumpy oatmeal.

"That's enough!" Poppa's shout shattered the stale kitchen air as he turned back to the stove.

Gina dropped her spoon, scattering sugar crystals, and when she tried to brush them together, she knocked over her glass of milk. She froze in place like a threatened rabbit. Milk streamed over the table edge onto Gina's school dress.

Alicia gave Gina a warning shake of the head and grabbed a dishrag from the sink.

Poppa spun around and stepped towards Gina.

"No, Poppa," Alicia said. "That was me … I spilled the milk. I'm sorry." She slid between Poppa and the back of Gina's chair.

He reached around Gina for Alicia's cereal bowl and heaved it into the sink. Shattering glass pinged against Alicia's ears.

Poppa shook his fist at Alicia. "There'll be no breakfast for you, girl."

The pained expression on Grandpa's face as he was forced to sit motionless, locked in an eternal silence in his wheelchair, made Alicia sick to her stomach. She couldn't have eaten the oatmeal if she'd tried.

"Come on, Gina. You need to change clothes now or we'll be late for school." Alicia pulled her sister out of the chair and didn't let go until they reached their bedroom.

Gina scrambled to quickly change. Mrs. Arnold's rules were law in the one-room schoolhouse; late-comers stayed after school, and then Poppa would punish the girls.

Yesterday, Alicia had asked if she could move her desk behind Gina's without telling the teacher the reason for the move: to protect Gina. Since the day Poppa smashed Alicia's bicycle, Gina had started to suck her thumb again, and some of the bigger boys, eighth graders, teased her and shot spitballs at her. Alicia wanted to block them. Instead of letting Alicia move, Mrs. Arnold rapped her knuckles with a ruler and told her to pay attention to the arithmetic problems on the blackboard. Alicia's head wasn't filled with division problems but rather plans to deal with Alphie, who often lurked behind the stand of church evergreens after school waiting for the sisters. Last Friday, he had followed them and pitched rocks at their feet, his mean ugly laugh bouncing off the sidewalk.

Today, she was ready. Over the weekend, she had fashioned a Y-shaped stick and a thick rubber band into a slingshot and had practiced with pebbles until her aim improved.

After school let out, Alphie was nowhere to be seen. Alicia wasn't sure if she was relieved or disappointed. While keeping an eye out for Alphie, Alicia attempted to convince Gina to hide her thumb in her fist every time she felt a need to suck it—especially around Poppa. That was one thing that Gina might do that Alicia couldn't pretend she had done.

At home, Momma, Donna, and Sarah huddled around the kitchen table. Something was wrong. Both girls shared the one empty chair and waited. Sarah spoke first.

"Anton tried to get out of his wheelchair this morning," Sarah said. "Shadow started barking and ran to Ilse. She had to call Slick to get Anton back in his chair. Ed was nowhere to be found."

"Pa was so agitated and upset. I'm afraid he might have another stroke," Momma said.

"When did it happen?" Alicia asked.

"Just after breakfast," Sarah said.

Alicia's heart sunk. Before his stroke, Grandpa would have stood up to Poppa. She now understood that Grandpa was aware of what was happening around him.

Alicia had been avoiding him out of sadness.

He must think I don't love him anymore.

Shame rose to the back of her throat.

"I don't know what I'm going to do." Momma's voice was filled with desperation. "I swear I don't. I need Clara here, and Ed's dead-set against her. I don't understand. Before the War, he was kind and loving. Now? What happened? What's going to happen to my family?" Momma's head swiveled from one friend to another. She seemed to shrink in her chair.

Gina's thumb slipped into her closed fist.

"Gina, let's go be with Grandpa," Alicia whispered. "He's probably lonesome."

Someone had moved him to the sofa. Alicia inhaled sharply. The left side of Grandpa's face was bruised purple; the lingering scab on his forehead had been scraped away. Alicia curled up beside him and slipped her arm through his immobile one.

I miss you; I need you.

"I'm sorry, Grandpa. Sorry for so many things." Alicia leaned her head against his shoulder.

Gina knelt in front of the coffee table. She turned the pages of Grandpa's *National Geographic Magazine* and told him about the pictures. Alicia slipped out the living room door, intending to pull the last of the onions. They rested on a board beside the garden, drying in the sun. The soil around the winter squash and Gina's pumpkins had been weeded. "I need to help more—even if they think I can't," she said to the ever-silent scarecrow.

The women were gone by the time Alicia returned. She set the table and sliced the last tomatoes from the garden. She placed sliced potatoes on a plate to fry for supper and arranged the cold meatloaf and cheese slices from the Ladies Aid. Poppa's car roared into the driveway.

He stormed past her without removing his work boots and coveralls, shouting angrily for Momma. "I forbid that girl—that Clara—in my house. Do you hear me?"

"What do you expect me to do? I can't handle all of this—Pa and now William. I can't. I can't."

The house shook with echoes of their argument. Alicia shut off the burner and called to Gina and Shadow to come with her.

"We need to borrow some grease from Sarah." Immediately, she regretted the lie.

"No, Gina, we don't need grease. I didn't want you in the house and hear them."

"I know," Gina said.

***

Poppa hadn't returned home by Alicia's bedtime, but the next morning he was ready with a list of rules for Clara. "Don't let her near my boy." Poppa paced the length of the kitchen. "If she touches him, so help me …" He retraced his steps. "Make sure she's gone before I get home for supper."

Momma stirred the oatmeal on the stove, keeping her back to Poppa.

"How is Clara going to help Momma if she can't touch William?" Gina asked.

Alicia kicked her sister under the table.

Poppa stepped towards Gina.

Alicia tipped her bowl of oatmeal with her elbow to distract him. She slid down in her chair, expecting a slap from him, but she realized, with Momma nearby, there would be no punishment.

Until later.

"Damnit, Alicia. Do you have to be so clumsy?" Poppa motioned with his finger for her to follow. He ignored Momma's pleas to stop.

Once outside, Poppa grabbed the back of her neck, squeezed hard, and steered her across the lawn to the car shed door.

Here it comes.

He released her neck, grasped her shoulders, and whirled her around to face him. "I know why you didn't take the bicycle. It's Clara. She's winning you over to her side. And now Gina, too. Well, that's going to change. Clara has one blue eye, one brown eye. That's a sure sign of evil." He leaned into her face. "Your duty is to spy on Clara and report back to me. I'm not letting her take my boy away. She's already making him sick."

Alicia felt herself float near the eaves of the car shed, able to look down on the two of them. He spoke in slow motion. She struggled to put sounds into words. Even after putting them together, they made no sense.

Clara is making William sick?

The question reached the end of her tongue and died.

"If she tries to get into my stuff—here or in the basement—or touch William, you will tell me, or both of you will be sorry in ways you can't know." Poppa fumbled with the door lock, jerked it open, and stepped into the darkness. Starlings, sheltered under the eaves, screeched and scattered.

An overpowering anger seized her. If Poppa thought he was going to scare her with pinches, slaps, or a knot on the head, he didn't know his own daughter. She vowed to never tell him when Clara took care of William. And she would find the hidden photograph album, discover his secrets in them, and find the answer to Momma's question—and hers—what had happened to Poppa.

Consumed with her own anger, she was opening the porch screen door before Poppa's words about William sunk in. Momma's concern that William slept all the time, refused to eat, and wasn't gaining weight … Did it all add up? Alicia was frightened for her baby brother. Suddenly, her search for Poppa's secret seemed unimportant. She rushed to find Momma and the truth.

In the shade-darkened living room, Grandpa sat on the sofa, his eyes seemingly fixed on his daughter who rocked back and forth, the chair creaking to some unknown rhythm. Worry etched her brow. Shadow, her nose on her front paws, lay on her rug beside William's bassinet.

Perhaps anticipating Alicia's question, Momma nodded her head towards Grandpa and mouthed the words "not now." She rose from the rocking chair, stooped over like the women pulling oxen with their shoulders in Grandpa's magazine, motioned Alicia into the kitchen, and leaned over the sink as if she was going to throw up.

Somehow Alicia found the courage to ask the question she dreaded. She took a deep breath. "Is William sick?"

"I'm taking him to see Doc Swenson in the morning." Momma's voice was a hollow, worried sound. "Thank goodness for Clara."

22

After school the next day, Alicia and Gina came home and found the family's world turned upside down. Thumb in her fist, Gina slipped out of the kitchen. Alicia drew up a chair next to Momma, afraid of what she might hear.

"William is a very, very sick little baby." Momma's face was the ashen color of fear. "Doc Swenson is getting him an appointment at the Mayo Clinic in Rochester. Soon. Very soon. I hope."

Alicia enveloped Momma in her arms, daughter holding mother, refusing to let her go until William whimpered from the living room.

Momma slowly unwrapped Alicia's arms. "He had a rough afternoon."

Suddenly, the room became too small for Alicia. Walls closed in, making it hard to breathe. Momma's words about William thundered in her head, dwarfing all worries about Poppa and Alphie.

In the three-day wait for the appointment, Poppa had twice returned home before Alicia's bedtime and cornered her to get his spy report. Both times she lied, telling him that Clara only cooked, cleaned, did the washing and ironing, and never fed, held, or changed William's diaper. He either believed her or had other things on his mind because he only commented with a grunt.

On Saturday, the fourth day, Momma sat next to Grandpa on the sofa, leaned forward to the coffee table, and listlessly stirred her cup of coffee. Alicia and Gina sat in the wingback chairs, quiet as Grandpa, their hands folded primly in their laps. William had cried most of the morning.

"My poor baby," Momma said, clasping one arm over her other arm across her breast as if trying to hold herself together. "I have a headache that won't quit."

Aware of a helplessness pervading her thoughts, Alicia knew she had to make some decisions. Unable to fix William, her main concern was to keep Gina from sliding into herself like Momma. She had renewed her determination to discover Poppa's secret after breakfast when he had torn the newspaper away from Momma's hands and had sworn at her.

As soon as they left for the Mayo Clinic, she would begin her search.

But first things first.

"Gina, William is finally sleeping like Grandpa. Let Momma rest, too. Clara's in the cellar doing the wash. Want to help hang pillowcases and towels?"

Gina nodded and came out of the chair to Alicia. She stuck her small hand into her sister's. "Shadow, come." The dog reluctantly left William's bassinet.

The day was hot—too hot for the middle of October. A warm wind blew, tinged with the knowledge that winter cold lurked on the other side. Summer had slipped away, and fall was fading. Squirrels scampered, buried acorns, and ignored Shadow.

Clara and Gina bent over the wicker basket, pulled up towels, and pinned them on the clothesline to sway in the breeze.

Clara called to Alicia and pointed at the telegraph-shaped wooden pole and a spider web taut and gleaming in the sun. "It's so pretty."

Wistfully, Alicia realized she seldom noticed anything beautiful. She had let problems and worries push aside her ability to see the good.

That's going to change.

"Alicia, there is a basket of Ed's coveralls in the basement still to be washed, and we're out of clothespins," Clara said.

"Why don't you two go to Graffie's and buy another package? Here's a half-dollar. I'll tell Ilse."

With a serious voice, trying to imitate Grandpa, Gina said, "We can shoot the breeze with Mr. Graffie."

Alicia smiled for the first time in ages.

A lifetime ago, the girls had walked to Graffie's, and since then, so much had happened—things she could no more control than the water of Cutters Creek crashing over the rock cliff. At least one thing she controlled: the protective cocoon around Gina, and it was working. So far.

Ahead of the girls, Shadow paused, occasionally sniffing the air. Graffie's parking lot was empty. His old sign, torn down by the tornado, was up but still hung by only one side. Graffie came out of the front door of his trading post, truck key in hand. "What do you need?"

Shadow wedged her head under Graffie's hand, looking for a treat. Alicia told him.

He went inside and came out with a package of clothes pins, two bottles of Orange Crush, and a bone. "On the house," he said when Alicia tried to pay him. "I'm on my way to see Anton and Clara, then up to Olivia for an auction at another closed POW camp. Ed mentioned he'd been up there to look around. You want a ride home?"

"No, thank you," Alicia said. Freedom away from home was too seldom, too great to cut short.

She and Gina crossed the empty hay field to the railroad tracks. "Watch me, Gina." Bottle in hand, package in the other, Alicia teetered on the steel rail and walked, arms outspread for balance. "Poppa would be mad as a hornet if he saw me."

What do I care? No matter what I do, I can't make him love me.

"You want to try?" Less steady than her sister, Gina leaned left, then right until she dropped her bottle of Orange Crush. It smashed on the steel rail, glass splintered, and orange soda pop sprayed Alicia.

"Oops," Gina said.

Alicia giggled; then Gina giggled—more and more until they bent over with laughter. It felt so good.

Finally, catching her breath, Alicia held her bottle to Gina. "Have mine. Look at Shadow. Do you think she's scolding us? She looks serious."

They followed the railroad tracks, jumping from tie to tie, to the tall gray grain elevator at the end of Main Street.

"Wait, Gina. Shadow is limping. Maybe she cut her paw on the glass."

The dog rolled on her side, and Alicia examined the paw while Gina waited in the cool shade of the grain elevator, away from grain-filled freight cars. "Just a pebble." Alicia glanced up.

Alphie had Gina by the back of her neck, steering her to an open boxcar.

Shadow scrambled to her feet, raced to them, barking and baring her teeth. Alphie let go of Gina when the dog lunged and knocked him to the gravel.

"Get off me, you damned mutt." Alphie drew his arms up to protect his face.

Alicia tugged Shadow away by her collar. "Good dog."

Alphie rose to his feet and backed away, his eyes on Shadow. "I'm not done with you yet."

A low, throaty growl came from Shadow.

Graffie slowly drove past.

Alicia turned around and wiped her sister's eyes with the hem of her blouse.

"I bet Alphie was scared silly," Gina said between sniffles.

When the sisters arrived home, Graffie was talking with Clara, his feet apart, a determined look on his face. Clara was both shaking her head and nodding, but with her back to Alicia, it was impossible to see her face. Graffie said a few more words, touched Clara's arm, climbed into his truck, and drove away.

"Gina, are you okay to go see Momma?" If Momma looked carefully at her daughter, she could tell Gina had been crying. "Don't tell her what happened. Momma's got enough to worry about."

The porch screen door closed behind Gina.

"Alphie," Clara said. "He's got himself in big trouble this time. Graffie got a call from his buddy at the sheriff's office; the sheriff is coming to arrest him. I'm going to find Slick and have him drive me out to the farm. I have to tell Pa and Ma before the sheriff gets there."

23

Doc Swenson called around noon the following Monday with an appointment time for William at the Mayo Clinic the next day: Tuesday, at 2 p.m. It was as if the whole house breathed a sigh of relief. Packed suitcases for Momma, Poppa, and William waited by the door, ready for Poppa's arrival. When he arrived, he pulled Alicia into the porch to tell her Gina was going along to the clinic. He told Alicia he'd already lost one daughter to that Clara and would be damned if he lost another. Gina protested, cried, but in the end, it did no good.

Momma hurriedly tossed Gina's clothing and Raggedy Ann into a paper grocery bag. Alicia carried William to the car, his blue eyes still and watchful, his breath warm against her cheek. "Bye, bye, sweet William."

Momma nestled him in her arms, and Alicia closed the door. The late afternoon sun reflected off the back window, hiding Gina from view.

Shadow lay on the grass, her nose pointing in the direction of the car as it faded from view; only when Slick arrived did she move.

***

Clara was unpacking in the small alcove off the girls' bedroom. She pushed her suitcase under the cot and sat down beside Alicia. Alicia couldn't wait any longer to ask about Alphie—worried he would take out his anger on her, or worse yet—Gina. "Can you … um … talk about Alphie?"

Clara looked out the window as if composing herself. "It's been going on all summer, I guess. Alphie breaking into Graffie's trading post, stealing thing—silly little things at first: seed packages, handful of nails, all the napkins from the holders—more like he wanted attention. And then the missing things got bigger—cost more: cigarettes, beer, a fillet knife from a locked cabinet. Graffie covered for him." Clara sighed. "Last week, he broke into Hinkle's Bar and was caught standing in the big plate glass window waving a beer bottle in each hand. Hinkle had him arrested. Pa refused to bail him out, so he's in jail until the judge sees him. I'd hoped Slick could … I guess nobody can fix anybody else." Clara stood and offered a hand to Alicia. "Guess I'd better get some supper going."

Clara's words left Alicia doubtful. Maybe discovering Poppa's album wouldn't fix anything, but Alicia knew she still had to try.

***

After an uneventful walk home from school, without a lurking Alphie, Alicia began her second search for Poppa's album. In her first search, Poppa's bedroom, she discovered nothing. Today, like a thief in the night, she slipped from the kitchen to the built-in buffet in the dining room and knelt in front of the bottom drawer where family albums and photographs were stored. A sepia photograph of Grandpa Anton and Grandma Molly was tucked in a dark green album with snapshots falling out: Johan and Clara, age about seven, beside a white-faced black cow at Clara's farm, and baby pictures of Gina and herself with Poppa at a carnival or county fair. Beneath the album lay Momma and Poppa's framed wedding picture that used to sit on Momma's piano until the piano had become a silent dinosaur in the living room. The glass was cracked from one corner of the tarnished frame to the other.

Are they the same Momma and Poppa?

Five albums were stacked in a corner of the drawer, one dark blue, two brown and two green, but not the green of Poppa's. Only slightly disappointed, she knew there were two other places to search: cellar and car shed, but one was locked.

The cellar stairs creaked, and dust floated in south window sunbeams over Grandpa's workbench where the family had huddled from the twister. Shelves—lined with the remaining jars of strawberry jam, a couple dozen empty mason jars, and six or seven bottles of dandelion wine—flanked Grandpa's workbench. Alicia stretched to pull the overhead light bulb chain. Hammers, chisels, wrenches, screwdrivers, and a yardstick hung from nails on a stained piece of wood behind the workbench. Nails, screws, nuts, and bolts filled wooden cubby holes. The rest of the cellar was a jumble of things: a huge coal-burning furnace, an octopus of pipes across the ceiling, a coal bin, a cistern for rainwater, a wash machine, two metal tubs for rinsing, and boxes slumping in corners.

I'll never find it.

Her determination matched her disappointment. She had to find a way into the locked car shed.

On the way up the steps, something soft touched against Alicia's cheek. Spider. She brushed the web away, and out of the corner of her eye saw a piece of paper dangling from a shelf across from the slop pail. With a chair from the kitchen, she climbed to eye level. Scissors, paste, and black corners to hold photographs in place lined the shelf. No album. She stood on tiptoes to better see. Just then the cellar door opened and Clara was backlit.

"I'm getting a new soap for Grandpa's shaving mug." Alicia surprised herself with the ease of the lie. "Slick said he was getting low."

The four days with Alphie in jail and Poppa away had settled them into a calm routine. Slick worked at the shop, Clara stayed at the house, and Alicia went to school. Nights, Alicia fell asleep listening to Slick and Clara talking softly and laughing downstairs.

On Saturday, Clara and Alicia packed a picnic lunch. Slick tied Grandpa's wheelchair on top of his jalopy, and the four of them and Shadow went fishing at Dead Coon Lake. Slick baited Grandpa's hook and dropped the line off the fishing dock. Grandpa was getting some movement back in his limp arm, and when a fish nibbled, Slick reeled and tugged on the rod with his hand over Grandpa's. The bullhead flopped on the dock. Tears filled Grandpa's eyes.

Alicia strolled away from the dock to collect the colored fall leaves to press between the pages of an old book. Lately, she had spent more time with Grandpa. Awkward at first, she told him stories about kids and school, complaining a time or two about Mrs. Arnold. She held back her fears and worries about William—a close, silent knot in her stomach. Momma had called, but only to say they would be home sometime Sunday afternoon. Tomorrow.

A bone-chilling rain fell all Sunday morning and into the afternoon. Slick had driven Clara home, and the house seemed lifeless without her. The more the day wore on, the more restless and agitated Grandpa became, seemingly fighting against his personal prison. Alicia went to read to him, but Slick shook his head. "I'll carry him upstairs and stay with him. You wait here for your folks."

Within the hour, Poppa drove into the driveway and parked. They were like a photograph caught in time; no one in the car made a move. Alicia dashed to Momma's door, took William into her arms, and sheltered him from the rain. Momma sagged like a rag doll. With his back to all of them, Poppa walked towards the house, stilted like an old man.

"Poppa. Wait. Help me."

He returned, lifted William from Alicia's arms without a glance at his pale, expressionless wife.

Not knowing if Momma needed a friend or a nurse, Alicia raced down the path to Donna's house, praying she was home from the hospital. Drenched and shivering, she pounded on Donna's door.

"Momma," she gasped.

Donna slammed the door shut and ran with Alicia to the car. The passenger door was still open, and half of Momma's suit was soaking wet. They wrapped Momma's arms over their shoulders and with slow, halting steps helped her into the house. Poppa rushed past them, heading outside. Slick was rocking William.

Alicia stopped short. "Momma? Where's Gina?"

Momma looked around, perplexed. "Is she still in the car?"

Alicia ran back out into the rain. Gina was curled into a small ball in the corner of the backseat, her face a stark white. Alicia crawled into the car beside her sister. After long minutes of coaxing, Gina slowly crawled out, followed Alicia into the house, and ran through the kitchen as if being chased by a wild animal.

A slight tapping sound on the porch door, and Sarah and Joe came into the kitchen.

"Bill called me after Donna rushed out," Sarah said. "Sit, Alicia. Fresh coffee. Bless that Slick." She set the table with four cups and poured coffee into each one.

Joe looked around the four cups and four females. "Uh, I guess I'll go help Ed with the suitcases."

Momma stared off to a distant place; worry clotted her eyes. A deep breath and she whispered, "I don't understand all of what the doctors at the Mayo Clinic explained to us, but it boils down to … his heart isn't working right. And his best chance … maybe his only chance … is an experimental operation at the University of Iowa." A long mournful sound came from Momma. "My baby, my poor, poor baby …"

The awful truth of Momma's words slammed into Alicia's heart like a fist and cemented her to the chair.

No, Momma!

Across the table, Donna and Sarah each grasped one of Momma's hands. Slick gently tugged Momma's hands from her friends, one at a time, and wrapped them around a sleeping William. Momma drew the baby to her breast. Slick quietly left the house.

In the dining room, Shadow was barking. Alicia went to quiet her, knowing the dog never barked when William slept.

The dining room and living rooms were empty, but Shadow continued to growl at the window.

Joe was carrying Momma's suitcase, but Poppa grabbed the leather straps, and in a tug-of-war, the suitcase split open. Baby clothes flew into the air and fell to the ground like leaves in a wind storm. Joe dropped his half of the suitcase, backed away palms up, turned, and disappeared down the hill to his gas station.

Poppa shook his fist at Joe's back, kicked his half of the suitcase across the wet yard, got into his car, and drove away.

Alicia returned to the kitchen.

"What's the ruckus?" Sarah asked.

Another lie hovered above her head like a comic balloon—except this wasn't funny. Alicia lifted her coffee cup from the table and sipped the cold liquid. "Nothing. Shadow must've spotted a squirrel too close to the window. Joe and Poppa left."

She swallowed her anger, went outside, and gathered the empty suitcase halves and rain-soaked baby clothes. On bent knees, she folded each diaper and tiny undershirt, and with arms loaded, she carried them to the back of the house—all the time engulfed in the sweet smell of baby William.

What's wrong with Poppa? It was, perhaps, the millionth time she had asked herself.

24

Since Alicia knew Momma would never get the white tulips planted for Johan's tree, she had asked Slick for a ride to the cemetery.

The brilliant October sun shared the sky with blue-black clouds and cast long shadows through bare trees, etching the tombstones with jagged slashes.

Alicia shuddered in the chill of approaching darkness. "Slick, we're done. Time to go." She gathered the small spade, empty water jug, browned clumps of grass, and leftover tulip bulbs into a burlap gunny sack and tied the top with twine.

Slick stood and brushed dirt from his coveralls. "Have Ed and Ilse decided about the experimental operation?

"I don't think so." Information bottled up inside of Alicia threatened to explode: Momma and Poppa's arguments far into the night, slammed doors, sobbing ... The dark cloud of worry, the one she had held at bay while she and Slick had worked and talked, returned.

Since the return from the Mayo Clinic, a gray pallor had invaded their kitchen and spread through the rest of the house, collecting like dust on every face. Neighbors came to call, hesitating at the kitchen door as if something contagious lurked inside. Grandpa's eyes rimmed with tears each time Slick helped him hold William. Momma pulled away from the girls and disappeared into her own sad, small world. The sunbeam that was Gina had diminished, faded as Alicia watched with horror. Alicia's plan to be a lightning rod for

Poppa's anger had failed. No matter what either of them did, he punished both of them. At times, he seemed to imagine or make up things that she and Gina either had done wrong or had not done at all. Alicia had figured that if she stayed away from Gina as much as possible that would cut Gina's punishments in half. And she hadn't invited her to the cemetery because Poppa had ordered Gina to stay in her room after school anyway until he came home.

"Ed's said nothing—treats me like I've become a stranger to him. Or he pulls his disappearing act." Slick's hand grazed the cold marble top of Grandma Molly's headstone. He opened his mouth as if to say more but stopped.

"Do you know where he goes?" she asked.

Slick shook his head.

Back home, Alicia tossed the gunny sack and spade under the porch, away from Poppa's sight and possible anger. In the kitchen, scorched potatoes assaulted her nose.

"There you are," Momma said. "I've been worried about you and Gina." She stared over Alicia's shoulder. "Isn't Gina with you?"

"No. Don't you remember? Poppa said she had to go to our room after school because she spilled water all over the floor trying to fill Shadow's bowl."

"But she's not home. At least, I don't think she is, but where could she be? I ... I ... guess I wasn't paying attention. William was spitting up all afternoon. And Clara had to work at Graffie's." She brushed aside the hair half covering her face. "I don't understand. Gina always does what Poppa tells her."

"I'll go upstairs and look again. Sometimes she likes to take Poppa's flashlight, crawl under the bed, and draw. Maybe she did and fell asleep." Or maybe she was hiding. Alicia had to worry more and more about her sister. Ever since her sister came home from the Mayo Clinic, Gina spent most of the night tossing, turning, and clutching Raggedy Ann.

Alicia took the steps two at a time and called softly at the top of the stairs. "Gina, all ye, all ye, in free." In their bedroom, she lifted the corner of their pink bedspread and peered underneath. Empty darkness. "I know you're hiding from me." Alicia searched Momma's bedroom. Next she searched Grandpa's bedroom and closet. The smell of moth balls reminded her of days spent playing dolls with Gina while Grandpa read in his chair by the window.

Alicia returned to her bedroom. "Gina, quit hiding from me. I'm getting mad." Gina's Raggedy Ann doll was propped against the pillow exactly as Gina had left it before school. Untouched. "How could Momma not know?" she asked the doll.

Raggedy Ann's coal black button eyes stared blankly.

"Why am I always talking to things that can't answer me back?" Alicia raised and lowered her shoulders, trying to lift the panic resting there. "Poppa can't find out she disobeyed him—he just can't."

Momma was behind Grandpa's wheelchair, a hand resting on his shoulder.

"I'll find her," Alicia said.

And it better be soon.

She hurried down the path by Grandpa's garden to Donna's house and knocked on the door between the white and yellow potted mums. Donna answered the door dressed in her nurse uniform.

"Hi, Alicia." Donna's face went from smiling to concern. "Is something wrong? William?"

"No, I just need to find Gina before supper. Did you see her after school?"

"Yes, as a matter of fact. Gina stopped by about an hour ago. She asked if I had a pencil she could borrow for a secret. I gave her a nickel and sent her to Bill's store." Donna tilted Alicia's chin. "Are you *sure* everything's okay?"

"Yes. Thanks." Alicia ran along Depot Road, past the hotel, and onto Main Street to Bill's store. The bell tinkled when she entered. Bill looked up from the meat counter where he was weighing hamburger for Mrs. Oldenburg. Alicia grabbed at the stitch in her side. They seemed to talk forever.

She searched every aisle, and then paced back and forth in front of the dry goods counter, counting the minutes until Mrs. Oldenburg left.

"Well," Bill said, "how lucky can I get? Two Drake girls in one afternoon. Gina bought a pencil and left in a hurry with that little tablet she always carries. What can I do for you?"

"Did she say where she was going?" Alicia asked.

"Joe's gas station."

"Oh, no! Gotta go. Bye."

Dust swirled in the wind along Center Street. Alicia raced the setting sun. Poppa would be hopping mad if he knew Gina went to Joe's gas station.

When Alicia arrived at the gas station, Joe was locking up. "Is Gina here?"

"She was. Left about fifteen, twenty minutes ago." He pointed at the metal stool by the door. "Sit, catch your breath. Is she hiding from you?"

Alicia trusted Joe. "I don't think so. She was supposed to stay in her room, but she's not there. Momma's worried. I'm getting worried, too."

Joe pocketed the key. "Well, Gina spent some time on that there stool, writing in her little tablet for a good while. Every once in a while, she glanced up the street. Probably worried Ed would find her. Alphie and his pa came, so I gassed up their car, took the money inside, and when I came out, she was gone. I can't imagine she's gone too far." In spite of his reassurance, worry lines crossed his brow.

"Alphie's out of jail?" Alicia's panic level doubled. Now she was worried and scared.

"Looks like it."

"Do you know where she went?"

Joe stroked his chin. "Wait a minute. I do believe she said she was going to the post office. It might still be open. I'll go home and see if Sarah knows anything and come back here. If you haven't found her, I'll help look."

If only I had my bicycle.

She ran back downtown, hurried past the closed post office, raced along Main Street, and turned right onto Depot Road to the depot. She hoped Postmaster Simpson was still there lining up mail bags for the nine o'clock Great Northern passenger train. The only car at the station belonged to depot agent, Mr. Oldenburg. Alicia cupped her hands around her eyes and put her nose to the window. He was tapping on the telegraph machine. She stuck her head inside after he waved to her. The wooden benches gleamed, and the smell of fresh wax filled the empty waiting room. The Regulator clock ticked away the time. Mr. Oldenburg kept tapping, and Alicia backed out the door, knowing she had to tell Poppa.

No matter the punishment—Gina had to be found.

Streetlights flickered a warning of encroaching darkness. She hesitated outside the shop. Slick opened the door as she reached for the handle. She told him what had happened and asked if he would search two unchecked places—the cemetery and Cutters Creek. Alicia went cold with images flashing of a bloody Gina lying in a ditch beside the highway.

"I'll do anything for your family." Slick ran out the door.

"Poppa?" Alicia called. He came out from the back bays, holding a rag reeking of gasoline and with his coveralls stained with oil and grease. Behind him, his tools lay in disarray.

"We can't find Gina."

Poppa strode towards her. She clinched her eyes shut. "What do you mean—you can't find her. Bullshit!" He took a step closer. "She's home. I told her not to leave her room after school." He stormed around her. "What kind of mischief are you up to? Is Clara outside?" He stomped to the plate glass window in front of the shop.

She followed. "Poppa …" He didn't turn to face her. "No, Poppa she isn't. Please listen." Alicia raised her voice as if Poppa had gone deaf. "Gina is not home. Momma doesn't know where she is, and I've looked everywhere."

"Damn that mother of yours. Her duty was to keep an eye on Gina. How can I trust her now to keep Clara from my son?"

She pushed the words out of her mouth one at a time. "Poppa ... please ... help ... me..."

A car backfired outside. White-faced Poppa dropped the gasoline-soaked rag and went behind the counter, shaking. Quiet returned outside, and his tremors stopped. He turned to the Timmer Auto Supply mirror. His face hardened into a stone sculpture and then he saluted himself. "I'll organize the men, and we'll mount a search mission. Where was she last spotted, soldier? With Clara? I knew it would come to this."

"Soldier?" She shivered. "Poppa!"

No response. He went into the bathroom and returned wearing his Army uniform jacket.

Alicia fled from the shop and nearly knocked Momma down with the door. "Poppa! He's acting crazy. He's pretending he's back in the Army, and he's mad at you." The words tumbled out. "Gina was at Joe's station and he was the last person who saw her. If Poppa finds out ..."

Slick drove up and got out of his car. "You didn't find her," Alicia said.

Slick shook his head. Alicia wished she could wake herself up from another nightmare.

Poppa had followed Alicia outside. He gave no sign that he even recognized Momma. "Slick, get some men and meet me at the north end of town by Joe's Station. We'll start with the dump, spread out, and work our way south to the depot. Got it, Private?"

Without missing a beat, Slick answered, "Sir. Yes, sir. Permission to take the women and children to safety."

"Permission granted." Poppa saluted and disappeared back into the shop.

"Let's go." Slick held the door for Momma and Alicia. Shadow raced past them and leaped into the back seat of Slick's jalopy.

"I called Clara at Graffie's," Momma said. "Gina wasn't there either, but Clara closed the trading post and came right over. She's with Pa and William. Alicia, we have to find Gina. Soon. With Ed acting this way, I … I … " Momma held Alicia's hand in a death grip so tight it felt like the bones would break, but Alicia didn't pull away. In the growing darkness, familiar trees, bushes, and signs took the shape of monsters. Gina would be scared, and Alicia was running out of places to search. Slick drove into Joe's gas station, and after Momma and Alicia got out, he sped away to get some men to help in the search.

"I've been waiting for you," Joe said, shaking his head. "Sarah hasn't seen her all day, but when I came back, I saw this paper floating in the breeze near the stool where Gina had been sitting." He handed it to Momma.

Momma walked to the light of the white crown gas pump with Alicia standing next to her. "Alicia, this is gibberish." Written on the Rainbow Tablet paper in Gina's neat print were the letters: AIRS, ARIZI, and ARIZ, each one with a straight line drawn through.

"Arizona," Alicia said.

"Arizona?" Momma took back the piece of paper, held it in her palm, and squinted. "I don't understand. What does this mean?"

Alicia shrugged. She reached for an answer, but fear blocked the way.

"I don't want to scare you none," Joe said, "but the car I gassed up before Alphie and his pa got here was from Arizona. Noticed 'cause not too many of them this far away."

"Oh, dear God, no." Joe caught Ilse as she slumped to her knees and guided her to the stool. "First Pa, then William, and now this." She was pale, a specter in the light from the white crown gas pump.

"Momma, I'm sure Gina's okay." Bit by bit, Alicia realized that Gina had probably tried spelling Arizona for her license plate list, but, and it was a big but, that still didn't solve the mystery of Gina's whereabouts. Fullerton wasn't that big.

Poppa's car screeched to a halt at the Highway 16 stop sign to the left of Joe's station. Bill immediately went to Poppa. A dozen men and older boys gathered by Slick and milled around beneath a streetlight. Smoke rose from their cigarettes into the still night air. Poppa motioned the crowd to him. The men parted as Momma walked to Poppa and adjusted his uniform jacket collar.

"I'll go over and give Ed a description of the car," Joe said.

Slick put a hand on Joe's arm. "Better let me," he said. Alphie's pa was with the men, but not Alphie. Her worry escalated.

"Men," Poppa said, "my daughter is missing and I suspect a kidnapping. We gotta get searching right now. We're looking for a ten year old black Nash with Arizona plates. If you spot it, keep your weapons holstered; Gina might be in that car."

The men glanced at each other. Several backed away.

"Weapons?" someone in the crowd questioned.

Poppa continued. "Ah, I meant to say he might have a weapon. Spread out in a straight line and proceed to Lester's cornfield just south of town." Flashlights clicked, and they moved forward in a nearly straight line with Shadow barking and leading the way.

"I'm going home so Ed doesn't find Clara with Baby William," Momma said.

Slick and Alicia walked with her up the hill, his flashlight shining over uneven grass. Through the lit kitchen window, she saw Clara holding William, and Grandpa sitting in his wheelchair across the table. "Alicia, go with Slick and find Gina. Please."

"Don't worry, Momma."

As if words could fix anything.

"Did you check the car shed?" Slick asked.

"No."

The side door creaked as Slick pushed it open and darkness confronted them.

"Gina?" Slick shined his flashlight, lighting the hayloft and layers and layers of undisturbed spider webs. He led the way to Poppa's foot locker. The dust was smeared and the lock hung open. "What the … Ed left this unlocked? With his pistol in there?" He lifted the lid and moved some things aside. "Oh, shit." He looked up at Alicia. "It's gone."

25

"A pistol? Poppa had a gun in his foot locker?" Alicia shuddered and stumbled into sticky spider webs that clung to her cheeks and hair.

Slick cupped his hands around his mouth and yelled. "Gina, are you in here?"

Silence.

"Do you think she … Poppa …"

"I don't know what to think except that we better find her before Ed." Slick guided her outside where the dark of night matched the dark of the car shed. "Do you have any ideas?"

"Well, maybe. I've been thinking since we left Joe's … You know about our sister secret and the license plates. The rules are that she has to see the plates, I spell them, and then she can write them in her Rainbow Tablet. That's why the torn page had all the different spellings. Spellings? That's it! The post office has a United States map on the wall. That's why she stopped there. But that doesn't tell me where she is or why she's not home." Alicia's good mood quickly dissipated.

"Keep thinking. Since it was a secret between you two, did she ever hide the list?"

"No, not really. I'm not sure. Everything's been crazy since they came back from the clinic, and I've been staying away from Gina because if Poppa punishes me and if Gina's around, he punishes her, too—when Momma's not around. This morning she asked me to go to Joe's with her after school to find new license plates, and I said no because Poppa told her to stay in her room after school and, besides, if Poppa found out we went to Joe's, we'd both be in for it. Poppa's more angry than ever since he and Joe fought over Momma's suitcase."

"Maybe she wanted to hide the list from Ed, because if he saw it, he'd know you went to Joe's. Any idea where she would hide the list from Ed?"

The puzzle pieces fell in place. "Oh no. Gina is at the lumber yard. I took her there one time. She promised me she'd never go there without me. But why didn't she come home? Poppa's already mad at her."

The high catwalk, jumbled stacks of wood.

Alicia looked up at Slick. Her growing fear was reflected in his eyes.

"Let's go," he said.

Alicia put her hand on Slick's jacket sleeve. "We can't let Poppa know."

***

Glass from shattered lumber yard lights crunched underfoot. "Straight ahead," Alicia said. "That's where they left the door unlocked. I took Gina in there."

She pulled the metal handle. The door didn't budge. She pulled harder as if her determination could open it.

Slick shined the flashlight on the door frame. It had collapsed on the door, wedging it in place except for a small opening—just large enough for Gina to slip through.

Alicia swallowed hard.

Slick gave her the flashlight, put his back to it, and shoved. No movement. "Stay here. I'll be right back."

Alicia put her ear to the door and listened for shouts or crying. Silence. She envisioned a broken, shattered Gina on the concrete floor. Fear and guilt crushed her chest. A dark shape rounded the corner.

Poppa?

Alicia drew herself closer to the shadowed door frame and held her breath.

"It's me," Slick called out. "I, uh, borrowed a crowbar from Mr. Oldenburg's garage. Aim the flashlight on the door and stand back." He wedged the crowbar between the door and frame and pushed. The wood groaned, but Slick's effort created an opening large enough for them to squeeze through single file.

Overhead, a moonless sky shrouded the open center of the lumber yard. A downdraft of cold air scattered the new wood smell.

"Where did you and Gina go?"

Alicia touched Slick's arm. "This way."

The beam from the flashlight arched over stack after stack of wood, the light catching on sharp wooden corners along a concrete walkway. At the bottom of the steps to the second floor, Alicia called to Gina.

Halfway up the steps to the upper tier of wood, the flashlight went out. Alicia slapped the metal tube against her hand. It came on. "Gina, it's me. Alicia. Can you hear me? Where are you?"

A sound like the meow of a tiny kitten answered.

Alicia cocked her head to hear. The meowing grew louder, became a cry. "Up there."

Slick raced ahead with Alicia close behind, shining the light ahead of him. "Squirt, call my name so I can find you."

"Slick," Gina cried out. A low rumbling echoed from a stack of lumber.

"Everything's going to be okay now, Squirt." His voice was calm, gentle like Grandpa's on Decoration Day. "But you've got to promise to stay still, okay? Remember, the picture show we saw? The hero always saves the pretty girl."

Beside Slick, Alicia slowly moved the tunnel of light back and forth, searching the dark depth of the stacked wood until she caught Gina's face in the beam. The boards had collapsed into a jumble. Gina perched on a wide plank next to a wooden railing that separated the stacks of wood.

"Alicia!" Gina called. The plank teetered.

"Easy, Gina. I know you're scared, but you can't move. I'm coming to get you. Alicia, let me have the flashlight." Slick illuminated the railing that separated wood stacks and paused over the nails holding it in place and the long drop to the concrete floor beneath. "It's not the sturdiest," he whispered to Alicia. "I will get her out. I can reach her if I inch my way along the bottom railing without disturbing the boards close to her. Take the flashlight and shine it on my hands until I get a good hold on the middle railing, then down on my feet. Alternate as I move."

The flashlight wobbled in Alicia's trembling hand. She needed both hands to steady it.

Slick moved with painstaking slowness. At the edge, where he might have disappeared into complete darkness, a board crashed to the concrete floor.

Gina screamed.

Hand over hand, Slick came back to the landing. "We'll have to try something else or get Ed and the men up here."

"No. I'm going to get her. I'm not as big and heavy as you. She's my sister." For Alicia, that explained everything.

"I know you can do it," Slick said.

The quiet calm of his voice reassured Alicia.

"First," he said, "I'm going down to get the rope hanging I saw on a pole. You wait."

In the dark silent time, everything stopped—even Gina's crying. Alicia wondered if that was good or bad.

"Gina, we're still here."

Gina started to cry again.

"I'm cold and I want to go home."

"Hush. Everything is going to be okay. I promise."

What if it isn't? What will Momma do?

Questions and fears filled her head, but Alicia focused on listening for Slick.

The landing creaked with Slick's weight. He circled her waist twice with the rope. "Navy knots. They'll hold." He wrapped the other end around himself and lifted her to the bottom of the three railings. "Be careful."

Another whimper fueled her determination to rescue her sister—no matter what might happen later.

"Gina, here I come." The distance between them felt chasm-like. The urge to rush washed over her. At a snail's pace, she moved closer. "Gina," she said with as much authority in her voice as she could muster. "Listen to me—every single word—and do exactly what I say. Be as still as a church mouse—no wiggling." When Alicia was halfway to her sister, the railing shifted. Alicia gripped the upper railing, and with her feet on the bottom railing, slid inches closer to the small dark mound that was her sister.

"Slowly, very slowly, reach out and put your arms around my neck."

Gina sat as still as if she hadn't heard a word.

Alicia fought to keep panic from her voice. "We have to get out of here before the lumber and you and me crash to the floor."

"I can't," Gina said. "I wet my pants, and I can't leave my Rainbow Tablet."

"I don't care about your wet pants. Listen to me! Poppa can't find you here. Now put your tablet in your mouth like Shadow with a bone and do what I said." Alicia ignored Slick's questions called from the landing.

Holding the railing with one hand, Alicia stretched her head and shoulders closer to Gina, lightly touching the edge of a plank with a free hand for balance.

With the slightest of movement, Gina leaned towards Alicia and wrapped her small, cold arms around her sister's neck.

"Hang on, Gina. Hang on tight." She lifted Gina with the free hand and righted herself parallel to the railing. The board Gina had been sitting on crashed to the concrete floor. Gina's legs dangled mid-air. With more strength than Alicia thought possible, she pulled herself and Gina close enough to the railing to grasp with her second hand. "Now wrap your legs around my waist."

Gina's heart thumped against her own.

Alicia inched her way back, moving a single foot, a single hand-hold at a time until they reached Slick. He pried Gina away from Alicia, set her down, and helped Alicia to safety. She dove to Gina, wanting never to let her go.

Slick touched Alicia's shoulder. She was barely able to see him through a curtain of tears.

"You gave us quite a scare, Squirt." Slick tried to separate the girls, but they clung to each other. He backed away and untied the rope around his waist. "Alicia, Let's get her home before anyone thinks to look here."

Reluctantly, Alicia stood so Slick could untie the rope from her waist. He scooped Gina into his arms, and the three of them raced back home.

Slick set Gina on the ground. "Go inside, and, Squirt, do exactly what Alicia tells you," he said and disappeared into the dark.

Alicia shut the outside door to the cellar and stared at the steps between them and the closed kitchen door. *We're home, but now what?*

Gina tugged at the back of Alicia's blouse and finally found her voice. "Don't tell Poppa on me. Please."

Alicia cringed. She still had Poppa to deal with and another lie to make up. "No, I won't, but don't you ever dare to go there again. Do you hear me? I mean it."

Gina hung her head.

Alicia peeked into the kitchen. Empty. A pot boiled on the stove. Alicia turned down the heat on the burner and led Gina through the dining room. William slept in his bassinet, and Grandpa snoozed in his chair. The girls crept past Momma's closed door. In their own room, Alicia helped Gina out of her wet dungarees and fumbled for a dry pair of panties in a bureau.

"Why did you go to the lumber yard? You promised me."

"I wanted to hide my list of license plates. To surprise you when I had all of them. I wanted to make you like me again."

Alicia's plan to protect Gina by staying away had failed. "You silly goose, Gina. Of course I like you." She tickled her sister.

Gina giggled. "Stop. I have to pee."

Alicia turned on the bathroom light. Gina's bare bottom was covered with fading purple, green, and yellow welts.

Poppa!

When Gina sat on the toilet, Alicia crouched to look Gina in the eye. "Poppa did that, didn't he? When?"

Eyes looking away, Gina nodded slightly and quickly.

"Please tell me."

Gina hesitated, and then finally blurted: "At the Mayo Clinic. In our hotel room. Momma was gone and I woke baby William up to sing him a song and Poppa spanked me with his belt."

Alicia steeled herself against spewing the anger boiling inside her. "Did you tell Momma?" Alicia was afraid that Momma knew and had done nothing and also afraid she didn't know.

"No. Poppa said if I told her, he would spank Momma with the belt, too." Gina propelled herself head first into Alicia's arms, knocking both of them on the floor. "I'm scared of Poppa."

She sighed. "Gina, Poppa's been hurting me for a long time, too, and it's getting worse since William got sick. I thought if I stayed away from you, he might not start hurting you. Then I had to do things to make him madder at me than he was at you. I was wrong. It didn't do any good. Now I'm going to take care of you—no matter what. Remember what Johan, I mean Slick said about doing what I told you?"

Where did that come from?

Alicia removed the cross necklace, put it around Gina's neck, and clasped her sister's small hands in hers. "Go put your nightgown on, take Raggedy Ann, and hide in Grandpa's closet under the quilt like we used to."

"Alicia, sometimes we have to lie, don't we?"

"Yes, sometimes."

Each and every day from now on.

"Now scoot before Poppa gets home. Stay there until I come and get you."

Alicia took the stairs slowly, thinking of an explanation for Momma.

I hate lying to Momma, but I gotta keep her out of it. Or the shell that is Momma will crack open. Someday he's going to pay for this.

"Momma?"

"In the kitchen. Did you find Gina?" Panic filled Momma's voice and face.

Alicia hesitated and waited for an open field to plant her lies. She looked Momma straight in the eye. "I came home to look for her one more time. When I went upstairs to the bathroom, I thought I heard a noise in Grandpa's closet. Gina was there asleep with Raggedy Ann under the quilt."

"But …" Momma looked unsure, uneasy.

Alicia forced a smile. "Poppa will be happy that she is safe. Let's go get her. I told her everyone was looking for her, and now she's afraid you're mad at her. Listen. William is fussing." They walked into the living room to his bassinet. Momma kissed her fingers, touched his head, picked him up, held him close to her breast, and rocked him gently in her arms.

"Mad? I'm so relieved that she's okay. I thought …" Relief in her voice shifted to worry. "Your Poppa is going to blame me for not watching her."

Before Poppa came home, I never lied.

"No, Momma. He won't blame you because you're going to tell him what I said, and he'll blame me because I didn't find her. 'Alicia, you got the whole town riled up. Shamed me—made me look like a fool.' That's what he'll say."

"I can't let you take the blame."

"Yes, you can, Momma. And you will. For everybody's sake."

The kitchen door slammed. Alicia and Momma jumped. Shadow raced to William, her tail between her legs.

"Ilse, we can't find her anywhere. I'm calling the sheriff."

"Ed, in here. By William's bassinet. Gina is home. She never left." Momma's face flushed with the lie.

He threw his Army jacket on the floor. "I'll see to her."

Alicia bolted for the stairs, but it felt like running in Dead Coon Lake with water up to her neck. She jumped ahead of Poppa and stood on the middle step—face to face. "I did it, Poppa. For a joke. I told her to hide, and then I told everyone she was lost." He pushed her against the banister. The wood dug into her back. She stretched her leg across the step to the opposite wall to block him. He put both hands on her waist.

He's going to throw me down the steps.

Poppa's eyes disappeared into slits. "You have betrayed me and mocked me for the last time. You're the enemy." He dropped his hands and stomped down the steps, shaking the house in his wake.

Red-hot anger filled her.

Enemy? If it's a war he wants, then Poppa has his war.

26

A hard, killing frost ravaged Grandpa's garden: pumpkin and winter squash vines had withered and shrunk; now they lay browned and brittle on the cold ground. Inside the house, Momma was like those lifeless plants. She spent her days gripping William's bassinet so hard that it left a wicker imprint on her hand when Clara or Alicia coaxed her away. Poppa's red-hot anger burned out and then reappeared ice cold. He spent more days away from home and Fullerton, and those days were like brief glimpses of sun through the clouded sky. Gina seldom smiled or laughed, and when she did, it was only fleeting. Alicia was afraid to fall asleep, afraid of the nightmares sitting on the edge of her bed waiting for her, afraid for Gina who sleep-walked into the closet in search of the bathroom, afraid Poppa might appear as Alicia changed Gina's wet nightgown.

In the mornings, Clara washed the nightgown. Neither said a word to Momma.

Last night, around suppertime, Doc Swenson had stopped by with more information from the Mayo Clinic about an experimental operation tried in Boston and now at the University of Iowa that could possibly help William. He would contact the hospital if Momma and Poppa agreed.

Poppa had come home after Alicia was in bed. After his first shout, she crossed her arms in front of her chest, held herself tightly. She knew the argument to follow, but she was unable to move away from the adjoining bedroom walls.

"I heard enough about experiments when I was in Germany. What the hell are you thinking? Nobody's touching my boy." Poppa's voice roared through the walls.

"Then William is going to die," Momma shouted back.

She'd spoken Alicia's worst fears.

What is wrong with Poppa that he won't even try?

She buried her face in her pillow and sobbed softly, trying not to wake Gina.

***

Alicia awoke with a start. Gina was sitting beside her on the bed, fully dressed, listless as Raggedy Ann clutched to her stomach.

"Gina! What happened now?" Alarmed, Alicia's eyes checked Gina's arms and legs for new bruises.

Gina turned her head to show a huge chunk of missing hair from the left side of her head. "I fell asleep with gum in my mouth and it got tangled in my curls and I cut it out."

"We have to get out of here before Poppa sees you. Maybe Sarah can fix it."

Alicia quickly dressed, hurried downstairs, spread strawberry jam on two slices of bread, and yelled for her sister from the dining room doorway. "Gina, hurry up!"

Too late. Alicia heard Poppa's boots stomping down the stairs. He came into the room, holding Gina's long curls so tightly they pulled back her eyelids. Tears streamed down Gina's cheeks, but her thumb was hidden in her fist.

"Alicia, what the hell have you done now?" Poppa asked. He swiveled Gina's head. "She looks like a goddamn refugee from one of those *Life Magazine* pictures." He shoved Gina away. "Goddamnit, Alicia. You'd better straighten up and fly right before you ruin this whole family."

"What's left to ruin?" she muttered.

He grabbed Alicia's arm and jerked her towards him. "Don't you sass me, girl." Poppa snapped his fingers and whistled for Shadow. The dog remained steadfast beside the girls. He wrapped his hand around the dog's collar and pulled her behind him. Shadow's paws scraped across the linoleum floor and out the door.

Gina dove into her sister's arms. Her pale, tear-stained face looked up at Alicia. "Why's Poppa like this? Why can't he be like the old Poppa? I hate him," she whispered between sobs.

Alicia shrugged her shoulders and shook her head. "I don't know either." The answer had to be in the photo album. The car shed was the only place she hadn't searched, and for good reason. Since Slick had told her about the missing pistol, the car shed key never left Poppa's chain of keys. There had to be another way in, she figured; it's an old converted barn. The search would come later, but for now, Gina needed her. She gently unwound Gina's arms and dried her sister's tears with the dish towel draped over the sink.

"Stay here, Gina. I need to tell Momma something."

Momma sat beside Grandpa on his bed and helped him cradle William in his arms. Grandpa's stiff hand lay on the baby's heart. One more thing in a growing list of what Grandpa could no longer fix.

"Momma, me and Gina are going to Sarah's house so she can fix Gina's hair."

Lost in her sadness, Momma nodded without looking up, reminding Alicia, once again that she, Alicia, was on her own.

Alicia was wiping the last of the jam from Gina's face when Clara knocked and came into the kitchen with two bottles of milk from her farm. "What's wrong?"

"I got gum in my hair, and I cut it out. Poppa got mad and shoved me and I cried," Gina said. "Now we're going to Sarah's to fix it. Poppa said I looked like someone in a magazine, but he didn't say it nice."

"Well, he's wrong," Clara said. "You're beautiful—even with the missing hair."

It was Alicia's turn to ask what was wrong. "Clara?"

"Alphie," Clara said. Sadness ringed her voice. "We all tried to help him—Johan, Slick, even me. I know, I know …

but he's still my brother. His choice was jail or join up. So … Pa signed the papers, and he left yesterday for the Army."

Alicia was caught in the middle of her feelings: relieved that Alphie was gone and sad for Clara. "I told Momma we're going to Sarah's. Be back in a while." There was nothing more she could say.

Sarah was on her knees beside a bunch of tulip bulbs in the flower garden surrounding the birdbath. She stood, removed her garden gloves, rubbed her knees, and smiled. Flicker raced to Gina and wound his long cat tail around her legs. "What brings you girls here? Oh, I see." She tilted Gina's head back, forth, up, and down. "Hmm. Let's go inside. See what I can do."

Alicia hesitated at the bottom porch step. "Can Gina stay here for a while? Momma knows we're here."

"Sure, come along, Gina."

Alicia waited at the street to make sure Sarah and Gina went inside. Gina was safe, giving Alicia time to search for the albums. She skirted Poppa's shop, approaching from the back alley. The bay doors were down, the front dark. Timing was perfect.

To stay hidden, she detoured by Joe's station. She climbed the tall maple that hung over the outhouse attached to the car shed. Hanging onto a thick branch, she lowered her feet to the roof of the outhouse. Then, holding onto the peaked roof, she made her way to a broken window with a crumbling wooden frame and shards of glass still embedded along the sides. She kicked away the remaining glass and climbed inside. Alicia waited for her eyes to adjust to the dark hayloft. A musty odor clung to rafters. An old horse-drawn plow was pushed into a corner, and rusted rakes and shovels were tied to the wall with spider webs. She tested her footing and then crept across the loft, avoiding gaping holes, to the ladder leading down to the mud-hardened floor.

Poppa's dark green foot locker was wedged under a wooden, make-shift work bench beside a three-legged milk stool. She sneezed wet dots on the dusty foot locker. Alicia's courage diminished as possible consequences began to dominate her thoughts. She gulped.

Now or never. For my family ... for myself.

She knelt, opened the front two latches, and lifted the still unlocked lid. She breathed a sigh of relief: no gun. Worry replaced relief.

Where is the gun?

Poppa's green album was on top of everything. Alicia carefully lifted it onto her lap and opened it. Black corners that once held photographs were empty. She turned the pages, but only one snapshot remained: Poppa, Cal, and three other soldiers in front of a burned-out building. No one smiled. She set the album aside and reached between layers of blankets they had used for Shadow and under the Army uniform Poppa had worn on Decoration Day, its jacket missing. In the far corner, she found another green album. Pasted inside were newspaper articles: June 18, 1946, War Trials at Nuremburg, Germany, to end soon; June 29, 1946, a WWII veteran in Houston who committed suicide with a German Luger pistol, a War souvenir; September 24, 1946 a "blue baby" dies after an operation performed for the first time in Minneapolis; October 1, 1946, verdict reached at Nuremberg War criminal trials, 21 convicted; October 5, 1946, a German POW walked out of a POW camp in northern Minnesota. Except for the article on the blue baby, nothing made sense. She shoved the album back into its hiding place.

Saturday slipped into Sunday, into Sunday night; Poppa still hadn't returned. Worry filled Momma's face. Cigarette after cigarette filled ashtrays. Momma told the girls she was going to call Doc Swenson to contact the University of Iowa and make an appointment. Poppa would have to be told.

The next morning Poppa was still not home when Alicia and Gina came downstairs for breakfast. The girls had coats on and were ready to leave for school when Poppa burst through the door. He turned, locked it, and lean against the frame.

"Don't want Clara walking in on us. This weekend, I drove to Olivia to check out the POW camp there." He lowered his voice to a conspiratorial whisper. "It's going to be closed, and some of the German POWs are going to come looking for me."

It was as if everyone held their collective breaths, drawing all the air from the room. "I saw Clara there. Saturday. In that town. I know she's spying on me for POWs."

Momma's mouth formed a big round circle, but no sound came out. Grandpa struggled to stand. Gina broke the silence. "But Poppa, Clara was here all day."

His eyebrows scrunched together. He tilted his head like Shadow when she doesn't understand what's being said. "How can that be? I was so sure …" He turned to face the door and twisted the knob. The key fell to the floor, but he seemed not to notice. Momma gave William to Alicia, went to the door, picked up the key, and unlocked it. Poppa rushed out.

27

The family waited to hear from the University of Iowa doctors. The retreating sun pulled color from leafless trees and left gray shadows haunting the kitchen. Alicia stared out the west window, trying to will the fading sunlight into the darkened corners of the room. She remembered taking William outside into the sunshine. Momma had smiled when she held her brother close to smell a rose blossom, his tiny arms and legs lost in his blue sleeper. "I love you," Alicia had whispered.

Momma, still in her bathrobe, her hair stringy, unwashed, wound her hands beneath the sleeves' frayed edges.

Gina, dressed in her angel Halloween costume, followed by Clara, came into the kitchen, and turned on the ceiling light switch. "Why are you sitting in the dark?" Gina asked.

The telephone rang: Two shorts, one long. The sharp rings halted everyone in place like a game of freeze tag until Momma knocked over her chair, lunging for the receiver. She cleared her throat and leaned into the mouthpiece.

"Hello?" She grasped the back of the chair. "Yes, it is." Momma nodded to the girls. "Yes, William is four months old." She reached up and touched the wall for support. "The doctors at the Mayo Clinic said he was born with it."

Alicia's hand gripped the table's edge. Fear and anticipation laced the kitchen silence.

"You will? Tomorrow afternoon? Yes, yes, we can." She motioned to Clara for Gina's Rainbow Tablet and scribbled something on a blue page. "I've got the hospital address written down. Thank you, doctor. Thank you." She hung up the receiver and slumped onto the chair beside the telephone. "Dear God, thank you."

"That was a doctor at University of Iowa Hospital. He said to bring William in tomorrow for some tests. We need to leave right away." She lifted the receiver and turned the side crank on the telephone. A long and a short. She spoke quietly. "Slick, I need to talk to Ed. Right away." Her brows knit together while she listened. "Do you know where he is?" She shook her head a couple of times and hung up. "Where could he be? Now that we need him." She sighed and it seemed as if all of her newly found strength drained away.

"I'll go look for him," Clara said.

A look passed between the two women, and Alicia understood.

"That's not a good idea, Clara," Momma said.

Clara hugged Momma. "I'll be careful, Ilse." Clara closed the door to the porch, but not before ushering in the cold night air.

The eternal wait for news from the university hospital had ended, but the clock in the living room ticked its warning of fleeting time. "Gina," Momma said, "help Alicia find William's diaper bag and my suitcase."

Alicia kissed William's forehead and gently laid the sleeping baby in his bassinet.

Out of earshot of Momma, Gina squeezed Alicia's hand—hard. "I don't want to go, Alicia."

The fear in her sister's voice chilled Alicia. Gina's bruises from Poppa's belt had faded to pale yellow but not the memory. Since the trip to the Mayo Clinic, Poppa's anger had simmered like a pot of boiling lard, constantly breaking the surface. Gina was not going on this trip, Alicia decided. Her determination matched Gina's desperation.

***

An hour later, Clara returned with Slick. Neither had found Poppa. By six o'clock, Momma had stopped calling around to find him. Only the howling wind disturbed the silence. Clara started a kettle of potato soup and left with Slick, having plans to return after Momma and Poppa left. Another hour passed, and the kitchen door opened and slammed into the radiator. Shadow raced ahead of Poppa but stopped at Momma and sat at her side.

"Where have you been?" Momma asked. "We've been looking all over for you. The university hospital in Iowa City called; they will see William tomorrow. We have to leave. Now." Her words came out fast and sharp.

Alicia interrupted before Poppa could speak. "Can Gina stay home so she doesn't miss Halloween?" She spoke to Momma, but her eyes were on Poppa. He seemed not to hear. "That would be better for her than sitting alone in a hospital waiting room. Clara and Slick will be here to take care of Grandpa, and I'll take care of Gina." She held her breath while squeezing Gina's shoulders, willing her to be quiet.

"Gina will be fine here with you," Momma said.

"I'll go. But no one is experimenting on my boy." With that proclamation, Poppa stalked out of the kitchen.

The smell of cedar clung to Momma's woolen winter coat laid across a chair next to the diaper bag and suitcase lined up beside the door. She dressed William, covering his blue sleeper with the still-too-large yellow sweater Donna had knit for him. Momma paced the kitchen linoleum like a caged tiger. "Ed, hurry up," she called more than once.

Alicia and Gina hunched in chairs in the semi-dark living room, hoping not to attract Poppa's attention. He passed them without a word or a glance. His coveralls were gone, and he wore dark trousers and a white shirt under his Army uniform jacket.

The girls headed outside and stood in the dark shadows of the elm trees. Poppa loaded the suitcase, slammed the trunk, and started up the Buick. He honked. Momma carried

William. She paused at the car door, turned back to the house, and slipped into the passenger seat. The headlights flashed. Poppa gunned the motor, spinning gravel in the car's wake. The car shrunk as it disappeared down the highway, lost from view in the tornado-like swirl of dead, dry leaves beneath the streetlight.

Alicia led Gina by the hand back into the living room. Alarmed, she ran to Grandpa who was stretched across the sofa as if he had thrown his body at the window facing the driveway. The fallen lace curtain lay like a veil across his face. Alicia righted him and leaned against his useless arm the same way she did when they used to listen to "Fibber McGee and Molly" radio show. That life had been drained and replaced with something else—hard, metallic. Neither liked nor wanted, but necessary for survival.

***

Alicia awoke to the smell of burnt toast. She scrambled into her dungarees and a blouse and raced to the kitchen.

Gina stood on a kitchen chair, tears dripping into the sink as she scraped. No one else was in sight.

Alicia took the toast and examined it.

"With some strawberry jam, it's going to taste good." She knew Gina was worried about wasting food. Poppa had warned them often enough, but there was more. Alicia wondered how much her sister knew or understood. She buttered the scraped toast and slathered some of Momma's strawberry jam corner to corner. She poured herself a cup of coffee. On the kitchen counter was an assortment of things: two brown paper grocery bags, paper, Gina's crayons, the jar of paste, and scissors.

"Why don't you and me make bags for trick or treating?" Alicia asked. "One for you and one for William. I'm too old this year."

They drew and colored ghosts, jack-o-lanterns, and blue cats for William's trick-or-treat bag. "Gina, you know William is very, very sick."

Gina nodded.

Alicia tucked a stray curl behind Gina's ear. "The doctors are going to try really, really hard to fix his heart." These were all the words she could speak.

Gina kept her head down, her tongue moving in unison with the color crayon in her hand until Alicia became silent. At that moment, Clara and Slick, pushing Grandpa in his wheelchair, came into the kitchen with a huge pumpkin on Grandpa's lap blanket.

"Squirt, draw the happiest face on this pumpkin, and I'll carve it for you." Slick placed it on the floor and sat beside it. Gina brought him one of Poppa's newspapers for the seeds and sat beside him.

"We stopped to visit Sarah, and she gave us some fresh-baked rolls." Clara lifted the dish towel covering a large blue bowl.

The aroma of cinnamon warmed the kitchen. "Did Ilse call?" Slick asked.

Alicia shook her head.

The rest of the day stretched on and on: minutes seemed like hours; hours like weeks. Wait and worry replaced conversation. Outside the dining room windows, a single, lost bird searched for its southbound flock. Slick had gone to the basement to shovel coal into the furnace, but nothing erased the chill in the air.

28

Halloween dawned cold, brittle, and gray. Momma had called the night before after the girls were in bed, talked to Clara, told her the tests were finished, and that the doctors were willing to go ahead with the operation later that morning. Somehow Poppa had been persuaded to agree.

Rain beat against the window, sad and angry. Clara, Gina, Slick, and Shadow left for Clara's farm home to pick up warm clothing. Grandpa dozed in his wheelchair, leaving Alicia alone with her fears and her worries. The ticking of a clock pounded against her ears. If the past three days had been difficult, today was going to be without measure. School was out of the question.

***

Shadow led everyone into the house. Not interested in the warm smell of roasted chicken in a pot Clara carried, Shadow plopped down on her rug next to William's empty bassinet, head on her front paws, her eyes listless. Gina joined the dog and rested her head on Shadow's back. Alicia covered them with a quilt and went to the kitchen with Clara, Grandpa, and Slick. Like smoke from a waning fire, lethargy crept over each of them, their faces cloaked in unrecognizable masks. And so the morning and afternoon passed, Donna, Sarah, and Bill slipped through the house with quiet words, barely heard and little understood.

At dusk, still no word.

Rain became drizzle, as if unable to give up its hold, blurring the world outside. Time to go trick-or-treating, but Alicia barely managed enough energy to help Gina slide her angel costume over her sweater and jacket. Clara's tightly stitched angel wings looked as if they might withstand the howling winds.

Gina clutched two Halloween sacks, one with white ghosts pasted on the front and the other pasted with blue cats. Like every Halloween Alicia remembered, the first stop was at Bill and Donna's house. They followed the pathway bordering Grandpa's garden.

"Don't be afraid, Alicia," Gina said when they passed the garden scarecrow swaying in the wind. Somehow, Gina knew it wasn't the scarecrow that Alicia feared. And she was right.

They walked up Donna's steps, and Gina knocked on the slightly ajar front door. The porch light flipped on and the door opened wide.

"Trick or treat," Gina said in a small, sad voice.

"Look at you," Donna said. "The prettiest angel that ever walked the earth." She put an apple in the bag.

"Can I have one for William, too?" Gina opened the second bag.

Donna placed another apple inside William's bag. Bill put his arm around Donna's shoulder and turned her away from the girls.

"I want to go to Sarah's house and then home," Gina said.

Slick's car was waiting for them in front of Sarah's house. Drizzle had disappeared, and the dark sky and clouds, black as midnight, hid the waning moon.

"Get in, Alicia. Get in, Squirt. I'm taking you home."

"Momma called," Alicia said.

Slick nodded. A premonition swept over Alicia. She shivered, but not from the cold. "Please hurry," she told Slick.

Clara raced to the car. "The central operator has been trying to reach you. I came downstairs to answer the telephone and found Anton had fallen again. Trying to reach the telephone, I guess. We got him back in his wheelchair, and I sent Slick to look for you. Come on, Gina. I've got hot cocoa waiting for you."

Alicia ran to the telephone, picked up the receiver, and cranked one long turn for the operator. When the operator came on, Alicia identified herself.

"Mrs. Drake has been calling long distance from Iowa City for you," the operator said. "Stay close to the telephone. She said she'd call back in a few minutes."

Alicia felt as if she were watching herself in a picture show in a kitchen that looked like her own but wasn't. She held her face close to the mouthpiece, her hand inches from the earpiece, ready to grab it. A short ring. Another short ring, followed by one long. Alicia picked up the earpiece. "Momma? Momma?"

Momma's tear-soaked voice spoke. "Alicia … I'm so sorry …" A heart-wrenching sob.

Alicia reached out and touched the wooden telephone box, as if to touch Momma.

"I have some very, very bad news."

A gasping sound.

"William passed away."

"Noooooooooooo …"

Poppa's voice thundered in the background. "Wait until I get my hands on those sons-of-bitches. They are going to be so goddamn sorry they took my boy. And Clara the hell better be long gone."

"Hush, Ed," Momma murmured. "I have to go before your Poppa … I'll be home tomorrow. We have to make … some funeral arrangements. I'll need to take some of William's clothes to the undertaker. Oh, God, I can't believe this is happening. My poor baby …"

Cemented in place, Alicia listened as Momma struggled. Her sobs gradually diminishing until she seemed to find her voice. "Ask Clara to call Pastor Anderson and … and tell him. Ed, Wait. Stop!"

Alicia stared at the disconnected silent earpiece and turned to a pale Clara whose mouth moved, but Alicia heard no words.

Clara gently removed the earpiece, hung it up, and wrapped her arms around Alicia. "Pastor Anderson needs to be called," Alicia said. She put her hand up to stop Clara's unspoken offer. "I need to do it."

Clara nodded.

In the living room, Grandpa, Slick, and Gina raised their faces to her. The pain in their faces matched the pain in her heart.

Alicia sat down beside Grandpa and covered his hand with hers. "I'm so, so sorry. William passed away."

Grandpa struggled to move, to speak. Tears flowed from his eyes.

Gina snuggled close to Grandpa, patting his other hand. "Don't cry," she said. "Baby William is going to be happy in heaven with Uncle Johan. Slick told me so, and he said it's beautiful there."

Outside, Shadow began a sad, disquieting howl.

A knock at the porch door startled Alicia. Bill slowly walked to them, leaning on his cane as if he needed support. Concern filled his eyes. "I'm so sorry. I rubbernecked when the operator rang you up so many times. I had to know. We all loved that precious baby. How can I help?"

Clara answered. "We'll be all right for tonight, but ask Sarah and Donna to come over tomorrow when they can. I'll stay as long as I dare, but I'd better be gone when Ed gets home."

"So. It has come to that." Bill shook his head. "If there's a problem with Ed, come and get me. Donna will be here as soon as she gets off work." He looked around the room at each person but uttered nothing else before he left.

Slick went with Alicia back into the kitchen. Alicia rang the operator and asked her to ring Pastor Anderson. The minister wanted to drive over, but she persuaded him that they would be fine.

How will we ever be fine again?

When she returned to the living room, Gina was asleep, thumb in mouth, her head in Grandpa's lap hugging Raggedy Ann. Clara carried Gina upstairs, and Slick helped Grandpa to bed. Alicia turned off the ten o'clock news on the radio. The silence was tomb-like. Slick returned alone. After he tucked the extra quilt from the sofa around Alicia, he sat in the chair next to hers. "We have to talk."

"No," she said. "Not now."

"Yes. I wish I didn't have to bring this up. With everything else." Slick leaned forward, his elbows on his legs, and rubbed his hands together like Grandpa used to do. "It's Ed." Slick hesitated, as if choosing his words. "I don't know what William's death will do to him. I don't know what he's capable of anymore." His eyes seemed to be imploring her. "I can't and I won't stand by and see anybody hurt. I came to Fullerton to help you."

She had no answer, but she knew he was right. Poppa's plan to make everything "right again" had died with William. She did know, however, that the problem was hers to solve.

It's between me and Poppa.

She sighed and stood. The quilt slipped from her shoulders, replaced by the weight of tomorrow. "I'm going to bed. Gina might wake up and need me."

Alicia peeked into the alcove where Clara pretended to sleep. In her own bed, Alicia tucked Raggedy Ann into her sister's arm. Gina stirred and put her thumb back into her mouth. Alicia placed her face into the pillow to muffle her sobs until no tears were left. She sat up and stared out the west window. Dark clouds assaulted the waning moon and stole away her sleep. When the morning sun rose and struck the blue-gray clouds off to the west, she finally fell asleep.

29

In the living room, chairs from the kitchen and dining room lined the walls—just like Poppa's homecoming party.

Gina sat in the lone chair at the kitchen table with her and William's trick-or-treat bags lined up in front of her fort-like. It reminded Alicia of Poppa's newspaper, paste, and scissor barricade back in July. She brushed a strand of Gina's hair out of her eyes and hooked it around her ear. Gina stirred her bowl of oatmeal, but didn't take a bite.

"Is Momma home yet?" Alicia asked.

"Not yet," Donna said. Donna's eyes were red above the half circles of purple. "People have been stopping by with food all morning. I don't know what to do with it." She looked like she was going to start crying again.

Sarah took the speckled blue roaster from Donna and set it on the stove. "Donna, you need to go home and get some rest. You've been up all night." She ushered Donna to the kitchen door. "We've all got some rough waters ahead. The girls are going to need our help." The porch door closed, and Sarah bent to wrap an arm around Alicia's shoulders. "Would you like some oatmeal?"

The smell of food turned Alicia's stomach. "No, thank you." She eased into the dining room behind Pastor Anderson who talked to Bill in hushed tones. Shadow lay beside William's empty bassinet, refusing to move. In his wheelchair, Grandpa's head was bent as if in prayer. Alicia slipped out the living room door and met Mrs. Oldenburg walking towards her with a cake pan. Their eyes met. Mrs.

Oldenburg's were rimmed with tears. Alicia remembered that Mrs. Oldenburg's boy had been killed in the War. A Gold Star Mother.

Is there a star for Momma, too?

Alicia walked around to the north side of the house to avoid everyone. The harsh wind stung her face, and the bruised purple sky threatened more rain. Brown blades of grass quivered. She couldn't open her mind wide enough to think about Poppa and what he might do now. "Are any of us safe?" she asked. The fear behind that question made her light-headed.

The kitchen window framed Gina, and Alicia's heart tightened. Gina must have spotted her because she came out the back cellar door with two jackets. They walked around to the west side. Dead leaves covered the yard, and their jack-o-lantern mocked them with its smile. Gina shivered, and Alicia drew her sister close on the bench.

"Slick left," Gina said.

Alicia nodded.

"Clara, too. Why does Poppa hate her so much?" Gina lowered her head. "He said she was bad like the devil, and if she ever hurt William, he'd hurt her, too." Gina looked up, her face white, panic stricken. "He really didn't say hurt, he said kill."

Alicia pulled Gina closer.

"Clara didn't make William dead," Gina said in muffled tones.

"Of course not. Clara would never have hurt William."

Is he crazy?

"Remember we talked about how sick William was and the doctors tried very, very hard to fix him." Alicia's arms ached to hold him again, to see his blue eyes, his sweet smile. "Gina, I miss him so much already." That emptiness, stretching forever into the future, was beyond her comprehension.

"Me, too." At that moment, Gina flinched.

Alicia looked up to see Poppa's car turn into the driveway.

Momma got out of the car and steadied herself with the door. Her face, the color of gunmetal, blended into the gray eastern sky behind her, obscuring her from view. Poppa stayed in the car. Puffs of cigarette smoke exploded from the open window.

30

William's funeral was held three days later. The sky opened and heaven wept.

31

The finality of the church bell's peel—one for each car as it had driven away from the church to the cemetery—echoed across the prairie. A sound Alicia knew would never leave her.

Now most of those same dark cars, still in funeral procession, lined her driveway. Only the hearse remained at the gravesite. Men, like silent sentinels, lined the sidewalk just outside the porch door. They smoked and shuffled from foot to foot, their trouser legs wet from the tall cemetery grass.

Pheasant hunters had remained silent during the funeral and burial. But now their blasts echoed across fields of corn stubble and open prairie, shattering the silence.

How much will the noise upset Poppa?

Men removed their hats as Momma, Poppa, and Gina entered the house. Right behind them, Slick and Bill carried Grandpa. Joe followed, set the wheelchair on the porch, and left. Joe and Clara were staying away, taking no chance to provoke Poppa.

Alicia hesitated in the backseat of Poppa's car as long as she dared. When she finally walked to the house, the same men removed their hats for her.

The porch door creaked on its hinges.

Alicia traced the outline of the kitchen with her eyes: a tuna-crusted, hot dishpan teetered on the sink's edge; a sharp knife lay beside Donna's sour milk chocolate cake; a stack of lipstick-smeared cups lined the table. She searched for herself in that kitchen—the one lost forever. Alicia was weightless and invisible. Everyone appeared blurred as if seen through Momma's sheer curtains. Voices seemed to come from far away.

She moved through the dining room where tree shadows slashed the wall. In the living room, someone had moved the sofa back in front of the leaded glass window where William's casket had rested. Pastor and Mrs. Anderson sat in the wingback chairs that replaced the baskets of golden mums left at the cemetery. The smell of roses lingered from William's pink bouquet—the one with a white ribbon and BROTHER in gold letters. The house seemed too big for itself.

Hushed words of sorry, sorry, sorry floated around the room, landing here and there. Donna and Sarah flanked Momma on the sofa; their white hankies, crumpled in black funeral dress sleeves, fluttered out to catch tears. Momma leaned over the coffee table, placed her hand on it, and stood. In the dim lamplight, her eyes were empty. She walked to the bassinet and caressed its edge. Poppa followed her, pulled her hand away. Momma jerked from his grasp, reached into the bassinet, picked up William's tiny blue blanket, and crushed it to her breast. Without a word or backward glance, she climbed the stairs, out of sight. Shadow traced Momma's steps.

Poppa paced, scattering his cigarette ashes on the rug. He spun around, his fingers pointing at everyone in the living and dining rooms. He spoke in an anger-rubbed voice. "Look at you. Having a good time while my baby's cold and dead in the ground!"

Gina lunged into Alicia's arms.

"Get out of here, you hypocrites. Every one of you thinks I deserve this."

The room was locked in time as if captured by a camera: coffee cups stopped midway to mouths; a plate halted mid-air on its way to the floor; silence blurred all sounds until, outside, a shotgun blast rattled the living room window. Poppa sunk to his knees. Donna and Pastor Anderson rushed to him, but before they reached him, he stood and shoved Donna aside with one hand and swung at the minister with the other. Bill grabbed Poppa's flaying hands and shoved him back. Poppa stumbled and caught himself on the back of Grandpa's wheelchair.

"I'm going to take care of this." He spit the words. "My way." Poppa's footsteps thundered across the floor. The house shook in the wake of a slammed door. The roar of Poppa's car balanced the silence in the house.

Undistinguishable sounds gurgled from Grandpa. He struggled, fell forward out of his wheelchair, and crumpled to the rug. Slick lifted him back into his wheelchair and stroked his hand. A multitude of voices joined, each trying to speak above someone else.

Pastor Anderson adjusted his white collar, raised his hand, and cleared his throat. "Quiet down, please. All this chaos is frightening the girls. Donna and Sarah, will you stay and clean up and watch the girls? The rest of us should leave and let Ilse get some rest." He walked to the wheelchair and placed his hands on Grandpa's shoulders. "I'll go look for Ed. That poor man is grief stricken."

Slick's eyes met Alicia's, and she realized the depth of Slick's warning the night William died. Slick quickly moved, followed by Sarah, worked his way through the departing men and women, and touched the minister's sleeve. "Pastor Anderson, I don't think that's a good idea, at least not right now."

Sarah nodded her head, and the three of them spoke quietly.

"I'll go look for him," Slick said.

"Wait," Alicia said. She unwound Gina's arms and placed Gina's hand in Sarah's. "I'll walk out with you."

Outside on the lawn, the air was sharp, cold, promising snow. The last of the mourners' cars disappeared on Depot Road, and when they were alone, Alicia finally asked the question that was tying a knot in her stomach. "Do you know what Poppa meant about fixing things?"

Before he answered, Gina's story of Poppa's threat of harming Clara flashed across her mind. "Oh no." She grabbed Slick's arm. "Have you seen Clara today? I … I'm afraid Poppa's going to hurt her …" She couldn't say more. She could hardly breathe.

"Goddamn him," Slick said. His face was grim, stone carved. "I talked to Clara last night. Ilse had called her after they brought William's casket home, and Graffie drove her here after Ed went to bed. She came to say goodbye to William. She said she'd stay home today. I'll go make sure she's all right before I go look for Ed. Maybe he'll have cooled down, but I doubt it." He placed his hands on Alicia's shoulders. "You need to be very careful—all of you."

Sarah, Donna, and Gina were washing the last of the dishes. "Gina, let's go see if Momma is resting." Alicia took her sister's hand.

They passed Grandpa's open bedroom door. He was sitting up, staring at his bureau.

At Johan's picture.

Momma was in the girls' bed, but William's blue baby blanket lay on the floor just out of reach. Alicia picked it up, folded it, and tucked it into Momma's arms. Tears slid silently down Momma's cheeks. The girls tiptoed down the stairs.

Sarah held out Gina's jacket. "Alicia, Joe just got a call from his sister, and I need to catch the train to Willmar tonight. Gina, come with me, and we'll make a warm bed for Flicker under the porch. That cat refused to be locked up inside." She sighed. "Gina, I could really …" Gina grabbed the jacket and was out the door before Sarah finished. "Use your help."

Donna dried her hands, folded the dish towel and hung it on the oven handle. "Are you sure you don't want me to stay here with you?"

Alicia shook her head.

"Well, then, you promise to call me if you need *anything* or have *any* problems? Bill will be home before I leave for my shift at the hospital … there's plenty of food … Slick will be back to help with Anton …"

"I'll be fine." Donna's concern felt warm, comforting.

Alicia waited ten, maybe fifteen minutes to make sure Donna didn't return.

Is Poppa's pistol back in his locker?

She insisted a reluctant Shadow go with her to the car shed. The door was unlocked, the interior dark in the encroaching night. Spider webs laced the window; everywhere the musty smell of things ending lingered. Poppa's locker was locked.

Now What?

32

Cold air laced with the smell of coffee wafted up the stairs. White roses frosted the stair landing window. The sight in the living room horrified Alicia. William's baby clothes lay in haphazard piles. His blue and white sleepers with drawstring bottoms that had covered his tiny feet, his yellow sweater and booties, his baptismal gown and bonnet—it was all there. William's favorite pink, blue, and yellow rattled lay crushed. Baby powder, white and smelling of William, covered piles of diapers, baby bottles, safety pins and yellow blankets. William's bassinet was missing and so was Shadow.

The slam of a car door drew Alicia to the living room window. Beneath a low, gray-black sky, Poppa, dressed in full uniform, carried William's bassinet to his car, stuffed it into the car's trunk, and strode back to the house. Alicia ducked out of sight and crawled behind the sofa, hoping that neither Momma nor Gina would wake up.

Silently, Poppa carried armful after armful of William's things to the trunk and the backseat of the car. A smell, a stink, surrounded Poppa, growing stronger with each trip to and from the car. Alicia dared to peer around the sofa, knowing to trust her eyes, but not quite able to believe what she was witnessing. What Poppa was doing didn't make sense. When all traces of William were gone, Poppa spun around, a grim smile on his face. But then, as if remembering something, he knelt, opened the bottom buffet drawer, and grabbed handfuls of photographs. One photograph slid from the last fistful of snapshots he rammed into the pocket of his pants.

When Poppa's car started, she eased out from behind the sofa, rose slowly beneath the window frame, parted the lace curtains, and watched, stunned, as Poppa's car backed out of the driveway onto Depot Road and turned left towards the highway. She raced to the window on the stair landing and used her palm to melt the ice rose. His car turned into the town dump. Shadow escaped from the car, circled Poppa, and stood between him and the dump. She jumped, knocking him down. Poppa kicked her, picked her up, and shoved the dog into the car.

Alicia raced to the dropped photograph and picked up a single snapshot of Momma, William, Gina, and Alicia that Cal had taken with his Kodak on the Fourth of July. She hurriedly opened the buffet door above the drawer Poppa had left open and slid the picture behind Momma's good china gravy boat in the darkest corner, closed the door, and went to wake Momma.

Still in her black funeral dress, Momma bolted upright when Alicia whispered her name. "What's wrong?"

Alicia had no words to give to her mother. Instead, she walked to the open door and waited. In the hallway, she took her Momma's hand and led her down the steps.

Seemingly dazed, Ilse followed her daughter until they reached the dining room corner where William's bassinet had been for three months. A sob caught in Momma's throat. Alicia wrapped her arms around Momma, and the two of them stood quietly for a very long time.

"Ed did this," Momma said, life draining from her voice.

Unwilling to separate, they walked together into the kitchen. When Momma sat, Alicia poured a cup of coffee for Momma and added cream. It curdled with a sweet, sick smell. Alicia poured it down the sink and took two cups from the cupboard and fresh milk from the refrigerator. She poured one for Momma and one for herself. With slow, deliberate motions, like Gina's mechanical bear, Momma clutched the cup, lifted it, sipped, set it down, lifted, sipped, and set it down. Repeating, repeating. Even after the cup was empty.

Slick entered the kitchen and hung his coat. "Starting to snow. Mr. Oldenburg got a warning telegraph from someone over in South Dakota that a blizzard is on its way." His eyes darted from Momma to daughter with a questioning look. "What did Ed do?"

Alicia tilted her head towards the dining room, not yet ready to deal with its emptiness. Momma needed her.

Slick bolted through the doorway and came back, leading Gina by the hand.

She tugged away and ran to her sister. "Poppa?" she asked in a small, frightened voice.

Alicia eased Gina into her lap, raised her face to meet Slick's, and mouthed the word *Clara.*

"God, what is this going to do to Anton? I'll go after Ed. Somebody's got to stop him before …" Slick went to Momma and placed his hand on her shoulder, but his eyes were on Alicia. "Alicia, will you and Gina make some oatmeal and take it and some coffee upstairs to Anton and help him eat? He'll be … better off upstairs in case Ed … "

When the sisters returned, Momma paced the kitchen, and then sat slumped in her chair, seemingly unaware of her daughters. A minute later, she exploded from her chair and charged to the door. She beat it with her fists. "How could he be so cruel? He took everything that touched my baby. God, I feel so empty."

Alicia leaped to her Momma, grabbed the fists, and locked them at Momma's side. "Stop, Momma, please! You're scaring Gina." Alicia knew it would ease Momma's pain if she told her about William's baby blanket and photograph, but Alicia also knew that Momma would want to hold them, and when Poppa came home, he'd rip them away.

"Gina I'm so sorry," Momma said. "I didn't mean to frighten you." She wrapped Gina in the folds of her funeral dress and rocked her daughter.

The outside door blew open and slammed against the radiator. Poppa stormed into the kitchen, his shirt half in and half out of his pants. A wild look in his eyes scared Alicia, but she still moved between him and Momma. Momma sidestepped Alicia and rammed herself into Poppa. She beat on his chest as hard as she had beaten the wood door. Her knuckles, scraped from pounding the door, left blood on his Army jacket. "Why did you take my baby's things? Why do you have to be so cruel to anyone who loves you?"

"I had to get rid of it—all of it. That Clara. She contaminated everything. Thought she had me fooled … roped my own daughter into betraying me." His voice lowered to a conspiratorial whisper. "*Clara* was at the POW camp. I know it for a fact." Poppa looked left, right, behind, and bent into Alicia's face. She swallowed hard before the smell of his breath gagged her. "Graffie is in on it, too. That's where she got the poison to slowly kill my baby. I'm sure of it."

He looked thoughtful. "Are you the enemy, too, Ilse?" In a swift motion, Poppa slammed Momma into the corner of the table. She collapsed to the floor, blood streaming from her head.

A low growl erupted from Shadow's throat. She bared her teeth and charged Poppa, snarling and snapping.

"Damn, dog." Poppa kicked her. "The old eye for an eye. Now, I'm going to even the score before they come after me." Dishes rattled with the force of Poppa's words. He ripped the telephone off of the wall. And then he was gone.

Alicia and Gina ran to Momma and lifted her from the floor. She clung to the table for support. The front of her dress was blood soaked. "Oh my God," she cried, her face whiter than the snow beginning to fall outside the window. "I've got to stop him." Her legs faltered with her first step.

"No, Momma. You've got to stay here and protect Gina."

"Poppa would never …"

"But he did. On the Mayo trip he used his belt on her." Momma's face changed from white to a crimson anger. "Oh my God, no …"

"Gina, get a clean dishrag for Momma's head. "I'll go get Joe. Then I'll find Slick and Clara." Shadow rose to follow, but Alicia told her to stay. The dog sat down beside Gina.

Snowflakes, big and soft, floated down from the sky. In another time and universe, she and Gina would be outside catching them on their tongues.

Alicia caught up with Joe at the bottom of the hill. He locked the station door. "Weather's coming in. Not going to be too many customers today."

She raced to him, half sliding on the collecting snow. "Joe, Momma needs you right away. Poppa's gone crazy."

"I'm on my way."

Alicia ran up Center Street. The parking lot was empty and the shop dark. She tried to think where Slick might have gone. Debating her choices, she heard Slick's car come out of the alley. He was alone. She climbed into the car and asked Slick if had found Clara. He shook his head. She told him what Poppa had said about Clara, words rushing out, bumping against each other.

"We'll check Graffie's. First, I'd better check for Ed's pistol in the car shed." His car fishtailed on the way to Alicia's house. He bolted, leaving the car door open. Snow billowed into the car, falling heavier, thicker, collecting on trees, lawn, and Slick until he vanished through the car shed door. He came back on a dead run. "The foot locker's open. Ed's pistol is gone."

33

Slick speeds down Depot Road; his car careens onto the highway. His hard-set jaw, a mirror of Alicia's, reflects fear fused with anger. Underneath the railroad bridge, two smashed cars block the highway to Graffie's. Slick's car fishtails to a stop on the icy pavement. One hand on the gear shift, one on the steering wheel, he slams the car into reverse. He charges backward to Depot Road, up the hill past Alicia's driveway, hits the brakes, slides into a half-circle turn towards the grain elevator and depot, crosses the railroad tracks, and bounces over frozen ruts of the cornfield. He comes to a halt at the back door of the Trading Post.

In the white-out snowstorm, it seems as if the sun has abandoned the world. Wind drives the snow sideways, covers Clara, and pelts the sweater she clutches at her throat. Above her, the awning hangs precariously, weighted with snow.

Alicia rolls down her window, yells into the storm. "Clara, get in the car. Poppa's after you."

Clara climbs in, and Alicia slides next to Slick, giving Clara a share of the meager car heat.

"What's wrong? What happened?" Worry etches lines on Clara's face.

The horror of what is happening and might happen in the next few hours strikes Alicia like a sledgehammer to her stomach.

"Ed's gone over the edge, Clara," Slick says. "He's threatened to get you. His German Luger pistol is gone."

Clara turns to Alicia. A word forms on her lips without sound. *Pistol?*

Slick continues. "He has to be stopped. One way or another." On Main Street, Slick drives behind the two-story railroad hotel, away from discovery. "I have to find him before he finds you two. I'll go find Bill and Graffie. Ed has to be calmed down … the pistol taken away …" Slick shakes his head. "Him doing that to Ilse … threatening his girls and Clara …" He slams his fist against the dashboard, shouting: "Goddamnit. Ed used to be a good man …" Slick drives away from the shelter of the hotel through the back alley, makes a left turn past Bill's darkened store windows, stops the car, and turns off the engine, seemingly lost in thought.

"Bill's at home," Alicia says. "Poppa ripped the telephone from the wall so Bill can't know what's happening. But we better hide Clara first, 'cause if Poppa sees her, he won't calm down." The truth of these words rocks Alicia. "I'll take Clara to the lumber yard. Then, I'm going with you."

Clara's hand touches Alicia.

Concern? A warning?

Neither matter to Alicia. "He's my Poppa."

Gusting wind clears the snow-plastered windshield for a moment. "Oh no. Gina!" Alicia screams.

Gina and Shadow—snow-covered ghosts—walk towards the car. Clara climbs out, lifts Gina into the front seat beside Alicia, and crawls into the back with Shadow. Slick starts the car. Gina's clothes are soaked through. Her face, hands, and legs are scarlet. The car smells of wet wool.

Alicia turns her back to Slick, slips Gina's shirt and undershirt over her head, pulls down her dungarees, and wraps her in the blanket that Clara slides into the front seat. "Why are you here?" Alicia removes Gina's shoes and anklets and rubs her feet.

Gina's chattering teeth make it hard to understand. "Poppa came back home and pounded on the locked door. Momma hid me behind the cellar door, but Poppa got inside 'cause I heard him swear at Joe and Momma, and then he screamed, 'Where's that traitor, Alicia?' And Momma didn't tell him and then she screamed. I was so scared, I don't 'member what they said. I came out when Poppa slammed the door. Joe was on the floor and Momma was crying, trying to wake him up." Gina buried her face in Alicia's arms. "Momma told me to stay in the cellar and hide, but I didn't listen. I snuck out to find you, and Shadow showed me." Tears and snot trickle down Gina's face.

Alicia wipes them away with her coat sleeve.

"Alicia … I'm so scared … of Poppa."

Alicia pulls Gina closer, not knowing how much of her sister's shivering is cold and how much is fear.

"When I get my hands on that son of a bitch, so help me, God …" Slick says.

"If Poppa finds Gina with me and Clara …" The rest is unspeakable. "Where can Gina be safe? Donna's probably stranded at the hospital; Sarah's out of town; if Gina goes home, Poppa will find her." She pauses thinking. "I know what we can do, Gina, but you have to promise to listen and do everything I say. All right?"

Gina nods, shaking more wet snow from drooping curls.

"Remember yesterday when you and Sarah made a blanket bed for Flicker under her porch—that secret place Momma cat hid her kittens last summer?"

A second nod from Gina.

"Slick will take you there, and you crawl under the blankets with Flicker and stay there. It's very important that nobody but Slick, Clara, and me know you're there."

Alicia reaches down, unties her shoes, pulls her anklets off, and puts the warm stockings on Gina's feet. Alicia slips her own shoes back on, aware of how cold they had become. She starts to remove her coat.

"My jacket is bigger and warmer. Keep yours on." Slick wraps his jacket around the blanketed Gina, dwarfing her. "Gina," Slick says, "I'm going to make sure your Momma and Joe are all right. Then me, Bill, and Graffie will find your Poppa and help him. Then I'll come and rescue you just like

Alicia did at the lumber yard. But you need to be as quiet as a church mouse. Promise?"

Gina nods, her eyes trusting.

Another round of anger surges through Alicia.

How little she is. I couldn't bear it if something happens to her.

Slick's car fades into the snow that merges land and sky. Alicia and Clara crouch along the side of the single, snow-covered car in front of the darkened Cozy Café. They wind around boulder-sized snow drifts forming in the park and pause for breath behind the band shell. Obscured by evergreen trees, they make their way to the lumber yard. Memories sting like the howling wind.

She shivers in the mind-numbing cold. The lumber yard building's side door is closed, not locked. Clara and Alicia put their backs to it, shove it open, and enter.

Snow clots the opening overhead, and in the faint light, they walk into deep shadows of lumber piles. With Slick's flashlight in hand, an eerie cone of light leads Alicia and Clara to the steps. They pause on the second floor landing. Here the wind shrieks like a demonic choir. As they burrow into the stacked lumber, the pile shifts and groans. The new wood smell sickens Alicia.

"Tell me again, exactly what happened," Clara says.

Alicia tells her of finding Poppa with William's clothes and how he destroyed all traces of her baby brother. Then, in the dark silence, truth pours out of her: the hurt Poppa inflicted on her—on Gina—his strange behavior, and her search for his secret.

Anger fuses into a steel knot of rage. She has one goal: stop Poppa.

"Let Slick and Bill handle Ed," Clara implores, as if reading Alicia's thoughts.

Satisfied that Clara is well hidden, Alicia slips from her grasp, and lowers herself from the stack of lumber. With her feet on the landing, she turns on the flashlight. Hesitates. "Listen." She stuffs the flashlight in her jacket to hide its beam. Faintly at first, and then louder and louder, work boots thump against the steps. Closer and closer. Boards shift and rumble.

Poppa reaches the landing. He sighs as if he's tired. "Thought you'd be safe here, did you? I know all about this hiding place. I've been outside, waiting for you."

Caught, she removes the flashlight and shines it on Poppa, away from Clara. He is sitting on the upturned nail barrel and leaning against the railing. She doesn't recognize him: spittle foams from the corners of his mouth; dark stubble hides his face; his eyes stare through her, cold and dark. Lowering the flashlight from his face, her body turns ice cold when the beam glints off the pistol in his other hand. "Tell her to come out. I just want to talk to her." His voice is low, pleading, coating the lie Alicia hears.

"No, Poppa."

"Goddamnit. I want to tell her I'm sorry."

Alicia senses Clara close behind her and whispers, "No, Clara."

"Ed, I'll come out if you let Alicia go." She moves a step forward, but Alicia catches Clara's arm in a death hold. Lumber shifts.

"I'll have to think about that. That girl consorted with the enemy. You." Poppa rises slowly, comes to full height like a dark giant from a nightmare. "Maybe I'll hold a court-martial for her." A hollow laugh follows. "I fooled you pretty good. All that spying … and you never found out. Hate to think what those judges might have done—about her and her baby." He jabs his finger at Alicia. "Turn off the damn light." He orders.

Alicia refuses. "Baby? Judges?"

"At Nuremburg. The hangings. Crimes against humanity. I committed a crime against humanity. I was so close to you, Clara, I saw your two different color eyes. I didn't mean to kill you … I didn't mean to kill your baby. I swear to God I'm not a killer. I was just a goddamn mechanic." A long sob catches in his throat like a ragged cry. "They cursed me when they gave me this medal." He jerks the medal from his uniform and heaves it. "A medal for killing a mother and her baby. But your baby's face … it keeps haunting my nightmares—crying. Then it was William's face …" Poppa kicks the nail barrel. It smashes through the railing. A thundering anger explodes from him. "Why couldn't you stay dead, Clara? Why did you take my baby—*my boy*, *my hope*—from me? Nothing is ever going to be right again. I might as well be dead. All of us dead."

Poppa lunges at Clara and slams the pistol against her forehead. Blood streams from a gash. It spatters Poppa's ice-coated uniform. Clara crumples into a heap, one arm dangling over the twenty-foot drop to the concrete. He stands over her, his pistol in hand, pointing at her, his voice calm as a prayer. "It's going to be over soon."

Alicia walks to him, places her hands on his out-stretched arm, moves it down to his side. She moves closer, lays her head on his shoulder, and whispers, "Poppa, stop, please, Poppa."

His body goes rigid, his head swirls left and right. "Alicia? Alicia? Where are we?"

"Give me the gun, Poppa. Please." She pleads, grasps the cold barrel in one hand. "We can fix things. You and me. Like with Shadow. Now … give … me … the gun."

He jerks the gun free, stares at the pistol in his hand, stares at blood gushing from Clara's head. "Nooooo. This can't be happening again." He shoves Alicia against the stack of lumber. "Stay away from me. I'm sorry, so sorry. Tell Ilse, tell Gina. And her."

The pistol is aimed at Alicia's heart. She steps closer.

Poppa staggers back, away from his daughter. Closer and closer to the broken railing.

"No, Poppa. Stop! I love you!"

The wooden railing protests, gives way, and Poppa topples through space. His plea for forgiveness echoes past Alicia, rises through the open roof, catches in the wind, and carries across the prairie.

"Poppa!" Alicia stumbles down the steps to her Poppa. She cradles his head in her lap, closes his eyes, and brushes strands of hair from his face.

He looks like my Poppa, not the one who came home from the War.

The blizzard outside holds no meaning. Snowflakes, soft and large, continue to fall; flakes merge with a young woman's tears, shrouding her and her Poppa with the sounds of silence.

34

In the distance, a man walks away into the swirling snow. At his heel, dark as a shadow, a dog follows.

AUTHOR'S NOTE

I extend my sincere apologies to all Minnesotans for rearranging the geography of our great state.

I wrote this book in loving memory of my baby brother, Michael Lee Wixon (July 16, 1950 – October 25, 1950), however all of the characters within are fictional.

ACKNOWLEDGEMENTS

A grand thank you to my two sons, Chris and Mike, for their love, encouragement, inspiration, and wise words that helped make this dream a reality.

David Pierce and Linda Busby Parker, both mentors in the MTSU (Middle Tennessee State University) Write Program, guided me through the darkness and confusion that is a story at its beginning. Thanks for the lantern! A special thank you to Jennifer Chesak, editor extraordinaire, who edited my novel with grace and skill.

Thank you to the men in my family who served: My great-uncles John Anderson, Martin Ofstad, and Giles Ofstad; my father Walt Wixon, my uncles Glen Anderson, Lyle Anderson, Marvin Anderson, Keith Wixon, Kenneth Wixon, and Wallace Wixon; and my brothers Kim Wixon and Michael A. Wixon.

And to all the men and woman who have served—thank you for your sacrifice and service.

ABOUT THE AUTHOR

Alberta Tolbert, a born-and-raised Minnesotan, has lived in six states and is now firmly planted in Tennessee with her husband, Vic. Her journey crossed the great Midwest, and she writes stories linked to its places and people.

CPSIA information can be obtained
at www.ICGtesting.com
Printed in the USA
FFOW02n0109031016
28127FF